P. G. WODEHOUSE

Very Good, Jeeves

arrow books

17 19 20 18 16

Arrow Books
20 Vauxhall Bridge Road
London SW1V 2SA

Arrow Books is part of the Penguin Random House group of companies
whose addresses can be found at global.penguinrandomhouse.com

Penguin
Random House
UK

First published in Great Britain by Herbert Jenkins Ltd in 1930
First published by Arrow Books in 2008

www.penguin.co.uk

A CIP catalogue record for this book is available from the British Library.

ISBN 9780099513728

Typeset by SX Composing DTP, Rayleigh, Essex

Printed and bound in Great Britain by Clays Ltd, Elcograf S.p.A.
Penguin Random House is committed to a sustainable future for
our business, our readers and our planet. This book is made from
Forest Stewardship Council® certified paper.

MIX
Paper from
responsible sources
FSC® C018179

Mr Wodehouse's

IDYLLIC WORLD CAN NEVER STALE.

He will continue to release future generations from captivity that may be more irksome than our own. He has made a world for us to live in and delight in'

Evelyn Waugh

'THE ULTIMATE IN COMFORT READING

because nothing bad ever happens in P. G. Wodehouse land. Or even if it does, it's always sorted out by the end of the book. For as long as I'm immersed in a P. G. Wodehouse book, it's possible to keep the real world at bay and live in a far, far nicer, funnier one where happy endings are the order of the day'

Marian Keyes

'You should read Wodehouse when you're well and when you're poorly; when you're travelling, and when you're not; when you're feeling clever, and when you're feeling utterly dim. Wodehouse
ALWAYS LIFTS YOUR SPIRITS,
no matter how high they happen to be already'

Lynne Truss

'P. G. Wodehouse remains the greatest chronicler of
A CERTAIN KIND OF ENGLISHNESS,
that no one else has ever captured quite so sharply, or with quite as much wit and affection'

Julian Fellowes

'Not only the funniest English novelist who ever wrote but one of our finest stylists.
His world is **PERFECT**, his stories are
PERFECT, his writing is **PERFECT**.
What more is there to be said?'

Susan Hill

'One of my (few) proud boasts is that I once spent a day interviewing P. G. Wodehouse at his home in America. He was exactly as I'd expected: a lovely, modest man. He could have walked out of one of his own novels. It's dangerous to use the word

GENIUS

to describe a writer, but I'll risk it with him'

John Humphrys

'The

INCOMPARABLE AND TIMELESS

genius – perfect for readers of all ages, shapes and sizes!'

Kate Mosse

'COMPULSORY READING

for anyone who has a pig, an aunt – or a sense of humour!'

Lindsey Davis

'A genius ...

ELUSIVE, DELICATE BUT LASTING.

He created such a credible world that, sadly, I suppose, never really existed but what a delight it always is to enter it and the temptation to linger there is sometimes almost overwhelming'

Alan Ayckbourn

'I've recorded all the Jeeves books, and I can tell you this: it's like singing Mozart. The perfection of the phrasing is

A PHYSICAL PLEASURE.

I doubt if any singer in the English language has more perfect music'

Simon Callow

'I constantly find myself drooling with admiration at the

SUBLIME

way Wodehouse plays with the English language'

Simon Brett

'To pick up a Wodehouse novel is to find oneself in the presence of genius – no writer has ever given me so much

PURE ENJOYMENT'

John Julius Norwich

'P. G. Wodehouse is

THE GOLD STANDARD OF ENGLISH WIT'

Christopher Hitchens

'Wodehouse is so

UTTERLY, PROPERLY, SIMPLY FUNNY'

Adele Parks

'To dive into a Wodehouse novel is to swim in some of the most

ELEGANTLY TURNED PHRASES

in the English language'

Ben Schott

'P. G. Wodehouse should be prescribed to treat depression. Cheaper, more effective than valium and far, far more

ADDICTIVE'

Olivia Williams

'My only problem with Wodehouse is deciding which of his

ENCHANTING

books to take to my desert island'

Ruth Dudley Edwards

'Quite simply,

THE MASTER OF COMIC WRITING

at work'

Jane Moore

Pelham Grenville Wodehouse (always known as 'Plum') wrote more than ninety novels and some three hundred short stories over 73 years. He is widely recognised as the greatest 20th-century writer of humour in the English language.

Wodehouse mixed the high culture of his classical education with the popular slang of the suburbs in both England and America, becoming a 'cartoonist of words'. Drawing on the antics of a near-contemporary world, he placed his Drones, Earls, Ladies (including draconian aunts and eligible girls) and Valets, in a recently vanished society, whose reality is transformed by his remarkable imagination into something timeless and enduring.

Perhaps best known for the escapades of Bertie Wooster and Jeeves, Wodehouse also created the world of Blandings Castle, home to Lord Emsworth and his cherished pig, the Empress of Blandings. His stories include gems concerning the irrepressible and disreputable Ukridge; Psmith, the elegant socialist; the ever-so-slightly-unscrupulous Fifth Earl of Ickenham, better known as Uncle Fred; and those related by Mr Mulliner, the charming raconteur of The Angler's Rest, and the Oldest Member at the Golf Club.

Wodehouse collaborated with a variety of partners on straight plays and worked principally alongside Guy Bolton on providing the lyrics and script for musical comedies with such composers as George Gershwin, Irving Berlin and Cole Porter. He liked to say that the royalties for 'Just My Bill', which Jerome Kern incorporated into *Showboat*, were enough to keep him in tobacco and whisky for the rest of his life.

In 1936 he was awarded the Mark Twain Prize for 'having made an outstanding and lasting contribution to the happiness of the world'. He was made a Doctor of Letters by Oxford University in 1939 and in 1975, aged 93, he was knighted by Queen Elizabeth II. He died shortly afterwards, on St Valentine's Day.

To have created so many characters that require no introduction places him in a very select group of writers, led by Shakespeare and Dickens.

Very Good, Jeeves

CONTENTS

TO

E. PHILLIPS OPPENHEIM

The question of how long an author is to be allowed to go on recording the adventures of any given character or characters is one that has frequently engaged the attention of thinking men. The publication of this book brings it once again into the foreground of national affairs.

It is now some fourteen summers since, an eager lad in my early thirties, I started to write Jeeves stories: and many people think this nuisance should now cease. Carpers say that enough is enough. Cavillers say the same. They look down the vista of the years and see these chronicles multiplying like rabbits, and the prospect appals them. But against this must be set the fact that writing Jeeves stories gives me a great deal of pleasure and keeps me out of the public-houses.

At what conclusion, then, do we arrive? The whole thing is undoubtedly very moot.

From the welter of recrimination and argument one fact emerges – that we have here the third volume of a series. And what I do feel very strongly is that, if a thing is worth doing, it is worth doing well and thoroughly. It is perfectly possible, no doubt, to read *Very Good, Jeeves!* as a detached effort – or, indeed, not to read it at all: but I like to think that this country contains men of spirit who will not rest content till they have dug down into the old oak chest and fetched up the sum necessary for the purchase of its two predecessors – *The Inimitable Jeeves* and *Carry On, Jeeves!* Only so can the best results be obtained. Only so will allusions in the present volume to incidents occurring in the previous volumes become intelligible, instead of mystifying and befogging.

We do you these two books at the laughable price of half-a-crown apiece, and the method of acquiring them is simplicity itself.

All you have to do is to go to the nearest bookseller, when the following dialogue will take place:

YOURSELF: Good morning, Mr Bookseller.
BOOKSELLER: Good morning, Mr Everyman.
YOURSELF: I want *The Inimitable Jeeves* and *Carry On, Jeeves!*
BOOKSELLER: Certainly, Mr Everyman. You make the easy
    payment of five shillings, and they will be delivered at your
    door in a plain van.
YOURSELF: Good morning, Mr Bookseller.
BOOKSELLER: Good morning, Mr Everyman.

Or take the case of a French visitor to London, whom, for want of a better name, we will call Jules St Xavier Popinot. In this instance the little scene will run on these lines:

AU COIN DE LIVRES

POPINOT: Bon jour, Monsieur le marchand de livres.
MARCHAND: Bon jour, Monsieur. Quel beau temps aujourdhui,
    n'est-ce-pas?
POPINOT: Absolument. Eskervous avez le *Jeeves Inimitable* et
    le *Continuez, Jeeves!* du maitre Vodeouse?

MARCHAND: Mais certainement, Monsieur.

POPINOT: Donnez-moi les deux, s'il vous plait.

MARCHAND: Oui, par exemple, morbleu. Et aussi la plume,
l'encre, et la tante du jardinière?

POPINOT: Je m'en fiche de cela. Je désire seulement le Vodeouse.

MARCHAND: Pas de chemises, de cravats, ou le tonic pour les
cheveux?

POPINOT: Seulement le Vodeouse, je vous assure.

MARCHAND: Parfaitement, Monsieur. Deux-et-six pour chaque
bibelot – exactement cinq roberts.

POPINOT: Bon jour, Monsieur.

MARCHAND: Bon jour, Monsieur.

As simple as that.

See that the name 'Wodehouse' is on every label.

P. G. W.

It was the morning of the day on which I was slated to pop down to my Aunt Agatha's place at Woollam Chersey in the county of Herts for a visit of three solid weeks; and, as I seated myself at the breakfast table, I don't mind confessing that the heart was singularly heavy. We Woosters are men of iron, but beneath my intrepid exterior at that moment there lurked a nameless dread.

'Jeeves,' I said, 'I am not the old merry self this morning.'

'Indeed, sir?'

'No, Jeeves. Far from it. Far from the old merry self.'

'I am sorry to hear that, sir.'

He uncovered the fragrant eggs and b., and I pronged a moody forkful.

'Why – this is what I keep asking myself, Jeeves, – why has my Aunt Agatha invited me to her country seat?'

'I could not say, sir.'

'Not because she is fond of me.'

'No, sir.'

'It is a well-established fact that I give her a pain in the neck. How it happens I cannot say, but every time our paths cross, so to speak, it seems to be a mere matter of time before I perpetrate some ghastly floater and have her hopping after me with her hatchet. The result being that she regards me as a worm and an outcast. Am I right or wrong, Jeeves?'

'Perfectly correct, sir.'

'And yet now she has absolutely insisted on my scratching all previous engagements and buzzing down to Woollam Chersey. She must have some sinister reason of which we know nothing. Can you blame me, Jeeves, if the heart is heavy?'

'No, sir. Excuse me, sir, I fancy I heard the front-door bell.'

He shimmered out, and I took another listless stab at the e. and bacon.

'A telegram, sir,' said Jeeves, re-entering the presence.

'Open it, Jeeves, and read contents. Who is it from?'

'It is unsigned, sir.'

'You mean there's no name at the end of it?'

'That is precisely what I was endeavouring to convey, sir.'

'Let's have a look.'

I scanned the thing. It was a rummy communication. Rummy. No other word.

As follows:

Remember when you come here absolutely vital meet perfect strangers.

We Woosters are not very strong in the head, particularly at breakfast-time; and I was conscious of a dull ache between the eyebrows.

'What does it mean, Jeeves?'

'I could not say, sir.'

'It says "come here". Where's here?'

'You will notice that the message was handed in at Woollam Chersey, sir.'

'You're absolutely right. At Woollam, as you very cleverly spotted, Chersey. This tells us something, Jeeves.'

'What, sir?'

'I don't know. It couldn't be from my Aunt Agatha, do you think?'

'Hardly, sir.'

'No; you're right again. Then all we can say is that some person unknown, resident at Woollam Chersey, considers it absolutely vital for me to meet perfect strangers. But why should I meet perfect strangers, Jeeves?'

'I could not say, sir.'

'And yet, looking at it from another angle, why shouldn't I?'

'Precisely, sir.'

'Then what it comes to is that the thing is a mystery which time alone can solve. We must wait and see, Jeeves.'

'The very expression I was about to employ, sir.'

I hit Woollam Chersey at about four o'clock, and found Aunt Agatha in her lair, writing letters. And, from what I know of her, probably offensive letters, with nasty postscripts. She regarded me with not a fearful lot of joy.

'Oh, there you are, Bertie.'

'Yes, here I am.'

'There's a smut on your nose.'

I plied the handkerchief.

'I am glad you have arrived so early. I want to have a word with you before you meet Mr Filmer.'

'Who?'

'Mr Filmer, the Cabinet Minister. He is staying in the house. Surely even you must have heard of Mr Filmer?'

'Oh, rather,' I said, though as a matter of fact the bird was completely unknown to me. What with one thing and another, I'm not frightfully up in the personnel of the political world.

'I particularly wish you to make a good impression on Mr Filmer.'

'Right-ho.'

'Don't speak in that casual way, as if you supposed that it was perfectly natural that you would make a good impression upon him. Mr Filmer is a serious-minded man of high character and purpose, and you are just the type of vapid and frivolous wastrel against which he is most likely to be prejudiced.'

Hard words, of course, from one's own flesh and blood, but well in keeping with past form.

'You will endeavour, therefore, while you are here not to display yourself in the *rôle* of a vapid and frivolous wastrel. In the first place, you will give up smoking during your visit.'

'Oh, I say!'

'Mr Filmer is president of the Anti-Tobacco League. Nor will you drink alcoholic stimulants.'

'Oh, dash it!'

'And you will kindly exclude from your conversation all that is suggestive of the bar, the billiard-room, and the stage-door. Mr Filmer will judge you largely by your conversation.'

I rose to a point of order.

'Yes, but why have I got to make an impression on this – on Mr Filmer?'

'Because,' said the old relative, giving me the eye, 'I particularly wish it.'

Not, perhaps, a notably snappy come-back as come-backs go; but it was enough to show me that that was more or less that; and I beetled out with an aching heart.

I headed for the garden, and I'm dashed if the first person I saw wasn't young Bingo Little.

Bingo Little and I have been pals practically from birth.

Born in the same village within a couple of days of one another, we went through kindergarten, Eton, and Oxford together; and, grown to riper years we have enjoyed in the old metrop. full many a first-class binge in each other's society. If there was one fellow in the world, I felt, who could alleviate the horrors of this blighted visit of mine, that bloke was young Bingo Little.

But how he came to be there was more than I could understand. Some time before, you see, he had married the celebrated authoress, Rosie M. Banks; and the last I had seen of him he had been on the point of accompanying her to America on a lecture tour. I distinctly remembered him cursing rather freely because the trip would mean his missing Ascot.

Still, rummy as it might seem, here he was. And aching for the sight of a friendly face, I gave tongue like a bloodhound.

'Bingo!'

He spun round; and, by Jove, his face wasn't friendly after all. It was what they call contorted. He waved his arms at me like a semaphore.

''Sh!' he hissed. 'Would you ruin me?'

'Eh?'

'Didn't you get my telegram?'

'Was that *your* telegram?'

'Of course it was my telegram.'

'Then why didn't you sign it?'

'I did sign it.'

'No, you didn't. I couldn't make out what it was all about.'

'Well, you got my letter.'

'What letter?'

'My letter.'

'I didn't get any letter.'

'Then I must have forgotten to post it. It was to tell you that I was down here tutoring your Cousin Thomas, and that it was essential that, when we met, you should treat me as a perfect stranger.'

'But why?'

'Because, if your aunt supposed that I was a pal of yours, she would naturally sack me on the spot.'

'Why?'

Bingo raised his eyebrows.

'Why? Be reasonable, Bertie. If you were your aunt, and you knew the sort of chap you were, would you let a fellow you knew to be your best pal tutor your son?'

This made the old head swim a bit, but I got his meaning after awhile, and I had to admit that there was much rugged good sense in what he said. Still, he hadn't explained what you might call the nub or gist of the mystery.

'I thought you were in America,' I said.

'Well, I'm not.'

'Why not?'

'Never mind why not. I'm not.'

'But why have you taken a tutoring job?'

'Never mind why. I have my reasons. And I want you to get it into your head, Bertie – to get it right through the concrete – that you and I must not be seen hobnobbing. Your foul cousin was caught smoking in the shrubbery the day before yesterday, and that has made my position pretty tottery, because your aunt said that, if I had exercised an adequate surveillance over him, it couldn't have happened. If, after that, she finds out I'm a friend of yours, nothing can save me from being shot out. And it is vital that I am not shot out.'

'Why?'

'Never mind why.'

At this point he seemed to think he heard somebody coming, for he suddenly leaped with incredible agility into a laurel bush. And I toddled along to consult Jeeves about these rummy happenings.

'Jeeves,' I said, repairing to the bedroom, where he was unpacking my things, 'you remember that telegram?'

'Yes, sir.'

'It was from Mr Little. He's here, tutoring my young Cousin Thomas.'

'Indeed, sir?'

'I can't understand it. He appears to be a free agent, if you know what I mean; and yet would any man who was a free agent wantonly come to a house which contained my Aunt Agatha?'

'It seems peculiar, sir.'

'Moreover, would anybody of his own free-will and as a mere pleasure-seeker tutor my Cousin Thomas, who is notoriously a tough egg and a fiend in human shape?'

'Most improbable, sir.'

'These are deep waters, Jeeves.'

'Precisely, sir.'

'And the ghastly part of it all is that he seems to consider it necessary, in order to keep his job, to treat me like a long-lost leper. Thus killing my only chance of having anything approaching a decent time in this abode of desolation. For do you realize, Jeeves, that my aunt says I mustn't smoke while I'm here?'

'Indeed, sir?'

'Nor drink.'

'Why is this, sir?'

'Because she wants me – for some dark and furtive reason which she will not explain – to impress a fellow named Filmer.'

'Too bad, sir. However, many doctors, I understand, advocate such abstinence as the secret of health. They say it promotes a freer circulation of the blood and insures the arteries against premature hardening.'

'Oh, do they? Well, you can tell them next time you see them that they are silly asses.'

'Very good, sir.'

And so began what, looking back along a fairly eventful career, I think I can confidently say was the scaliest visit I have ever experienced in the course of my life. What with the agony of missing the life-giving cocktail before dinner; the painful necessity of being obliged, every time I wanted a quiet cigarette, to lie on the floor in my bedroom and puff the smoke up the chimney; the constant discomfort of meeting Aunt Agatha round unexpected corners; and the fearful strain on the morale of having to chum with the Right Hon. A. B. Filmer, it was not long before Bertram was up against it to an extent hitherto undreamed of.

I played golf with the Right Hon. every day, and it was only by biting the Wooster lip and clenching the fists till the knuckles stood out white under the strain that I managed to pull through. The Right Hon. punctuated some of the ghastliest golf I have ever seen with a flow of conversation which, as far as I was concerned, went completely over the top; and, all in all, I was beginning to feel pretty sorry for myself when, one night as I was in my room listlessly donning the soup-and-fish in preparation for the evening meal, in trickled young Bingo and took my mind off my own troubles.

For when it is a question of a pal being in the soup, we Woosters no longer think of self; and that poor old Bingo was knee-deep in the bisque was made plain by his mere appearance – which was that of a cat which has just been struck by a half-brick and is expecting another shortly.

'Bertie,' said Bingo, having sat down on the bed and diffused silent gloom for a moment, 'how is Jeeves's brain these days?'

'Fairly strong on the wing, I fancy. How is the grey matter, Jeeves? Surging about pretty freely?'

'Yes, sir.'

'Thank Heaven for that,' said young Bingo, 'for I require your soundest counsel. Unless right-thinking people take strong steps through the proper channels, my name will be mud.'

'What's wrong, old thing?' I asked, sympathetically.

Bingo plucked at the coverlet.

'I will tell you,' he said. 'I will also now reveal why I am staying in this pest-house, tutoring a kid who requires not education in the Greek and Latin languages but a swift slosh on the base of the skull with a black-jack. I came here, Bertie, because it was the only thing I could do. At the last moment before she sailed to America, Rosie decided that I had better stay behind and look after the Peke. She left me a couple of hundred quid to see me through till her return. This sum, judiciously expended over the period of her absence, would have been enough to keep Peke and self in moderate affluence. But you know how it is.'

'How what is?'

'When someone comes slinking up to you in the club and tells you that some cripple of a horse can't help winning even if it develops lumbago and the botts ten yards from the starting-post. I tell you, I regarded the thing as a cautious and conservative investment.'

'You mean you planked the entire capital on a horse?'

Bingo laughed bitterly.

'If you could call the thing a horse. If it hadn't shown a flash of speed in the straight, it would have got mixed up with the next race. It came in last, putting me in a dashed delicate position. Somehow or other I had to find the funds to keep me going, so that I could win through till Rosie's return without her knowing what had occurred. Rosie is the dearest girl in the world; but if you were a married man, Bertie, you would be aware that the best of wives is apt to cut up rough if she finds that her husband has dropped six weeks' housekeeping money on a single race. Isn't that so, Jeeves?'

'Yes, sir. Women are odd in that respect.'

'It was a moment for swift thinking. There was enough left from the wreck to board the Peke out at a comfortable home. I signed him up for six weeks at the Kosy Komfort Kennels at Kingsbridge, Kent, and tottered out, a broken man, to a tutoring job. I landed the kid Thomas. And here I am.'

It was a sad story, of course, but it seemed to me that, awful as it might be to be in constant association with my Aunt Agatha and young Thos, he had got rather well out of a tight place.

'All you have to do,' I said, 'is to carry on here for a few weeks more, and everything will be oojah-cum-spiff.'

Bingo barked bleakly.

'A few weeks more! I shall be lucky if I stay two days. You remember I told you that your aunt's faith in me as a guardian of her blighted son was shaken a few days ago by the fact that he was caught smoking. I now find that the person who caught him smoking was the man Filmer. And ten minutes ago young Thomas told me that he was proposing to inflict some hideous revenge on Filmer for having reported him to your aunt. I don't know what he is going to do, but if he does it, out I inevitably go on my left ear. Your aunt thinks the world of Filmer, and would sack me on the spot. And three weeks before Rosie gets back!'

I saw all.

'Jeeves,' I said.

'Sir?'

'I see all. Do you see all?'

'Yes, sir.'

'Then flock round.'

'I fear, sir—'

Bingo gave a low moan.

'Don't tell me, Jeeves,' he said, brokenly, 'that nothing suggests itself.'

'Nothing at the moment, I regret to say, sir.'

Bingo uttered a stricken woofle like a bull-dog that has been refused cake.

'Well, then, the only thing I can do, I suppose,' he said sombrely, 'is not to let the pie-faced little thug out of my sight for a second.'

'Absolutely,' I said. 'Ceaseless vigilance, eh, Jeeves?'

'Precisely, sir.'

'But meanwhile, Jeeves,' said Bingo in a low, earnest voice, 'you will be devoting your best thought to the matter, won't you?'

'Most certainly, sir.'

'Thank you, Jeeves.'

'Not at all, sir.'

I will say for young Bingo that, once the need for action arrived, he behaved with an energy and determination which compelled respect. I suppose there was not a minute during the next two days when the kid Thos was able to say to himself, 'Alone at last!' But on the evening of the second day Aunt Agatha announced that some people were coming over on the morrow for a spot of tennis, and I feared that the worst must now befall.

Young Bingo, you see, is one of those fellows who, once their fingers close over the handle of a tennis racket, fall into a sort of trance in which nothing outside the radius of the lawn exists for them. If you came up to Bingo in the middle of a set and told him that panthers were devouring his best friend in the kitchen garden, he would look at you and say, 'Oh, ah?' or words to that effect. I knew that he would not give a thought to young Thomas and the Right Hon. till the last ball had bounced, and, as I dressed for dinner that night, I was conscious of an impending doom.

'Jeeves,' I said, 'have you ever pondered on Life?'

'From time to time, sir, in my leisure moments.'

'Grim, isn't it, what?'

'Grim, sir?'

'I mean to say, the difference between things as they look and things as they are.'

'The trousers perhaps a half-inch higher, sir. A very slight adjustment of the braces will effect the necessary alteration. You were saying, sir?'

'I mean, here at Woollam Chersey we have apparently a happy, care-free country-house party. But beneath the glittering surface, Jeeves, dark currents are running. One gazes at the Right Hon. wrapping himself round the salmon mayonnaise at lunch, and he seems a man without a care in the world. Yet all the while a dreadful fate is hanging over him, creeping nearer and nearer. What exact steps do you think the kid Thomas intends to take?'

'In the course of an informal conversation which I had with the young gentleman this afternoon, sir, he informed me that he had been reading a romance entitled *Treasure Island*, and had been much struck by the character and actions of a certain Captain Flint. I gathered that he was weighing the advisability of modelling his own conduct on that of the Captain.'

'But, good heavens, Jeeves! If I remember *Treasure Island*, Flint was the bird who went about hitting people with a cutlass. You don't think young Thomas would bean Mr Filmer with a cutlass?'

'Possibly he does not possess a cutlass, sir.'

'Well, with anything.'

'We can but wait and see, sir. The tie, if I might suggest it, sir, a shade more tightly knotted. One aims at the perfect butterfly effect. If you will permit me—'

'What do ties matter, Jeeves, at a time like this? Do you realize that Mr Little's domestic happiness is hanging in the scale?'

'There is no time, sir, at which ties do not matter.'

I could see the man was pained, but I did not try to heal the wound. What's the word I want? Preoccupied. I was too preoccupied, don't you know. And distrait. Not to say careworn.

I was still careworn when, next day at half-past two, the revels commenced on the tennis lawn. It was one of those close, baking days, with thunder rumbling just round the corner; and it seemed to me that there was a brooding menace in the air.

'Bingo,' I said, as we pushed forth to do our bit in the first doubles, 'I wonder what young Thos will be up to this afternoon, with the eye of authority no longer on him?'

'Eh?' said Bingo, absently. Already the tennis look had come into his face, and his eye was glazed. He swung his racket and snorted a little.

'I don't see him anywhere,' I said.

'You don't what?'

'See him.'

'Who?'

'Young Thos.'

'What about him?'

I let it go.

The only consolation I had in the black period of the opening of the tourney was the fact that the Right Hon. had taken a seat among the spectators and was wedged in between a couple of females with parasols. Reason told me that even a kid so steeped in sin as young Thomas would hardly perpetrate any outrage on a man in such a strong strategic position. Considerably relieved, I gave myself up to the game; and was in the act of putting it across the local curate with a good deal of vim when there was a roll of thunder and the rain started to come down in buckets.

We all stampeded for the house, and had gathered in the drawing-room for tea, when suddenly Aunt Agatha, looking up from a cucumber-sandwich, said:

'Has anybody seen Mr Filmer?'

It was one of the nastiest jars I have ever experienced. What with my fast serve zipping sweetly over the net and the man of God utterly unable to cope with my slow bending return down the centre-line, I had for some little time been living, as it were, in another world. I now came down to earth with a bang: and my slice of cake, slipping from my nerveless fingers, fell to the ground and was wolfed by Aunt Agatha's spaniel, Robert. Once more I seemed to become conscious of an impending doom.

For this man Filmer, you must understand, was not one of those men who are lightly kept from the tea-table. A hearty trencherman, and particularly fond of his five o'clock couple of cups and bite of muffin, he had until this afternoon always been well up among the leaders in the race for the food-trough. If one thing was certain, it was that only the machinations of some enemy could be keeping him from being in the drawing-room now, complete with nose-bag.

'He must have got caught in the rain and be sheltering somewhere in the grounds,' said Aunt Agatha. 'Bertie, go out and find him. Take a raincoat to him.'

'Right-ho!' I said. My only desire in life now was to find the Right Hon. And I hoped it wouldn't be merely his body.

I put on a raincoat and tucked another under my arm, and was sallying forth, when in the hall I ran into Jeeves.

'Jeeves,' I said, 'I fear the worst. Mr Filmer is missing.'

'Yes, sir.'

'I am about to scour the grounds in search of him.'

'I can save you the trouble, sir. Mr Filmer is on the island in the middle of the lake.'

'In this rain? Why doesn't the chump row back?'

'He has no boat, sir.'

'Then how can he be on the island?'

'He rowed there, sir. But Master Thomas rowed after him and set his boat adrift. He was informing me of the circumstances a moment ago, sir. It appears that Captain Flint was in the habit of marooning people on islands, and Master Thomas felt that he could pursue no more judicious course than to follow his example.'

'But, good Lord, Jeeves! The man must be getting soaked.'

'Yes, sir. Master Thomas commented upon that aspect of the matter.'

It was a time for action.

'Come with me, Jeeves!'

'Very good, sir.'

I buzzed for the boathouse.

My Aunt Agatha's husband, Spenser Gregson, who is on the Stock Exchange, had recently cleaned up to an amazing extent in Sumatra Rubber; and Aunt Agatha, in selecting a country estate, had lashed out on an impressive scale. There were miles of what they call rolling parkland, trees in considerable profusion well provided with doves and what not cooing in no uncertain voice, gardens full of roses, and also stables, outhouses, and messuages, the whole forming a rather fruity *tout ensemble*. But the feature of the place was the lake.

It stood to the east of the house, beyond the rose garden, and covered several acres. In the middle of it was an island. In the middle of the island was a building known as the Octagon. And in the middle of the Octagon, seated on the roof and spouting water like a public fountain, was the Right Hon. A. B. Filmer. As we drew nearer, striking a fast clip with self at the oars and Jeeves handling the tiller-ropes, we heard cries of gradually increasing volume, if that's the expression I want; and presently, up aloft, looking from a distance as if he were perched on top of the bushes, I located the Right Hon. It seemed to me that even a Cabinet Minister ought to have had more sense than to stay right out in the open like that when there were trees to shelter under.

'A little more to the right, Jeeves.'

'Very good, sir.'

I made a neat landing.

'Wait here, Jeeves.'

'Very good, sir. The head gardener was informing me this morning, sir, that one of the swans had recently nested on this island.'

'This is no time for natural history gossip, Jeeves,' I said, a little severely, for the rain was coming down harder than ever and the Wooster trouser-legs were already considerably moistened.

'Very good, sir.'

I pushed my way through the bushes. The going was sticky and took about eight and elevenpence off the value of my Sure-Grip tennis shoes in the first two yards: but I persevered, and presently came out in the open and found myself in a sort of clearing facing the Octagon.

This building was run up somewhere in the last century, I have been told, to enable the grandfather of the late owner to have some quiet place out of earshot of the house where he could practise the fiddle. From what I know of fiddlers, I should imagine that he had produced some fairly frightful sounds there in his time: but they can have been nothing to the ones that were coming from the roof of the place now. The Right Hon., not having spotted the arrival of the rescue-party, was apparently trying to make his voice carry across the waste of waters to the house; and I'm not saying it was not a good sporting effort. He had one of those highish tenors, and his yowls seemed to screech over my head like shells.

I thought it about time to slip him the glad news that assistance had arrived, before he strained a vocal cord.

'Hi!' I shouted, waiting for a lull.

He poked his head over the edge.

'Hi!' he bellowed, looking in every direction but the right one, of course.

'Hi!'

'Hi!'

'Hi!'

'Hi!'

'Oh!' he said, spotting me at last.

'What-ho!' I replied, sort of clinching the thing. I suppose the conversation can't be said to have touched a frightfully high level up to this moment; but probably we should have got a good deal brainier very shortly − only just then, at the very instant when I was getting ready to say something good, there was a hissing noise like a tyre bursting in a nest of cobras, and out of the bushes to my left there popped something so large and white and active that, thinking quicker than I have ever done in my puff, I rose like a rocketing pheasant, and, before I knew what I was doing, had begun to climb for life. Something slapped against the wall about an inch below my right ankle, and any doubts I may have had about remaining below vanished. The lad who bore 'mid snow and ice the banner with the strange device 'Excelsior!' was the model for Bertram.

'Be careful!' yipped the Right Hon.

I was.

Whoever built the Octagon might have constructed it especially for this sort of crisis. Its walls had grooves at regular intervals which were just right for the hands and feet, and it wasn't very long before I was parked up on the roof beside the Right Hon., gazing down at one of the largest and shortest-tempered swans I had ever seen. It was standing below, stretching up a neck like a hosepipe, just where a bit of brick, judiciously bunged, would catch it amidships.

I bunged the brick and scored a bull's-eye.

The Right Hon. didn't seem any too well pleased.

'Don't tease it!' he said.

'It teased me,' I said.

The swan extended another eight feet of neck and gave an imitation of steam escaping from a leaky pipe. The rain continued to lash down with what you might call indescribable fury, and I was sorry that in the agitation inseparable from shinning up a stone wall at practically a second's notice I had dropped the raincoat which I had been bringing with me for my fellow-rooster. For a moment I thought of offering him mine, but wiser counsels prevailed.

'How near did it come to getting you?' I asked.

'Within an ace,' replied my companion, gazing down with a look of marked dislike. 'I had to make a very rapid spring.'

The Right Hon. was a tubby little chap who looked as if he had been poured into his clothes and had forgotten to say 'When!' and the picture he conjured up, if you know what I mean, was rather pleasing.

'It is no laughing matter,' he said, shifting the look of dislike to me.

'Sorry.'

'I might have been seriously injured.'

'Would you consider bunging another brick at the bird?'

'Do nothing of the sort. It will only annoy him.'

'Well, why not annoy him? He hasn't shown such a dashed lot of consideration for our feelings.'

The Right Hon. now turned to another aspect of the matter.

'I cannot understand how my boat, which I fastened securely to the stump of a willow-tree, can have drifted away.'

'Dashed mysterious.'

'I begin to suspect that it was deliberately set loose by some mischievous person.'

'Oh, I say, no, hardly likely, that. You'd have seen them doing it.'

'No, Mr Wooster. For the bushes form an effective screen. Moreover, rendered drowsy by the unusual warmth of the afternoon, I dozed off for some little time almost immediately I reached the island.'

This wasn't the sort of thing I wanted his mind dwelling on, so I changed the subject.

'Wet, isn't it, what?' I said.

'I had already observed it,' said the Right Hon. in one of those nasty, bitter voices. 'I thank you, however, for drawing the matter to my attention.'

Chit-chat about the weather hadn't gone with much of a bang, I perceived. I had a shot at Bird Life in the Home Counties.

'Have you ever noticed,' I said, 'how a swan's eyebrows sort of meet in the middle?'

'I have had every opportunity of observing all that there is to observe about swans.'

'Gives them a sort of peevish look, what?'

'The look to which you allude has not escaped me.'

'Rummy,' I said, rather warming to my subject, 'how bad an effect family life has on a swan's disposition.'

'I wish you would select some other topic of conversation than swans.'

'No, but, really, it's rather interesting. I mean to say, our old pal down there is probably a perfect ray of sunshine in normal circumstances. Quite the domestic pet, don't you know. But purely and simply because the little woman happens to be nesting—'

I paused. You will scarcely believe me, but until this moment, what with all the recent bustle and activity, I had clean forgotten that, while we were treed up on the roof like this, there lurked all the time in the background one whose giant brain, if notified of the emergency and requested to flock round, would probably be able to think up half-a-dozen schemes for solving our little difficulties in a couple of minutes.

'Jeeves!' I shouted.

'Sir?' came a faint respectful voice from the great open spaces.

'My man,' I explained to the Right Hon. 'A fellow of infinite resource and sagacity. He'll have us out of this in a minute. Jeeves!'

'Sir?'

'I'm sitting on the roof.'

'Very good, sir.'

'Don't say "Very good". Come and help us. Mr Filmer and I are treed, Jeeves.'

'Very good, sir.'

'Don't keep saying "Very good". It's nothing of the kind. The place is alive with swans.'

'I will attend to the matter immediately, sir.'

I turned to the Right Hon. I even went so far as to pat him on the back. It was like slapping a wet sponge.

'All is well,' I said. 'Jeeves is coming.'

'What can he do?'

I frowned a trifle. The man's tone had been peevish, and I didn't like it.

'That,' I replied with a touch of stiffness, 'we cannot say until we see him in action. He may pursue one course, or he may pursue another. But on one thing you can rely with the utmost confidence – Jeeves will find a way. See, here he comes stealing through the undergrowth, his face shining with the light of pure intelligence. There are no limits to Jeeves's brain-power. He virtually lives on fish.'

I bent over the edge and peered into the abyss.

'Look out for the swan, Jeeves.'

'I have the bird under close observation, sir.'

The swan had been uncoiling a further supply of neck in our direction; but now he whipped round. The sound of a voice speaking in his rear seemed to affect him powerfully. He subjected Jeeves to a short, keen scrutiny; and then, taking in some breath for hissing purposes, gave a sort of jump and charged ahead.

'Look out, Jeeves!'

'Very good, sir.'

Well, I could have told that swan it was no use. As swans go, he may have been well up in the ranks of the intelligentsia; but, when it came to pitting his brains against Jeeves, he was simply wasting his time. He might just as well have gone home at once.

Every young man starting life ought to know how to cope with an angry swan, so I will briefly relate the proper procedure. You begin by picking up the raincoat which somebody has dropped; and then, judging the distance to a nicety, you simply shove the raincoat over the bird's head; and, taking the boat-hook which you have prudently brought with you, you insert it underneath the swan and heave. The swan goes into a bush and starts trying to unscramble itself; and you saunter back to your boat, taking with you any friends who may happen at the moment to be sitting on roofs in the vicinity. That was Jeeves's method, and I cannot see how it could have been improved upon.

The Right Hon. showing a turn of speed of which I would not have believed him capable, we were in the boat in considerably under two ticks.

'You behaved very intelligently, my man,' said the Right Hon. as we pushed away from the shore.

'I endeavour to give satisfaction, sir.'

The Right Hon. appeared to have said his say for the time

being. From that moment he seemed to sort of huddle up and meditate. Dashed absorbed he was. Even when I caught a crab and shot about a pint of water down his neck he didn't seem to notice it.

It was only when we were landing that he came to life again.

'Mr Wooster.'

'Oh, ah?'

'I have been thinking of that matter of which I spoke to you some time back – the problem of how my boat can have got adrift.'

I didn't like this.

'The dickens of a problem,' I said. 'Better not bother about it any more. You'll never solve it.'

'On the contrary, I have arrived at a solution, and one which I think is the only feasible solution. I am convinced that my boat was set adrift by the boy Thomas, my hostess's son.'

'Oh, I say, no! Why?'

'He had a grudge against me. And it is the sort of thing only a boy, or one who is practically an imbecile, would have thought of doing.'

He legged it for the house; and I turned to Jeeves, aghast. Yes, you might say aghast.

'You heard, Jeeves?'

'Yes, sir.'

'What's to be done?'

'Perhaps Mr Filmer, on thinking the matter over, will decide that his suspicions are unjust.'

'But they aren't unjust.'

'No, sir.'

'Then what's to be done?'

'I could not say, sir.'

I pushed off rather smartly to the house and reported to Aunt Agatha that the Right Hon. had been salved; and then I toddled upstairs to have a hot bath, being considerably soaked from stem to stern as the result of my rambles. While I was enjoying the grateful warmth, a knock came at the door.

It was Purvis, Aunt Agatha's butler.

'Mrs Gregson desires me to say, sir, that she would be glad to see you as soon as you are ready.'

'But she has seen me.'

'I gather that she wishes to see you again, sir.'

'Oh, right-ho.'

I lay beneath the surface for another few minutes; then, having dried the frame, went along the corridor to my room. Jeeves was there, fiddling about with underclothing.

'Oh, Jeeves,' I said, 'I've just been thinking. Oughtn't somebody to go and give Mr Filmer a spot of quinine or something? Errand of mercy, what?'

'I have already done so, sir.'

'Good. I wouldn't say I like the man frightfully, but I don't want him to get a cold in the head.' I shoved on a sock. 'Jeeves,' I said, 'I suppose you know that we've got to think of something pretty quick? I mean to say, you realize the position? Mr Filmer suspects young Thomas of doing exactly what he did do, and if he brings home the charge Aunt Agatha will undoubtedly fire Mr Little, and then Mrs Little will find out what Mr Little has been up to, and what will be the upshot and outcome, Jeeves? I will tell you. It will mean that Mrs Little will get the goods on Mr Little to an extent to which, though only a bachelor myself, I should say that no wife ought to get the goods on her husband if the proper give and take of married life – what you might call the essential balance, as it were – is to be preserved.

Women bring these things up, Jeeves. They do not forget and forgive.'

'Very true, sir.'

'Then how about it?'

'I have already attended to the matter, sir.'

'You have?'

'Yes, sir. I had scarcely left you when the solution of the affair presented itself to me. It was a remark of Mr Filmer's that gave me the idea.'

'Jeeves, you're a marvel!'

'Thank you very much, sir.'

'What was the solution?'

'I conceived the notion of going to Mr Filmer and saying that it was you who had stolen his boat, sir.'

The man flickered before me. I clutched a sock in a feverish grip.

'Saying – what?'

'At first Mr Filmer was reluctant to credit my statement. But I pointed out to him that you had certainly known that he was on the island – a fact which he agreed was highly significant. I pointed out, furthermore, that you were a light-hearted young gentleman, sir, who might well do such a thing as a practical joke. I left him quite convinced, and there is now no danger of his attributing the action to Master Thomas.'

I gazed at the blighter spellbound.

'And that's what you consider a neat solution?' I said.

'Yes, sir. Mr Little will now retain his position as desired.'

'And what about me?'

'You are also benefited, sir.'

'Oh, I am, am I?'

'Yes, sir. I have ascertained that Mrs Gregson's motive in

inviting you to this house was that she might present you to Mr Filmer with a view to your becoming his private secretary.'

'What!'

'Yes, sir. Purvis, the butler, chanced to overhear Mrs Gregson in conversation with Mr Filmer on the matter.'

'Secretary to that superfatted bore! Jeeves, I could never have survived it.'

'No, sir. I fancy you would not have found it agreeable. Mr Filmer is scarcely a congenial companion for you. Yet, had Mrs Gregson secured the position for you, you might have found it embarrassing to decline to accept it.'

'Embarrassing is right!'

'Yes, sir.'

'But I say, Jeeves, there's just one point which you seem to have overlooked. Where exactly do I get off?'

'Sir?'

'I mean to say, Aunt Agatha sent word by Purvis just now that she wanted to see me. Probably she's polishing up her hatchet at this very moment.'

'It might be the most judicious plan not to meet her, sir.'

'But how can I help it?'

'There is a good, stout waterpipe running down the wall immediately outside this window, sir. And I could have the two-seater waiting outside the park gates in twenty minutes.'

I eyed him with reverence.

'Jeeves,' I said, 'you are always right. You couldn't make it five, could you?'

'Let us say ten, sir.'

'Ten it is. Lay out some raiment suitable for travel, and leave the rest to me. Where is this waterpipe of which you speak so highly?'

I checked the man with one of my glances. I was astounded and shocked.

'Not another word, Jeeves,' I said. 'You have gone too far. Hats, yes. Socks, yes. Coats, trousers, shirts, ties, and spats, absolutely. On all these things I defer to your judgement. But when it comes to vases, no.'

'Very good, sir.'

'You say that this vase is not in harmony with the appointments of the room – whatever that means, if anything. I deny this, Jeeves, *in toto*. I like this vase. I call it decorative, striking, and, all in all, an exceedingly good fifteen bob's worth.'

'Very good, sir.'

'That's that, then. If anybody rings up, I shall be closeted during the next hour with Mr Sipperley at the offices of *The Mayfair Gazette*.'

I beetled off with a fairish amount of restrained hauteur, for I was displeased with the man. On the previous afternoon, while sauntering along the Strand, I had found myself wedged into one of those sort of alcove places where fellows with voices like fog-horns stand all day selling things by auction. And, though I was still vague as to how exactly it had happened, I had somehow become the possessor of a large china vase with crimson dragons on it. And not only dragons, but birds, dogs, snakes, and a thing that looked like a leopard. This menagerie was now stationed on a bracket over the door of my sitting-room.

I liked the thing. It was bright and cheerful. It caught the eye. And that was why, when Jeeves, wincing a bit, had weighed in with some perfectly gratuitous art-criticism, I ticked him off with no little vim. *Ne sutor ultra* whatever-it-is, I would have said to him, if I'd thought of it. I mean to say, where does a valet get off, censoring vases? Does it fall within his province to knock the young master's chinaware? Absolutely not, and so I told him.

I was still pretty heartily hipped when I reached the office of *The Mayfair Gazette*, and it would have been a relief to my feelings to have decanted my troubles on to old Sippy, who, being a very dear old pal of mine, would no doubt have understood and sympathized. But when the office-boy had slipped me through into the inner cubbyhole where the old lad performed his editorial duties, he seemed so preoccupied that I hadn't the heart.

All these editor blokes, I understand, get pretty careworn after they've been at the job for awhile. Six months before, Sippy had been a cheery cove, full of happy laughter; but at that time he was what they call a free-lance, bunging in a short story here and a set of verses there and generally enjoying himself. Ever since he had become editor of this rag, I had sensed a change, so to speak.

To-day he looked more editorial then ever; so, shelving my own worries for the nonce, I endeavoured to cheer him up by telling him how much I had enjoyed his last issue. As a matter of fact, I hadn't read it, but we Woosters do not shrink from subterfuge when it is a question of bracing up a buddy.

The treatment was effective. He showed animation and verve.

'You really liked it?'

'Red-hot, old thing.'

'Full of good stuff, eh?'

'Packed.'

'That poem – Solitude?'

'What a gem!'

'A genuine masterpiece.'

'Pure tabasco. Who wrote it?'

'It was signed,' said Sippy, a little coldly.

'I keep forgetting names.'

'It was written,' said Sippy, 'by Miss Gwendolen Moon. Have you ever met Miss Moon, Bertie?'

'Not to my knowledge. Nice girl?'

'My God!' said Sippy.

I looked at him keenly. If you ask my Aunt Agatha she will tell you – in fact, she is quite likely to tell you even if you don't ask her – that I am a vapid and irreflective chump. Barely sentient, was the way she once described me: and I'm not saying that in a broad, general sense she isn't right. But there is one department of life in which I am Hawkshaw the detective in person. I can recognize Love's Young Dream more quickly than any other bloke of my weight and age in the Metropolis. So many of my pals have copped it in the past few years that now I can spot it a mile off on a foggy day. Sippy was leaning back in his chair, chewing a piece of indiarubber with a far-off look in his eyes, and I formed my diagnosis instantly.

'Tell me all, laddie,' I said.

'Bertie, I love her.'

'Have you told her so?'

'How can I?'

'I don't see why not. Quite easy to bring into the general conversation.'

Sippy groaned hollowly.

'Do you know what it is, Bertie, to feel the humility of a worm?'

'Rather! I do sometimes with Jeeves. But today he went too far. You will scarcely credit it, old man, but he had the crust to criticize a vase which—'

'She is so far above me.'

'Tall girl?'

'Spiritually. She is all soul. And what am I? Earthy.'

'Would you say that?'

'I would. Have you forgotten that a year ago I did thirty days without the option for punching a policeman in the stomach on Boat-Race night?'

'But you were whiffled at the time.'

'Exactly. What right has an inebriated jail-bird to aspire to a goddess?'

My heart bled for the poor old chap.

'Aren't you exaggerating things a trifle, old lad?' I said. 'Everybody who has had a gentle upbringing gets a bit sozzled on Boat-Race night, and the better element nearly always have trouble with the gendarmes.'

He shook his head.

'It's no good, Bertie. You mean well, but words are useless. No, I can but worship from afar. When I am in her presence a strange dumbness comes over me. My tongue seems to get entangled with my tonsils. I could no more muster up the nerve to propose to her than ... Come in!' he shouted.

For, just as he was beginning to go nicely and display a bit of eloquence, a knock had sounded on the door. In fact, not so much a knock as a bang – or even a slosh. And there now entered a large, important-looking bird with penetrating eyes, a Roman nose, and high cheek-bones. Authoritative. That's the word I want. I didn't like his collar, and Jeeves would have had a thing or two to say about the sit of his trousers; but, nevertheless, he was authoritative. There was something compelling about the man. He looked like a traffic-policeman.

'Ah, Sipperley!' he said.

Old Sippy displayed a good deal of agitation. He had leaped from his chair, and was now standing in a constrained attitude, with a sort of pop-eyed expression on his face.

'Pray be seated, Sipperley,' said the cove. He took no notice of me. After one keen glance and a brief waggle of the nose in my direction, he had washed Bertram out of his life. 'I have brought you another little offering – ha! Look it over at your leisure, my dear fellow.'

'Yes, sir,' said Sippy.

'I think you will enjoy it. But there is just one thing. I should be glad, Sipperley, if you would give it a leetle better display, a rather more prominent position in the paper than you accorded to my "Landmarks of Old Tuscany". I am quite aware that in a weekly journal space is a desideratum, but one does not like one's efforts to be – I can only say pushed away in a back corner among advertisements of bespoke tailors and places of amusement.' He paused, and a nasty gleam came into his eyes. 'You will bear this in mind, Sipperley?'

'Yes, sir,' said Sippy.

'I am greatly obliged, my dear fellow,' said the cove, becoming genial again. 'You must forgive my mentioning it. I would be the last person to attempt to dictate the – ha! – editorial policy, but— Well, good afternoon, Sipperley. I will call for your decision at three o'clock to-morrow.'

He withdrew, leaving a gap in the atmosphere about ten feet by six. When this had closed in, I sat up.

'What was it?' I said.

I was startled to observe poor old Sippy apparently go off his onion. He raised his hands over his head, clutched his hair, wrenched it about for a while, kicked a table with great violence, and then flung himself into his chair.

'Curse him!' said Sippy. 'May he tread on a banana-skin on his way to chapel and sprain both ankles!'

'Who was he?'

'May he get frog-in-the-throat and be unable to deliver the end-of-term sermon!'

'Yes, but who was he?'

'My old head master, Bertie,' said Sippy.

'Yes, but, my dear old soul—'

'Head master of my old school.' He gazed at me in a distraught sort of way. 'Good Lord! Can't you understand the position?'

'Not by a jugful, laddie.'

Sippy sprang from his chair and took a turn or two up and down the carpet.

'How do you feel,' he said, 'when you meet the head master of your old school?'

'I never do. He's dead.'

'Well, I'll tell you how I feel. I feel as if I were in the Lower Fourth again, and had been sent up by my form-master for creating a disturbance in school. That happened once, Bertie, and the memory still lingers. I can recall as if it were yesterday knocking at old Waterbury's door and hearing him say, "Come in!" like a lion roaring at an early Christian, and going in and shuffling my feet on the mat and him looking at me and me explaining – and then, after what seemed a lifetime, bending over and receiving six of the juiciest on the old spot with a cane that bit like an adder. And whenever he comes into my office now the old wound begins to trouble me, and I just say, "Yes, sir," and "No, sir," and feel like a kid of fourteen.'

I began to grasp the posish. The whole trouble with these fellows like Sippy, who go in for writing, is that they develop the artistic temperament, and you never know when it is going to break out.

'He comes in here with his pockets full of articles on "The Old School Cloisters" and "Some Little-Known Aspects of Tacitus", and muck like that, and I haven't the nerve to refuse them. And this is supposed to be a paper devoted to the lighter interests of Society.'

'You must be firm, Sippy. Firm, old thing.'

'How can I, when the sight of him makes me feel like a piece of chewed blotting-paper? When he looks at me over that nose, my *morale* goes blue at the roots and I am back at school again. It's persecution, Bertie. And the next thing that'll happen is that my proprietor will spot one of those articles, assume with perfect justice that, if I can print that sort of thing, I must be going off my chump, and fire me.'

I pondered. It was a tough problem.

'How would it be—?' I said.

'That's no good.'

'Only a suggestion,' I said.

'Jeeves,' I said, when I got home, 'surge round!'

'Sir?'

'Burnish the old bean. I have a case that calls for one of your best efforts. Have you ever heard of a Miss Gwendolen Moon?'

'Authoress of *Autumn Leaves. 'Twas on an English June*, and other works. Yes, sir.'

'Great Scott, Jeeves, you seem to know everything.'

'Thank you very much, sir.'

'Well, Mr Sipperley is in love with Miss Moon.'

'Yes, sir.'

'But fears to speak.'

'It is often the way, sir.'

'Deeming himself unworthy.'

'Precisely, sir.'

'Right! But that is not all. Tuck that away in a corner of the mind, Jeeves, and absorb the rest of the facts. Mr Sipperley, as you are aware, is the editor of a weekly paper devoted to the interests of the lighter Society. And now the head master of his old school has started calling at the office and unloading on him junk entirely unsuited to the lighter Society. All clear?'

'I follow you perfectly, sir.'

'And this drip Mr Sipperley is compelled to publish, much against his own wishes, purely because he lacks the nerve to tell the man to go to blazes. The whole trouble being, Jeeves, that he has got one of those things that fellows do get – it's on the tip of my tongue.'

'An inferiority complex, sir?'

'Exactly. An inferiority complex. I have one myself with regard to my Aunt Agatha. You know me, Jeeves. You know that if it were a question of volunteers to man the lifeboat, I would spring to the task. If anyone said, "Don't go down the coal-mine, daddy," it would have not the slightest effect on my resolution—'

'Undoubtedly, sir.'

'And yet – and this is where I want you to follow me very closely, Jeeves – when I hear that my Aunt Agatha is out with her hatchet and moving in my direction, I run like a rabbit. Why? Because she gives me an inferiority complex. And so it is with Mr Sipperley. He would, if called upon, mount the deadly breach, and do it without a tremor; but he cannot bring himself to propose to Miss Moon, and he cannot kick his old head master in the stomach and tell him to take his beastly essays on "The Old School Cloisters" elsewhere, because he has an inferiority complex. So what about it, Jeeves?'

'I fear I have no plan which I could advance with any confidence on the spur of the moment, sir.'

'You want time to think, eh?'

'Yes, sir.'

'Take it, Jeeves, take it. You may feel brainier after a night's sleep. What is it Shakespeare calls sleep, Jeeves?'

'Tired Nature's sweet restorer, sir.'

'Exactly. Well, there you are, then.'

You know, there's nothing like sleeping on a thing. Scarcely had I woken up next morning when I discovered that, while I slept, I had got the whole binge neatly into order and worked out a plan Foch might have been proud of. I rang the bell for Jeeves to bring me my tea.

I rang again. But it must have been five minutes before the man showed up with the steaming.

'I beg your pardon, sir,' he said, when I reproached him. 'I did not hear the bell. I was in the sitting-room, sir.'

'Ah?' I said, sucking down a spot of the mixture. 'Doing this and that, no doubt?'

'Dusting your new vase, sir.'

My heart warmed to the fellow. If there's one person I like, it's the chap who is not too proud to admit it when he's in the wrong. No actual statement to that effect had passed his lips, of course, but we Woosters can read between the lines. I could see that he was learning to love the vase.

'How does it look?'

'Yes, sir.'

A bit cryptic, but I let it go.

'Jeeves,' I said.

'Sir?'

'That matter we were in conference about yestereen.'

'The matter of Mr Sipperley, sir?'

'Precisely. Don't worry yourself any further. Stop the brain working. I shall not require your services. I have found the solution. It came on me like a flash.'

'Indeed, sir?'

'Just like a flash. In a matter of this kind, Jeeves, the first thing to do is to study – what's the word I want?'

'I could not say, sir.'

'Quite a common word – though long.'

'Psychology, sir?'

'The exact noun. It is a noun?'

'Yes, sir.'

'Spoken like a man! Well, Jeeves, direct your attention to the psychology of old Sippy. Mr Sipperley, if you follow me, is in the position of a man from whose eyes the scales have not fallen. The task that faced me, Jeeves, was to discover some scheme which would cause those scales to fall. You get me?'

'Not entirely, sir.'

'Well, what I'm driving at is this. At present this head master bloke, this Waterbury, is tramping all over Mr Sipperley because he is hedged about with dignity, if you understand what I mean. Years have passed; Mr Sipperley now shaves daily and is in an important editorial position; but he can never forget that this bird once gave him six of the juiciest. Result: an inferiority complex. The only way to remove that complex, Jeeves, is to arrange that Mr Sipperley shall see this Waterbury in a thoroughly undignified position. This done, the scales will fall from his eyes. You must see that for yourself, Jeeves. Take your own case. No doubt there are a number of your friends and relations who look up to you and respect you greatly. But suppose one night they were to see you, in an advanced state of intoxication, dancing the Charleston in your underwear in the middle of Piccadilly Circus?'

'The contingency is remote, sir.'

'Ah, but suppose they did. The scales would fall from their eyes, what?'

'Very possibly, sir.'

'Take another case. Do you remember a year or so ago the occasion when my Aunt Agatha accused the maid at that French hotel of pinching her pearls, only to discover that they were still in her drawer?'

'Yes, sir.'

'Whereupon she looked the most priceless ass. You'll admit that.'

'Certainly I have seen Mrs Spenser Gregson appear to greater advantage than at that moment, sir.'

'Exactly. Now follow me like a leopard. Observing my Aunt Agatha in her downfall; watching her turn bright mauve and listening to her being told off in liquid French by a whiskered hotel proprietor without coming back with so much as a single lift of the eyebrows, I felt as if the scales had fallen from my eyes. For the first time in my life, Jeeves, the awe with which this woman had inspired me from childhood's days left me. It came back later, I'll admit; but at the moment I saw my Aunt Agatha for what she was – not, as I had long imagined, a sort of man-eating fish at the very mention of whose name strong men quivered like aspens, but a poor goop who had just dropped a very serious brick. At that moment, Jeeves, I could have told her precisely where she got off; and only a too chivalrous regard for the sex kept me from doing so. You won't dispute that?'

'No, sir.'

'Well, then, my firm conviction is that the scales will fall from Mr Sipperley's eyes when he sees this Waterbury, this old head master, stagger into his office covered from head to foot with flour.'

'Flour, sir?'

'Flour, Jeeves.'

'But why should he pursue such a course, sir?'

'Because he won't be able to help it. The stuff will be balanced on top of the door, and the force of gravity will do the rest. I propose to set a booby-trap for this Waterbury, Jeeves.'

'Really, sir, I would scarcely advocate—'

I raised my hand.

'Peace, Jeeves! There is more to come. You have not forgotten that Mr Sipperley loves Miss Gwendolen Moon, but fears to speak. I bet you'd forgotten that.'

'No, sir.'

'Well, then, my belief is that, once he finds he has lost his awe of this Waterbury, he will be so supremely braced that there will be no holding him. He will rush right off and bung his heart at her feet, Jeeves.'

'Well, sir—'

'Jeeves,' I said, a little severely, 'whenever I suggest a plan or scheme or course of action, you are too apt to say "Well, sir," in a nasty tone of voice. I do not like it, and it is a habit you should check. The plan or scheme or course of action which I have outlined contains no flaw. If it does, I should like to hear it.'

'Well, sir—'

'Jeeves!'

'I beg your pardon, sir. I was about to remark that, in my opinion, you are approaching Mr Sipperley's problems in the wrong order.'

'How do you mean; the wrong order?'

'Well, I fancy sir, that better results would be obtained by first inducing Mr Sipperley to offer marriage to Miss Moon. In the event of the young lady proving agreeable, I think that Mr Sipperley would be in such an elevated frame of mind that he would have no difficulty in asserting himself with Mr Waterbury.'

'Ah, but you are then stymied by the question – How is he to be induced?'

'It had occurred to me, sir, that, as Miss Moon is a poetess and of a romantic nature, it might have weight with her if she heard that Mr Sipperley had met with a serious injury and was mentioning her name.'

'Calling for her brokenly, you mean?'

'Calling for her, as you say, sir, brokenly.'

I sat up in bed, and pointed at him rather coldly with the teaspoon.

'Jeeves,' I said, 'I would be the last man to accuse you of dithering, but this is not like you. It is not the old form, Jeeves. You are losing your grip. It might be years before Mr Sipperley had a serious injury.'

'There is that to be considered, sir.'

'I cannot believe that it is you, Jeeves, who are meekly suggesting that we should suspend all activities in this matter year after year, on the chance that some day Mr Sipperley may fall under a truck or something. No! The programme will be as I have sketched it out, Jeeves. After breakfast, kindly step out, and purchase about a pound and a half of the best flour. The rest you may leave to me.'

'Very good, sir.'

The first thing you need in matters of this kind, as every general knows, is a thorough knowledge of the terrain. Not know the terrain, and where are you? Look at Napoleon and that sunken road at Waterloo. Silly ass!

I had a thorough knowledge of the terrain of Sippy's office, and it ran as follows. I won't draw a plan, because my experience is that, when you're reading one of those detective stories and come to the bit where the author draws a plan of the Manor, showing room where body was found, stairs leading to passageway, and all the rest of it, one just skips. I'll simply explain in a few brief words.

The offices of *The Mayfair Gazette* were on the first floor of a mouldy old building off Covent Garden. You went in at a front door and ahead of you was a passage leading to the premises of Bellamy Bros, dealers in seeds and garden produce. Ignoring the Bros Bellamy, you proceeded upstairs and found two doors opposite you. One, marked Private, opened into Sippy's editorial sanctum. The other – sub-title: Inquiries – shot you into a small room where an office-boy sat, eating peppermints and reading the adventures of Tarzan. If you got past the office-boy, you went through another door and there you were in Sippy's room, just as if you had nipped through the door marked Private. Perfectly simple.

It was over the door marked Inquiries that I proposed to suspend the flour.

Now, setting a booby-trap for a respectable citizen like a head master (even of an inferior school to your own) is not a matter to be approached lightly and without careful preparation. I don't suppose I've ever selected a lunch with more thought than I did that day. And after a nicely-balanced meal, preceded by a couple of dry Martinis, washed down with half a bot. of a nice light, dry champagne, and followed by a spot of brandy, I could have set a booby-trap for a bishop.

The only really difficult part of the campaign was to get rid of the office-boy; for naturally you don't want witnesses when you're shoving bags of flour on doors. Fortunately, every man has his price, and it wasn't long before I contrived to persuade the lad that there was sickness at home and he was needed at Cricklewood. This done, I mounted a chair and got to work.

It was many, many years since I had tackled this kind of job, but the old skill came back as good as ever. Having got the bag so nicely poised that a touch on the door would do all that was necessary, I skipped down from my chair, popped off through Sippy's room, and went into the street. Sippy had not shown up yet, which was all to the good, but I knew he usually trickled in at about five to three. I hung about in the street, and presently round the corner came the bloke Waterbury. He went in at the front door, and I started off for a short stroll. It was no part of my policy to be in the offing when things began to happen.

It seemed to me that, allowing for wind and weather, the scales should have fallen from old Sippy's eyes by about three-fifteen, Greenwich mean time; so, having prowled around Covent Garden among the spuds and cabbages for twenty minutes or so, I retraced my steps and pushed up the stairs. I went in at the door marked Private, fully expecting to see old Sippy, and conceive of my astonishment and chagrin when I found on entering only the bloke Waterbury. He was seated at Sippy's desk, reading a paper, as if the place belonged to him.

And, moreover, there was of flour on his person not a trace.

'Great Scott!' I said.

It was a case of the sunken road, after all. But, dash it, how could I have been expected to take into consideration the possibility that this cove, head master though he was, would have had the cold nerve to walk into Sippy's private office instead of pushing in a normal and orderly manner through the public door?

He raised the nose, and focused me over it.

'Yes?'

'I was looking for old Sippy.'

'Mr Sipperley has not yet arrived.'

He spoke with a good deal of pique, seeming to be a man who was not used to being kept waiting.

'Well, how is everything?' I said, to ease things along.

He started reading again. He looked up as if he found me pretty superfluous.

'I beg your pardon?'

'Oh, nothing.'

'You spoke.'

'I only said "How is everything?" don't you know.'

'How is what?'

'Everything.'

'I fail to understand you.'

'Let it go,' I said.

I found a certain difficulty in boosting along the chit-chat. He was not a responsive cove.

'Nice day,' I said.

'Quite.'

'But they say the crops need rain.'

He had buried himself in his paper once more, and seemed peeved this time on being lugged to the surface.

'What?'

'The crops.'

'The crops?'

'Crops.'

'What crops?'

'Oh, just crops.'

He laid down his paper.

'You appear to be desirous of giving me some information about crops. What is it?'

'I hear they need rain.'

'Indeed?'

That concluded the small-talk. He went on reading, and I found a chair and sat down and sucked the handle of my stick. And so the long day wore on.

It may have been some two hours later, or it may have been about five minutes, when there became audible in the passage outside a strange wailing sound, as of some creature in pain. The bloke Waterbury looked up. I looked up.

The wailing came closer. It came into the room. It was Sippy, singing.

'—I love you. That's all that I can say. I love you, I lo-o-ve you. The same old—'

He suspended the chant, not too soon for me.

'Oh, hullo!' he said.

I was amazed. The last time I had seen old Sippy, you must remember, he had had all the appearance of a man who didn't know it was loaded. Haggard. Drawn face. Circles under the eyes. All that sort of thing. And now, not much more than twenty-four hours later, he was simply radiant. His eyes sparkled. His mobile lips were curved in a happy smile. He looked as if he had been taking as much as will cover a sixpence every morning before breakfast for years.

'Hullo, Bertie!' he said. 'Hullo, Waterbury old man! Sorry I'm late.'

The bloke Waterbury seemed by no means pleased at this cordial form of address. He froze visibly.

'You are exceedingly late. I may mention that I have been waiting for upwards of half an hour, and my time is not without its value.'

'Sorry, sorry, sorry, sorry, sorry,' said Sippy, jovially. 'You wanted to see me about that article on the Elizabethan dramatists you left here yesterday, didn't you? Well, I've read it, and I'm sorry to say, Waterbury, my dear chap, that it's N.G.'

'I beg your pardon?'

'No earthly use to us. Quite the wrong sort of stuff. This paper is supposed to be all light Society interest. What the *débutante* will wear for Goodwood, you know, and I saw Lady Betty Bootle in the Park yesterday – she is, of course, the sister-in-law of the Duchess of Peebles, "Cuckoo" to her intimates – all that kind of rot. My readers don't want stuff about Elizabethan dramatists.'

'Sipperley—!'

Old Sippy reached out and patted him in a paternal manner on the back.

'Now listen, Waterbury,' he said, kindly. 'You know as well as I do that I hate to turn down an old pal. But I have my duty to the paper. Still, don't be discouraged. Keep trying, and you'll do fine. There is a lot of promise in your stuff, but you want to study your market. Keep your eyes open and see what editors need. Now, just as a suggestion, why not have a dash at a light, breezy article on pet dogs. You've probably noticed that the pug, once so fashionable, has been superseded by the Peke, the griffon, and the Sealyham. Work on that line and—'

The bloke Waterbury navigated towards the door.

'I have no desire to work on that line, as you put it,' he said, stiffly. 'If you do not require my paper on the Elizabethan dramatists I shall no doubt be able to find another editor whose tastes are more in accord with my work.'

'The right spirit absolutely, Waterbury,' said Sippy, cordially. 'Never give in. Perseverance brings home the gravy. If you get an article accepted, send another article to that editor. If you get an article refused, send that article to another editor. Carry on, Waterbury. I shall watch your future progress with considerable interest.'

'Thank you,' said the bloke Waterbury, bitterly. 'This expert advice should prove most useful.'

He biffed off, banging the door behind him, and I turned to Sippy, who was swerving about the room like an exuberant snipe.

'Sippy—'

'Eh? What? Can't stop, Bertie, can't stop. Only looked in to tell you the news. I'm taking Gwendolen to tea at the Carlton. I'm the happiest man in the world, Bertie. Engaged, you know. Betrothed. All washed up and signed on the dotted line. Wedding, June the first, at eleven a.m. sharp, at St Peter's, Eaton Square. Presents should be delivered before the end of May.'

'But, Sippy! Come to roost for a second. How did this happen? I thought—'

'Well, it's a long story. Much too long to tell you now. Ask Jeeves. He came along with me, and is waiting outside. But when I found her bending over me, weeping, I knew that a word from me was all that was needed. I took her little hand in mine and—'

'What do you mean, bending over you? Where?'

'In your sitting-room.'

'Why?'

'Why what?'

'Why was she bending over you?'

'Because I was on the floor, ass. Naturally a girl would bend over a fellow who was on the floor. Good-bye, Bertie. I must rush.'

He was out of the room before I knew he had started. I followed at a high rate of speed, but he was down the stairs before I reached the passage. I legged it after him, but when I got into the street it was empty.

No, not absolutely empty. Jeeves was standing on the pavement, gazing dreamily at a brussels sprout which lay in the fairway.

'Mr Sipperley has this moment gone, sir,' he said, as I came charging out.

I halted and mopped the brow.

'Jeeves,' I said, 'what has been happening?'

'As far as Mr Sipperley's romance is concerned, sir, all, I am happy to report, is well. He and Miss Moon have arrived at a satisfactory settlement.'

'I know. They're engaged. But how did it happen?'

'I took the liberty of telephoning to Mr Sipperley in your name, asking him to come immediately to the flat, sir.'

'Oh, that's how he came to be at the flat? Well?'

'I then took the liberty of telephoning to Miss Moon and

informing her that Mr Sipperley had met with a nasty accident. As I anticipated, the young lady was strongly moved and announced her intention of coming to see Mr Sipperley immediately. When she arrived, it required only a few moments to arrange the matter. It seems that Miss Moon has long loved Mr Sipperley, sir, and—'

'I should have thought that, when she turned up and found he hadn't had a nasty accident, she would have been thoroughly pipped at being fooled.'

'Mr Sipperley had had a nasty accident, sir.'

'He had?'

'Yes, sir.'

'Rummy coincidence. I mean, after what you were saying this morning.'

'Not altogether, sir. Before telephoning to Miss Moon, I took the further liberty of striking Mr Sipperley a sharp blow on the head with one of your golf-clubs, which was fortunately lying in a corner of the room. The putter, I believe, sir. If you recollect, you were practising with it this morning before you left.'

I gaped at the blighter. I had always known Jeeves for a man of infinite sagacity, sound beyond belief on any question of ties or spats; but never before had I suspected him capable of strong-arm work like this. It seemed to open up an entirely new aspect of the fellow. I can't put it better than by saying that, as I gazed at him, the scales seemed to fall from my eyes.

'Good heavens, Jeeves!'

'I did it with the utmost regret, sir. It appeared to me the only course.'

'But look here, Jeeves. I don't get this. Wasn't Mr Sipperley pretty shirty when he came to and found that you had been soaking him with putters?'

'He was not aware that I had done so, sir. I took the precaution of waiting until his back was momentarily turned.'

'But how did you explain the bump on his head?'

'I informed him that your new vase had fallen on him, sir.'

'Why on earth would he believe that? The vase would have been smashed.'

'The vase was smashed, sir.'

'What!'

'In order to achieve verisimilitude, I was reluctantly compelled to break it, sir. And in my excitement, sir, I am sorry to say I broke it beyond repair.'

I drew myself up.

'Jeeves!' I said.

'Pardon me, sir, but would it not be wiser to wear a hat? There is a keen wind.'

I blinked.

'Aren't I wearing a hat?'

'No, sir.'

I put up a hand and felt the lemon. He was perfectly right.

'Nor I am! I must have left it in Sippy's office. Wait here, Jeeves, while I fetch it.'

'Very good, sir.'

'I have much to say to you.'

'Thank you, sir.'

I galloped up the stairs and dashed in at the door. And something squashy fell on my neck, and the next minute the whole world was a solid mass of flour. In the agitation of the moment I had gone in at the wrong door; and what it all boils down to is that, if any more of my pals get inferiority complexes, they can jolly well get rid of them for themselves. Bertram is through.

The letter arrived on the morning of the sixteenth. I was pushing a bit of breakfast into the Wooster face at the moment and, feeling fairly well-fortified with coffee and kippers, I decided to break the news to Jeeves without delay. As Shakespeare says, if you're going to do a thing you might just as well pop right at it and get it over. The man would be disappointed, of course, and possibly even chagrined: but, dash it all, a splash of disappointment here and there does a fellow good. Makes him realize that life is stern and life is earnest.

'Oh, Jeeves,' I said.

'Sir?'

'We have here a communication from Lady Wickham. She has written inviting me to Skeldings for the festives. So you will see about bunging the necessaries together. We repair thither on the twenty-third. Plenty of white ties, Jeeves, also a few hearty country suits for use in the daytime. We shall be there some little time, I expect.'

There was a pause. I could feel he was directing a frosty gaze at me, but I dug into the marmalade and refused to meet it.

'I thought I understood you to say, sir, that you proposed to visit Monte Carlo immediately after Christmas.'

'I know. But that's all off. Plans changed.'

'Very good, sir.'

At this point the telephone bell rang, tiding over very nicely what had threatened to be an awkward moment. Jeeves unhooked the receiver.

'Yes?... Yes, madam... Very good, madam. Here is Mr Wooster.' He handed me the instrument. 'Mrs Spenser Gregson, sir.'

You know, every now and then I can't help feeling that Jeeves is losing his grip. In his prime it would have been with him the work of a moment to have told Aunt Agatha that I was not at home. I gave him one of those reproachful glances, and took the machine.

'Hullo?' I said. 'Yes? Hullo? Hullo? Bertie speaking. Hullo? Hullo? Hullo?'

'Don't keep on saying Hullo,' yipped the old relative in her customary curt manner. 'You're not a parrot. Sometimes I wish you were, because then you might have a little sense.'

Quite the wrong sort of tone to adopt towards a fellow in the early morning, of course, but what can one do?

'Bertie, Lady Wickham tells me she has invited you to Skeldings for Christmas. Are you going?'

'Rather!'

'Well, mind you behave yourself. Lady Wickham is an old friend of mine.'

I was in no mood for this sort of thing over the telephone. Face to face, I'm not saying, but at the end of a wire, no.

'I shall naturally endeavour, Aunt Agatha,' I replied stiffly, 'to conduct myself in a manner befitting an English gentleman paying a visit—'

'What did you say? Speak up. I can't hear.'

'I said Right-ho.'

'Oh? Well, mind you do. And there's another reason why I particularly wish you to be as little of an imbecile as you can manage while at Skeldings. Sir Roderick Glossop will be there.'

'What!'

'Don't bellow like that. You nearly deafened me.'

'Did you say Sir Roderick Glossop?'

'I did.'

'You don't mean Tuppy Glossop?'

'I mean Sir Roderick Glossop. Which was my reason for saying Sir Roderick Glossop. Now, Bertie, I want you to listen to me attentively. Are you there?'

'Yes. Still here.'

'Well, then, listen. I have at last succeeded, after incredible difficulty, and in face of all the evidence, in almost persuading Sir Roderick that you are not actually insane. He is prepared to suspend judgement until he has seen you once more. On your behaviour at Skeldings, therefore——'

But I had hung up the receiver. Shaken. That's what I was. S. to the core.

Stop me if I've told you this before: but, in case you don't know, let me just mention the facts in the matter of this Glossop. He was a formidable old bird with a bald head and out-size eyebrows, by profession a loony-doctor. How it happened, I couldn't tell you to this day, but I once got engaged to his daughter, Honoria, a ghastly dynamic exhibit who read Nietzsche and had a laugh like waves breaking on a stern and rock-bound coast. The fixture was scratched owing to events occurring which convinced the old boy that I was off my napper; and since then he has always had my name at the top of his list of 'Loonies I have Lunched With'.

It seemed to me that even at Christmas time, with all the

peace on earth and goodwill towards men that there is knocking about at that season, a reunion with this bloke was likely to be tough going. If I hadn't had more than one particularly good reason for wanting to go to Skeldings, I'd have called the thing off.

'Jeeves,' I said, all of a twitter, 'do you know what? Sir Roderick Glossop is going to be at Lady Wickham's.'

'Very good, sir. If you have finished breakfast, I will clear away.'

Cold and haughty. No symp. None of the rallying-round spirit which one likes to see. As I had anticipated, the information that we were not going to Monte Carlo had got in amongst him. There is a keen sporting streak in Jeeves, and I knew he had been looking forward to a little flutter at the tables.

We Woosters can wear the mask. I ignored his lack of decent feeling.

'Do so, Jeeves,' I said proudly, 'and with all convenient speed.'

Relations continued pretty fairly strained all through the rest of the week. There was a frigid detachment in the way the man brought me my dollop of tea in the mornings. Going down to Skeldings in the car on the afternoon of the twenty-third, he was aloof and reserved. And before dinner on the first night of my visit he put the studs in my dress-shirt in what I can only call a marked manner. The whole thing was extremely painful, and it seemed to me, as I lay in bed on the morning of the twenty-fourth, that the only step to take was to put the whole facts of the case before him and trust to his native good sense to effect an understanding.

I was feeling considerably in the pink that morning. Everything had gone like a breeze. My hostess, Lady Wickham, was a beaky female built far too closely on the lines of my Aunt Agatha for comfort, but she had seemed matey enough on my arrival. Her daughter, Roberta, had welcomed me with a warmth which, I'm bound to say, had set the old heart-strings fluttering a bit. And Sir Roderick, in the brief moment we had had together, appeared to have let the Yule Tide Spirit soak into him to the most amazing extent. When he saw me, his mouth sort of flickered at one corner, which I took to be his idea of smiling, and he said 'Ha, young man!' Not particularly chummily, but he said it: and my view was that it practically amounted to the lion lying down with the lamb.

So, all in all, life at this juncture seemed pretty well all to the mustard, and I decided to tell Jeeves exactly how matters stood.

'Jeeves,' I said, as he appeared with the steaming.

'Sir?'

'Touching on this business of our being here, I would like to say a few words of explanation. I consider that you have a right to the facts.'

'Sir?'

'I'm afraid scratching that Monte Carlo trip has been a bit of a jar for you, Jeeves.'

'Not at all, sir.'

'Oh, yes, it has. The heart was set on wintering in the world's good old Plague Spot, I know. I saw your eye light up when I said we were due for a visit there. You snorted a bit and your fingers twitched. I know, I know. And now that there has been a change of programme the iron has entered into your soul.'

'Not at all, sir.'

'Oh, yes, it has. I've seen it. Very well, then, what I wish to impress upon you, Jeeves, is that I have not been actuated in this matter by any mere idle whim. It was through no light and airy caprice that I accepted this invitation to Lady Wickham's. I have been angling for it for weeks, prompted by many considerations. In the first place, does one get the Yule-tide spirit at a spot like Monte Carlo?'

'Does one desire the Yule-tide spirit, sir?'

'Certainly one does. I am all for it. Well, that's one thing. Now here's another. It was imperative that I should come to Skeldings for Christmas, Jeeves, because I knew that young Tuppy Glossop was going to be here.'

'Sir Roderick Glossop, sir?'

'His nephew. You may have observed hanging about the place a fellow with light hair and a Cheshire-cat grin. That is Tuppy, and I have been anxious for some time to get to grips with him. I have it in for that man of wrath. Listen to the facts, Jeeves, and tell me if I am not justified in planning a hideous vengeance.' I took a sip of tea, for the mere memory of my wrongs had shaken me. 'In spite of the fact that young Tuppy is the nephew of Sir Roderick Glossop, at whose hands, Jeeves, as you are aware, I have suffered much, I fraternized with him freely, both at the Drones Club and elsewhere. I said to myself that a man is not to be blamed for his relations, and that I would hate to have my pals hold my Aunt Agatha, for instance, against me. Broad-minded, Jeeves, I think?'

'Extremely, sir.'

'Well, then, as I say, I sought this Tuppy out, Jeeves, and hobnobbed, and what do you think he did?'

'I could not say, sir.'

'I will tell you. One night after dinner at the Drones he betted me I wouldn't swing myself across the swimming-bath by the ropes and rings. I took him on and was buzzing along in great style until I came to the last ring. And then I found that this fiend in human shape had looped it back against the rail, thus leaving me hanging in the void with no means of getting ashore to my home and loved ones. There was nothing for it but to drop into the water. He told me that he had often caught fellows that way: and what I maintain, Jeeves, is that, if I can't get back at him somehow at Skeldings – with all the vast resources which a country-house affords at my disposal – I am not the man I was.'

'I see, sir.'

There was still something in his manner which told me that even now he lacked complete sympathy and understanding, so, delicate though the subject was, I decided to put all my cards on the table.

'And now, Jeeves, we come to the most important reason why I had to spend Christmas at Skeldings. Jeeves,' I said, diving into the old cup once more for a moment and bringing myself out wreathed in blushes, 'the fact of the matter is, I'm in love.'

'Indeed, sir?'

'You've seen Miss Roberta Wickham?'

'Yes, sir.'

'Very well, then.'

There was a pause, while I let it sink in.

'During your stay here, Jeeves,' I said, 'you will, no doubt, be thrown a good deal together with Miss Wickham's maid. On such occasions, pitch it strong.'

'Sir?'

'You know what I mean. Tell her I'm rather a good chap. Mention my hidden depths. These things get round. Dwell on the fact that I have a kind heart and was runner-up in the Squash Handicap at the Drones this year. A boost is never wasted, Jeeves.'

'Very good, sir. But—'

'But what?'

'Well, sir—'

'I wish you wouldn't say "Well, sir" in that soupy tone of voice. I have had to speak of this before. The habit is one that is growing upon you. Check it. What's on your mind?'

'I hardly like to take the liberty—'

'Carry on, Jeeves. We are always glad to hear from you, always.'

'What I was about to remark, if you will excuse me, sir, was that I would scarcely have thought Miss Wickham a suitable—'

'Jeeves,' I said coldly, 'if you have anything to say against that lady, it had better not be said in my presence.'

'Very good, sir.'

'Or anywhere else, for that matter. What is your kick against Miss Wickham?'

'Oh, really, sir!'

'Jeeves, I insist. This is a time for plain speaking. You have beefed about Miss Wickham. I wish to know why.'

'It merely crossed my mind, sir, that for a gentleman of your description Miss Wickham is not a suitable mate.'

'What do you mean by a gentleman of my description?'

'Well, sir—'

'Jeeves!'

'I beg your pardon, sir. The expression escaped me inadvertently. I was about to observe that I can only asseverate—'

'Only what?'

'I can only say that, as you have invited my opinion—'

'But I didn't.'

'I was under the impression that you desired to canvass my views on the matter, sir.'

'Oh? Well, let's have them, anyway.'

'Very good, sir. Then briefly, if I may say so, sir, though Miss Wickham is a charming young lady—'

'There, Jeeves, you spoke an imperial quart. What eyes!'

'Yes, sir.'

'What hair!'

'Very true, sir.'

'And what *espièglerie*, if that's the word I want.'

'The exact word, sir.'

'All right, then. Carry on.'

'I grant Miss Wickham the possession of all these desirable qualities, sir. Nevertheless, considered as a matrimonial prospect for a gentleman of your description, I cannot look upon her as suitable. In my opinion Miss Wickham lacks seriousness, sir. She is too volatile and frivolous. To qualify as Miss Wickham's husband, a gentleman would need to possess a commanding personality and considerable strength of character.'

'Exactly!'

'I would always hesitate to recommend as a life's companion a young lady with quite such a vivid shade of red hair. Red hair, sir, in my opinion, is dangerous.'

I eyed the blighter squarely.

'Jeeves,' I said, 'you're talking rot.'

'Very good, sir.'

'Absolute drivel.'

'Very good, sir.'

'Pure mashed potatoes.'

'Very good, sir.'

'Very good, sir – I mean very good Jeeves, that will be all,' I said.

And I drank a modicum of tea, with a good deal of hauteur.

* * *

It isn't often that I find myself able to prove Jeeves in the wrong, but by dinner-time that night I was in a position to do so, and I did it without delay.

'Touching on that matter we were touching on, Jeeves,' I said, coming in from the bath and tackling him as he studied the shirt, 'I should be glad if you would give me your careful attention for a moment. I warn you that what I am about to say is going to make you look pretty silly.'

'Indeed, sir?'

'Yes, Jeeves. Pretty dashed silly it's going to make you look. It may lead you to be rather more careful in future about broadcasting these estimates of yours of people's characters. This morning, if I remember rightly, you stated that Miss Wickham was volatile, frivolous and lacking in seriousness. Am I correct?'

'Quite correct, sir.'

'Then what I have to tell you may cause you to alter that opinion. I went for a walk with Miss Wickham this afternoon: and, as we walked, I told her about what young Tuppy Glossop did to me in the swimming-bath at the Drones. She hung upon my words, Jeeves, and was full of sympathy.'

'Indeed, sir?'

'Dripping with it. And that's not all. Almost before I had finished, she was suggesting the ripest, fruitiest, brainiest scheme for bringing young Tuppy's grey hairs in sorrow to the grave that anyone could possibly imagine.'

'That is very gratifying, sir.'

'Gratifying is the word. It appears that at the girls' school where Miss Wickham was educated, Jeeves, it used to become necessary from time to time for the right-thinking element of the community to slip it across certain of the baser sort. Do you know what they did, Jeeves?'

'No, sir.'

'They took a long stick, Jeeves, and – follow me closely here – they tied a darning-needle to the end of it. Then at dead of night, it appears, they sneaked privily into the party of the second part's cubicle and shoved the needle through the bed-clothes and punctured her hot-water bottle. Girls are much subtler in these matters than boys, Jeeves. At my old school one would occasionally heave a jug of water over another bloke during the night-watches, but we never thought of effecting the same result in this particularly neat and scientific manner. Well, Jeeves, that was the scheme which Miss Wickham suggested I should work on young Tuppy, and that is the girl you call frivolous and lacking in seriousness. Any girl who can think up a wheeze like that is my idea of a helpmeet. I shall be glad, Jeeves, if by the time I come to bed to-night you have waiting for me in this room a stout stick with a good sharp darning needle attached.'

'Well, sir—'

I raised my hand.

'Jeeves,' I said. 'Not another word. Stick, one, and needle, darning, good, sharp, one, without fail in this room at eleven-thirty to-night.'

'Very good, sir.'

'Have you any idea where young Tuppy sleeps?'

'I could ascertain, sir.'

'Do so, Jeeves.'

In a few minutes he was back with the necessary informash.

'Mr Glossop is established in the Moat Room, sir.'

'Where's that?'

'The second door on the floor below this, sir.'

'Right ho, Jeeves. Are the studs in my shirt?'

'Yes, sir.'

'And the links also?'

'Yes, sir.'

'Then push me into it.'

The more I thought about this enterprise which a sense of duty and good citizenship had thrust upon me, the better it seemed to me. I am not a vindictive man, but I felt, as anybody would have felt in my place, that if fellows like young Tuppy are allowed to get away with it the whole fabric of Society and Civilization must inevitably crumble. The task to which I had set myself was one that involved hardship and discomfort, for it meant sitting up till well into the small hours and then padding down a cold corridor, but I did not shrink from it. After all, there is a lot to be said for family tradition. We Woosters did our bit in the Crusades.

It being Christmas Eve, there was, as I had foreseen, a good deal of revelry and what not. First, the village choir surged round and sang carols outside the front door, and then somebody suggested a dance, and after that we hung around chatting of this and that, so that it wasn't till past one that I got to my room. Allowing for everything, it didn't seem that it was going to be safe to start my little expedition till half-past two at the earliest: and I'm bound to say that it was only the utmost resolution that kept me from snuggling into the sheets and calling it a day. I'm not much of a lad now for late hours.

However, by half-past two everything appeared to be quiet. I shook off the mists of sleep, grabbed the good old stick-and-needle and toddled off along the corridor. And presently, pausing outside the Moat Room, I turned the handle, found the door wasn't locked, and went in.

I suppose a burglar – I mean a real professional who works at the job six nights a week all the year round – gets so that finding himself standing in the dark in somebody else's bedroom means absolutely nothing to him. But for a bird like me, who has had no previous experience, there's a lot to be said in favour of washing the whole thing out and closing the door gently and popping back to bed again. It was only by summoning up all the old bull-dog courage of the Woosters, and reminding myself that, if I let this opportunity slip another might never occur, that I managed to stick out what you might call the initial minute of the binge. Then the weakness passed, and Bertram was himself again.

At first when I beetled in, the room had seemed as black as a coal-cellar: but after a bit things began to lighten. The curtains weren't quite drawn over the window and I could see a trifle of the scenery here and there. The bed was opposite the window, with the head against the wall and the end where the feet were jutting out towards where I stood, thus rendering it possible after one had sown the seed, so to speak, to make a quick getaway. There only remained now the rather tricky problem of locating the old hot-water bottle. I mean to say, the one thing you can't do if you want to carry a job like this through with secrecy and dispatch is to stand at the end of a fellow's bed, jabbing the blankets at random with a darning-needle. Before proceeding to anything in the nature of definite steps, it is imperative that you locate the bot.

I was a good deal cheered at this juncture to hear a fruity snore from the direction of the pillows. Reason told me that a bloke who could snore like that wasn't going to be awakened by a trifle. I edged forward and ran a hand in a gingerly sort of way over the coverlet. A moment later I had found the bulge.

I steered the good old darning-needle on to it, gripped the stick, and shoved. Then, pulling out the weapon, I sidled towards the door, and in another moment would have been outside, buzzing for home and the good night's rest, when suddenly there was a crash that sent my spine shooting up through the top of my head and the contents of the bed sat up like a jack-in-the-box and said:

'Who's that?'

It just shows how your most careful strategic moves can be the very ones that dish your campaign. In order to facilitate the orderly retreat according to plan I had left the door open, and the beastly thing had slammed like a bomb.

But I wasn't giving much thought to the causes of the explosion, having other things to occupy my mind. What was disturbing me was the discovery that, whoever else the bloke in the bed might be, he was not young Tuppy. Tuppy has one of those high, squeaky voices that sound like the tenor of the village choir failing to hit a high note. This one was something in between the last Trump and a tiger calling for breakfast after being on a diet for a day or two. It was the sort of nasty, rasping voice you hear shouting 'Fore!' when you're one of a slow foursome on the links and are holding up a couple of retired colonels. Among the qualities it lacked were kindliness, suavity and that sort of dove-like cooing note which makes a fellow feel he has found a friend.

I did not linger. Getting swiftly off the mark, I dived for the door-handle and was off and away, banging the door behind me. I may be a chump in many ways, as my Aunt Agatha will freely attest, but I know when and when not to be among those present.

And I was just about to do the stretch of corridor leading to the stairs in a split second under the record time for the course, when something brought me up with a sudden jerk. One moment, I was all dash and fire and speed; the next, an irresistible force had checked me in my stride and was holding me straining at the leash, as it were.

You know, sometimes it seems to me as if Fate were going out of its way to such an extent to snooter you that you wonder if it's worth while continuing to struggle. The night being a trifle chillier than the dickens, I had donned for this expedition a dressing-gown. It was the tail of this infernal garment that had caught in the door and pipped me at the eleventh hour.

The next moment the door had opened, light was streaming through it, and the bloke with the voice had grabbed me by the arm.

It was Sir Roderick Glossop.

The next thing that happened was a bit of a lull in the proceedings. For about three and a quarter seconds or possibly more we just stood there, drinking each other in, so to speak, the old boy still attached with a limpet-like grip to my elbow. If I hadn't been in a dressing-gown and he in pink pyjamas with a blue stripe, and if he hadn't been glaring quite so much as if he were shortly going to commit a murder, the tableau would have looked rather like one of those advertisements you see in the magazines, where the experienced elder is patting the young man's arm, and saying to him, 'My boy, if you subscribe to the Mutt-Jeff Correspondence School of Oswego, Kan., as I did, you may some day, like me, become Third Assistant Vice-President of the Schenectady Consolidated Nail-File and Eyebrow Tweezer Corporation.'

'You!' said Sir Roderick finally. And in this connection I want to state that it's all rot to say you can't hiss a word that hasn't an 's' in it. The way he pushed out that 'You!' sounded like an angry cobra, and I am betraying no secrets when I mention that it did me no good whatsoever.

By rights, I suppose, at this point I ought to have said something. The best I could manage, however, was a faint, soft bleating sound. Even on ordinary social occasions, when meeting this bloke as man to man and with a clear conscience, I could never be completely at my ease: and now those eyebrows seemed to pierce me like a knife.

'Come in here,' he said, lugging me into the room. 'We don't want to wake the whole house. Now,' he said, depositing me on the carpet and closing the door and doing a bit of eyebrow work, 'kindly inform me what is this latest manifestation of insanity?'

It seemed to me that a light and cheery laugh might help the thing along. So I had a pop at one.

'Don't gibber!' said my genial host. And I'm bound to admit that the light and cheery hadn't come out quite as I'd intended.

I pulled myself together with a strong effort.

'Awfully sorry about all this,' I said in a hearty sort of voice. 'The fact is, I thought you were Tuppy.'

'Kindly refrain from inflicting your idiotic slang on me. What do you mean by the adjective "tuppy"?'

'It isn't so much an adjective, don't you know. More of a noun, I should think, if you examine it squarely. What I mean to say is, I thought you were your nephew.'

'You thought I was my nephew? Why should I be my nephew?'

'What I'm driving at is, I thought this was his room.'

'My nephew and I changed rooms. I have a great dislike for sleeping on an upper floor. I am nervous about fire.'

For the first time since this interview had started, I braced up a trifle. The injustice of the whole thing stirred me to such an extent that for a moment I lost that sense of being a toad under the harrow which had been cramping my style up till now. I even went so far as to eye this pink-pyjamaed poltroon with a good deal of contempt and loathing. Just because he had this craven fear of fire and this selfish preference for letting Tuppy be cooked instead of himself should the emergency occur, my nicely-reasoned plans had gone up the spout. I gave him a look, and I think I may even have snorted a bit.

'I should have thought that your man-servant would have informed you,' said Sir Roderick, 'that we contemplated making this change. I met him shortly before luncheon and told him to tell you.'

I reeled. Yes, it is not too much to say that I reeled. This extraordinary statement had taken me amidships without any preparation, and it staggered me. That Jeeves had been aware all along that this old crumb would be the occupant of the bed which I was proposing to prod with darning-needles and had let me rush upon my doom without a word of warning was almost beyond belief. You might say I was aghast. Yes, practically aghast.

'You told Jeeves that you were going to sleep in this room?' I gasped.

'I did. I was aware that you and my nephew were on terms of intimacy, and I wished to spare myself the possibility of a visit from you. I confess that it never occurred to me that such a visit was to be anticipated at three o'clock in the morning. What the devil do you mean,' he barked, suddenly hotting up, 'by prowling about the house at this hour? And what is that thing in your hand?'

I looked down, and found that I was still grasping the stick. I give you my honest word that, what with the maelstrom of emotions into which his revelation about Jeeves had cast me, the discovery came as an absolute surprise.

'This?' I said. 'Oh, yes.'

'What do you mean, "Oh, yes"? What is it?'

'Well, it's a long story—'

'We have the night before us.'

'It's this way. I will ask you to picture me some weeks ago, perfectly peaceful and inoffensive, after dinner at the Drones, smoking a thoughtful cigarette and—'

I broke off. The man wasn't listening. He was goggling in a rapt sort of way at the end of the bed, from which there had now begun to drip on to the carpet a series of drops.

'Good heavens!'

'—thoughtful cigarette and chatting pleasantly of this and that—'

I broke off again. He had lifted the sheets and was gazing at the corpse of the hot-water bottle.

'Did you do this?' he said in a low, strangled sort of voice.

'Er – yes. As a matter of fact, yes. I was just going to tell you—'

'And your aunt tried to persuade me that you were not insane!'

'I'm not. Absolutely not. If you'll just let me explain.'

'I will do nothing of the kind.'

'It all began—'

'Silence!'

'Right-ho.'

He did some deep-breathing exercises through the nose.

'My bed is drenched!'

'The way it all began—'

'Be quiet!' He heaved somewhat for awhile. 'You wretched, miserable idiot,' he said, 'kindly inform me which bedroom you are supposed to be occupying?'

'It's on the floor above. The Clock Room.'

'Thank you. I will find it.'

He gave me the eyebrow.

'I propose,' he said, 'to pass the remainder of the night in your room, where, I presume, there is a bed in a condition to be slept in. You may bestow yourself as comfortably as you can here. I will wish you good-night.'

He buzzed off, leaving me flat.

Well, we Woosters are old campaigners. We can take the rough with the smooth. But to say that I liked the prospect now before me would be paltering with the truth. One glance at the bed told me that any idea of sleeping there was out. A goldfish could have done it, but not Bertram. After a bit of a look round, I decided that the best chance of getting a sort of night's rest was to doss as well as I could in the arm-chair. I pinched a couple of pillows off the bed, shoved the hearth-rug over my knees, and sat down and started counting sheep.

But it wasn't any good. The old lemon was sizzling much too much to admit of anything in the nature of slumber. This hideous revelation of the blackness of Jeeves's treachery kept coming back to me every time I nearly succeeded in dropping off: and, what's more, it seemed to get colder and colder as the long night wore on. I was just wondering if I would ever get to sleep again in this world when a voice at my elbow said 'Good-morning, sir,' and I sat up with a jerk.

I could have sworn I hadn't so much as dozed off for even a

minute, but apparently I had. For the curtains were drawn back and daylight was coming in through the window and there was Jeeves standing beside me with a cup of tea on a tray.

'Merry Christmas, sir!'

I reached out a feeble hand for the restoring brew. I swallowed a mouthful or two, and felt a little better. I was aching in every limb and the dome felt like lead, but I was now able to think with a certain amount of clearness, and I fixed the man with a stony eye and prepared to let him have it.

'You think so, do you?' I said. 'Much, let me tell you, depends on what you mean by the adjective "merry". If, moreover, you suppose that it is going to be merry for you, correct that impression. Jeeves,' I said, taking another half-oz of tea and speaking in a cold, measured voice, 'I wish to ask you one question. Did you or did you not know that Sir Roderick Glossop was sleeping in this room last night?'

'Yes, sir.'

'You admit it!'

'Yes, sir.'

'And you didn't tell me!'

'No, sir. I thought it would be more judicious not to do so.'

'Jeeves—'

'If you will allow me to explain, sir.'

'Explain!'

'I was aware that my silence might lead to something in the nature of an embarrassing contretemps, sir—'

'You thought that, did you?'

'Yes, sir.'

'You were a good guesser,' I said, sucking down further Bohea.

'But it seemed to me, sir, that whatever might occur was all for the best.'

I would have put in a crisp word or two here, but he carried on without giving me the opp.

'I thought that possibly, on reflection, sir, your views being what they are, you would prefer your relations with Sir Roderick Glossop and his family to be distant rather than cordial.'

'My views? What do you mean, my views?'

'As regards a matrimonial alliance with Miss Honoria Glossop, sir.'

Something like an electric shock seemed to zip through me. The man had opened up a new line of thought. I suddenly saw what he was driving at, and realized all in a flash that I had been wronging this faithful fellow. All the while I supposed he had been landing me in the soup, he had really been steering me away from it. It was like those stories one used to read as a kid about the traveller going along on a dark night and his dog grabs him by the leg of his trousers and he says 'Down, sir! What are you doing, Rover?' and the dog hangs on and he gets rather hot under the collar and curses a bit but the dog won't let him go and then suddenly the moon shines through the clouds and he finds he's been standing on the edge of a precipice and one more step would have— well, anyway, you get the idea: and what I'm driving at is that much the same sort of thing seemed to have been happening now.

It's perfectly amazing how a fellow will let himself get off his guard and ignore the perils which surround him. I give you my honest word, it had never struck me till this moment that my Aunt Agatha had been scheming to get me in right with Sir Roderick so that I should eventually be received back into the fold, if you see what I mean, and subsequently pushed off on Honoria.

'My God, Jeeves!' I said, paling.

'Precisely, sir.'

'You think there was a risk?'

'I do, sir. A very grave risk.'

A disturbing thought struck me.

'But, Jeeves, on calm reflection won't Sir Roderick have gathered by now that my objective was young Tuppy and that puncturing his hot-water bottle was just one of those things that occur when the Yule-tide spirit is abroad – one of those things that have to be overlooked and taken with the indulgent smile and the fatherly shake of the head? I mean to say, Young Blood and all that sort of thing? What I mean is he'll realize that I wasn't trying to snooter him, and then all the good work will have been wasted.'

'No, sir. I fancy not. That might possibly have been Sir Roderick's mental reaction, had it not been for the second incident.'

'The second incident?'

'During the night, sir, while Sir Roderick was occupying your bed, somebody entered the room, pierced his hot-water bottle with some sharp instrument, and vanished in the darkness.'

I could make nothing of this.

'What! Do you think I walked in my sleep?'

'No, sir. It was young Mr Glossop who did it. I encountered him this morning, sir, shortly before I came here. He was in cheerful spirits and enquired of me how you were feeling about the incident. Not being aware that his victim had been Sir Roderick.'

'But, Jeeves, what an amazing coincidence!'

'Sir?'

'Why, young Tuppy getting exactly the same idea as I did. Or, rather, as Miss Wickham did. You can't say that's not rummy. A miracle, I call it.'

'Not altogether, sir. It appears that he received the suggestion from the young lady.'

'From Miss Wickham?'

'Yes, sir.'

'You mean to say that, after she had put me up to the scheme of puncturing Tuppy's hot-water bottle, she went away and tipped Tuppy off to puncturing mine?'

'Precisely, sir. She is a young lady with a keen sense of humour, sir.'

I sat there, you might say stunned. When I thought how near I had come to offering the heart and hand to a girl capable of double-crossing a strong man's honest love like that, I shivered.

'Are you cold, sir?'

'No, Jeeves. Just shuddering.'

'The occurrence, if I may take the liberty of saying so, sir, will perhaps lend colour to the view which I put forward yesterday that Miss Wickham, though in many respects a charming young lady—'

I raised the hand.

'Say no more, Jeeves,' I replied. 'Love is dead.'

'Very good, sir.'

I brooded for a while.

'You've seen Sir Roderick this morning, then?'

'Yes, sir.'

'How did he seem?'

'A trifle feverish, sir.'

'Feverish?'

'A little emotional, sir. He expressed a strong desire to meet you, sir.'

'What would you advise?'

'If you were to slip out by the back entrance as soon as you are dressed, sir, it would be possible for you to make your way across the field without being observed and reach the village, where you could hire an automobile to take you to London. I could bring on your effects later in your own car.'

'But London, Jeeves? Is any man safe? My Aunt Agatha is in London.'

'Yes, sir.'

'Well, then?'

He regarded me for a moment with a fathomless eye.

'I think the best plan, sir, would be for you to leave England, which is not pleasant at this time of the year, for some little while. I would not take the liberty of dictating your movements, sir, but as you already have accommodation engaged on the Blue Train for Monte Carlo for the day after to-morrow—'

'But you cancelled the booking?'

'No, sir.'

'I thought you had.'

'No, sir.'

'I told you to.'

'Yes, sir. It was remiss of me, but the matter slipped my mind.'

'Oh?'

'Yes, sir.'

'All right, Jeeves. Monte Carlo ho, then.'

'Very good, sir.'

'It's lucky, as things have turned out, that you forgot to cancel that booking.'

'Very fortunate indeed, sir. If you will wait here, sir, I will return to your room and procure a suit of clothes.'

Another day had dawned all hot and fresh and, in pursuance of my unswerving policy at that time, I was singing 'Sonny Boy' in my bath, when there was a soft step without and Jeeves's voice came filtering through the woodwork.

'I beg your pardon, sir.'

I had just got to that bit about the Angels being lonely, where you need every ounce of concentration in order to make the spectacular finish, but I signed off courteously.

'Yes, Jeeves? Say on.'

'Mr Glossop, sir.'

'What about him?'

'He is in the sitting-room, sir.'

'Young Tuppy Glossop?'

'Yes, sir.'

'In the sitting-room?'

'Yes, sir.'

'Desiring speech with me?'

'Yes, sir.'

'H'm!'

'Sir?'

'I only said H'm.'

And I'll tell you why I said H'm. It was because the man's

story had interested me strangely. The news that Tuppy was visiting me at my flat, at an hour when he must have known that I would be in my bath and consequently in a strong strategic position to heave a wet sponge at him, surprised me considerably.

I hopped out with some briskness and, slipping a couple of towels about the limbs and torso, made for the sitting-room. I found young Tuppy at the piano, playing 'Sonny Boy' with one finger.

'What ho!' I said, not without a certain hauteur.

'Oh, hullo, Bertie,' said young Tuppy. 'I say, Bertie, I want to see you about something important.'

It seemed to me that the bloke was embarrassed. He had moved to the mantelpiece, and now he broke a vase in rather a constrained way.

'The fact is, Bertie, I'm engaged.'

'Engaged?'

'Engaged,' said young Tuppy, coyly dropping a photograph frame into the fender. 'Practically, that is.'

'Practically?'

'Yes. You'll like her, Bertie. Her name is Cora Bellinger. She's studying for Opera. Wonderful voice she has. Also dark, flashing eyes and a great soul.'

'How do you mean, practically?'

'Well, it's this way. Before ordering the trousseau, there is one little point she wants cleared up. You see, what with her great soul and all that, she has a rather serious outlook on life: and the one thing she absolutely bars is anything in the shape of hearty humour. You know, practical joking and so forth. She said if she thought I was a practical joker she would never speak to me again. And unfortunately she appears to have heard about that little affair at the Drones – I expect you have forgotten all about that, Bertie?'

'I have not!'

'No, no, not forgotten exactly. What I mean is, nobody laughs more heartily at the recollection than you. And what I want you to do, old man, is to seize an early opportunity of taking Cora aside and categorically denying that there is any truth in the story. My happiness, Bertie, is in your hands, if you know what I mean.'

Well, of course, if he put it like that, what could I do? We Woosters have our code.

'Oh, all right,' I said, but far from brightly.

'Splendid fellow!'

'When do I meet this blighted female?'

'Don't call her "this blighted female", Bertie, old man. I have planned all that out. I will bring her round here to-day for a spot of lunch.'

'What!'

'At one-thirty. Right. Good. Fine. Thanks. I knew I could rely on you.'

He pushed off, and I turned to Jeeves, who had shimmered in with the morning meal.

'Lunch for three to-day, Jeeves,' I said.

'Very good, sir.'

'You know, Jeeves, it's a bit thick. You remember my telling you about what Mr Glossop did to me that night at the Drones?'

'Yes, sir.'

'For months I have been cherishing dreams of getting a bit of my own back. And now, so far from crushing him into the dust, I've got to fill him and fiancée with rich food and generally rally round and be the good angel.'

'Life is like that, sir.'

'True, Jeeves. What have we here?' I asked, inspecting the tray.

'Kippered herrings, sir.'

'And I shouldn't wonder,' I said, for I was in thoughtful mood, 'if even herrings haven't troubles of their own.'

'Quite possibly, sir.'

'I mean, apart from getting kippered.'

'Yes, sir.'

'And so it goes on, Jeeves, so it goes on.'

I can't say I exactly saw eye to eye with young Tuppy in his admiration for the Bellinger female. Delivered on the mat at one-twenty-five, she proved to be an upstanding light-heavy-weight of some thirty summers, with a commanding eye and a square chin which I, personally, would have steered clear of. She seemed to me a good deal like what Cleopatra would have been after going in too freely for the starches and cereals. I don't know why it is, but women who have anything to do with Opera, even if they're only studying for it, always appear to run to surplus poundage.

Tuppy, however, was obviously all for her. His whole demean-our, both before and during lunch, was that of one striving to be worthy of a noble soul. When Jeeves offered him a cocktail, he practically recoiled as from a serpent. It was terrible to see the change which love had effected in the man. The spectacle put me off my food.

At half-past two, the Bellinger left to go to a singing lesson. Tuppy trotted after her to the door, bleating and frisking a goodish bit, and then came back and looked at me in a goofy sort of way.

'Well, Bertie?'

'Well, what?'

'I mean, isn't she?'

'Oh, rather,' I said, humouring the poor fish.

'Wonderful eyes?'

'Oh, rather.'

'Wonderful figure?'

'Oh, quite.'

'Wonderful voice?'

Here I was able to intone the response with a little more heartiness. The Bellinger, at Tuppy's request, had sung us a few songs before digging in at the trough, and nobody could have denied that her pipes were in great shape. Plaster was still falling from the ceiling.

'Terrific,' I said.

Tuppy sighed, and, having helped himself to about four inches of whisky and one of soda, took a deep, refreshing draught.

'Ah!' he said. 'I needed that.'

'Why didn't you have it at lunch?'

'Well, it's this way,' said Tuppy. 'I have not actually ascertained what Cora's opinions are on the subject of the taking of slight snorts from time to time, but I thought it more prudent to lay off. The view I took was that laying off would seem to indicate the serious mind. It is touch-and-go, as you might say, at the moment, and the smallest thing may turn the scale.'

'What beats me is how on earth you expect to make her think you've got a mind at all – let alone a serious one.'

'I have my methods.'

'I bet they're rotten.'

'You do, do you?' said Tuppy warmly. 'Well, let me tell you, my lad, that that's exactly what they're anything but. I am handling this affair with consummate generalship. Do you remember Beefy Bingham who was at Oxford with us?'

'I ran into him only the other day. He's a parson now.'

'Yes. Down in the East End. Well, he runs a Lads' Club for the local toughs – you know the sort of thing – cocoa and back-gammon in the reading-room and occasional clean, bright entertainments in the Oddfellows' Hall: and I've been helping him. I don't suppose I've passed an evening away from the back-gammon board for weeks. Cora is extremely pleased. I've got her to promise to sing on Tuesday at Beefy's next clean, bright entertainment.'

'You have?'

'I absolutely have. And now mark my devilish ingenuity, Bertie. I'm going to sing, too.'

'Why do you suppose that's going to get you anywhere?'

'Because the way I intend to sing the song I intend to sing will prove to her that there are great deeps in my nature, whose existence she has not suspected. She will see that rough, un-lettered audience wiping the tears out of its bally eyes and she will say to herself "What ho! The old egg really has a soul!" For it is not one of your mouldy comic songs, Bertie. No low buffoonery of that sort for me. It is all about Angels being lonely and what not—'

I uttered a sharp cry.

'You don't mean you're going to sing "Sonny Boy"?'

'I jolly well do.'

I was shocked. Yes, dash it, I was shocked. You see, I held strong views on "Sonny Boy". I considered it a song only to be attempted by a few of the elect in the privacy of the bathroom. And the thought of it being murdered in open Oddfellows' Hall by a man who could treat a pal as young Tuppy had treated me that night at the Drones sickened me. Yes, sickened me.

I hadn't time, however, to express my horror and disgust, for at this juncture Jeeves came in.

'Mrs Travers has just rung up on the telephone, sir. She desired me to say that she will be calling to see you in a few minutes.'

'Contents noted, Jeeves,' I said. 'Now listen, Tuppy—'

I stopped. The fellow wasn't there.

'What have you done with him, Jeeves?' I asked.

'Mr Glossop has left, sir.'

'Left? How can he have left? He was sitting there—'

'That is the front door closing now, sir.'

'But what made him shoot off like that?'

'Possibly Mr Glossop did not wish to meet Mrs Travers, sir.'

'Why not?'

'I could not say, sir. But undoubtedly at the mention of Mrs Travers' name he rose very swiftly.'

'Strange, Jeeves.'

'Yes, sir.'

I turned to a subject of more moment.

'Jeeves,' I said, 'Mr Glossop proposes to sing "Sonny Boy" at an entertainment down in the East End next Tuesday.'

'Indeed, sir?'

'Before an audience consisting mainly of costermongers, with a sprinkling of whelk-stall owners, purveyors of blood-oranges, and minor pugilists.'

'Indeed, sir?'

'Make a note to remind me to be there. He will infallibly get the bird, and I want to witness his downfall.'

'Very good, sir.'

'And when Mrs Travers arrives, I shall be in the sitting-room.'

* * *

Those who know Bertram Wooster best are aware that in his journey through life he is impeded and generally snootered by about as scaly a platoon of aunts as was ever assembled. But there is one exception to the general ghastliness – viz., my Aunt Dahlia. She married old Tom Travers the year Bluebottle won the Cambridgeshire, and is one of the best. It is always a pleasure to me to chat with her, and it was with a courtly geniality that I rose to receive her as she sailed over the threshold at about two-fifty-five.

She seemed somewhat perturbed, and snapped into the agenda without delay. Aunt Dahlia is one of those big, hearty women. She used to go in a lot for hunting, and she generally speaks as if she had just sighted a fox on a hillside half a mile away.

'Bertie,' she cried, in the manner of one encouraging a bevy of hounds to renewed efforts. 'I want your help.'

'And you shall have it, Aunt Dahlia,' I replied suavely. 'I can honestly say that there is no one to whom I would more readily do a good turn than yourself; no one to whom I am more delighted to be—'

'Less of it,' she begged, 'less of it. You know that friend of yours, young Glossop?'

'He's just been lunching here.'

'He has, has he? Well, I wish you'd poisoned his soup.'

'We didn't have soup. And, when you describe him as a friend of mine, I wouldn't quite say the term absolutely squared with the facts. Some time ago, one night when we had been dining together at the Drones—'

At this point Aunt Dahlia – a little brusquely, it seemed to me – said that she would rather wait for the story of my life till she could get it in book-form. I could see now that she was definitely not her usual sunny self, so I shelved my personal grievances and asked what was biting her.

'It's that young hound Glossop,' she said.

'What's he been doing?'

'Breaking Angela's heart.' (Angela. Daughter of above. My cousin. Quite a good egg.)

'Breaking Angela's heart?'

'Yes ... Breaking ... Angela's ... HEART!'

'You say he's breaking Angela's heart?'

She begged me in rather a feverish way to suspend the vaudeville cross-talk stuff.

'How's he doing that?' I asked.

'With his neglect. With his low, callous, double-crossing duplicity.'

'Duplicity is the word, Aunt Dahlia,' I said. 'In treating of young Tuppy Glossop, it springs naturally to the lips. Let me just tell you what he did to me one night at the Drones. We had finished dinner—'

'Ever since the beginning of the season, up till about three weeks ago, he was all over Angela. The sort of thing which, when I was a girl, we should have described as courting—'

'Or wooing?'

'Wooing or courting, whichever you like.'

'Whichever *you* like, Aunt Dahlia,' I said courteously.

'Well, anyway, he haunted the house, lapped up daily lunches, danced with her half the night, and so on, till naturally the poor kid, who's quite off her oats about him, took it for granted that it was only a question of time before he suggested that they should feed for life out of the same crib. And now he's gone and dropped her like a hot brick, and I hear he's infatuated with some girl he met at a Chelsea tea-party – a girl named – now, what was it?'

'Cora Bellinger.'

'How do you know?'

'She was lunching here to-day.'

'He brought her?'

'Yes.'

'What's she like?'

'Pretty massive. In shape, a bit on the lines of the Albert Hall.'

'Did he seem very fond of her?'

'Couldn't take his eyes off the chassis.'

'The modern young man,' said Aunt Dahlia, 'is a congenital idiot and wants a nurse to lead him by the hand and some strong attendant to kick him regularly at intervals of a quarter of an hour.'

I tried to point out the silver lining.

'If you ask me, Aunt Dahlia,' I said, 'I think Angela is well out of it. This Glossop is a tough baby. One of London's toughest. I was trying to tell you just now what he did to me one night at the Drones. First having got me in sporting mood with a bottle of the ripest, he betted I wouldn't swing myself across the swimming-bath by the ropes and rings. I knew I could do it on my head, so I took him on, exulting in the fun, so to speak. And when I'd done half the trip and was going as strong as dammit, I found he had looped the last rope back against the rail, leaving me no alternative but to drop into the depths and swim ashore in correct evening costume.'

'He did?'

'He certainly did. It was months ago, and I haven't got really dry yet. You wouldn't want your daughter to marry a man capable of a thing like that?'

'On the contrary, you restore my faith in the young hound. I see that there must be lots of good in him, after all. And I want this Bellinger business broken up, Bertie.'

'How?'

'I don't care how. Any way you please.'

'But what can I do?'

'Do? Why, put the whole thing before your man Jeeves. Jeeves will find a way. One of the most capable fellers I ever met. Put the thing squarely up to Jeeves and tell him to let his mind play round the topic.'

'There may be something in what you say, Aunt Dahlia,' I said thoughtfully.

'Of course there is,' said Aunt Dahlia. 'A little thing like this will be child's play to Jeeves. Get him working on it, and I'll look in to-morrow to hear the result.'

With which, she biffed off, and I summoned Jeeves to the presence.

'Jeeves,' I said, 'you have heard all?'

'Yes, sir.'

'I thought you would. My Aunt Dahlia has what you might call a carrying voice. Has it ever occurred to you that, if all other sources of income failed, she could make a good living calling the cattle home across the Sands of Dee?'

'I had not considered the point, sir, but no doubt you are right.'

'Well, how do we go? What is your reaction? I think we should do our best to help and assist.'

'Yes, sir.'

'I am fond of my Aunt Dahlia and I am fond of my cousin Angela. Fond of them both, if you get my drift. What the misguided girl finds to attract her in young Tuppy, I cannot say,

Jeeves, and you cannot say. But apparently she loves the man – which shows it can be done, a thing I wouldn't have believed myself – and is pining away like—'

'Patience on a monument, sir.'

'Like Patience, as you very shrewdly remark, on a monument. So we must cluster round. Bend your brain to the problem, Jeeves. It is one that will tax you to the uttermost.'

Aunt Dahlia blew in on the morrow, and I rang the bell for Jeeves. He appeared looking brainier than one could have believed possible – sheer intellect shining from every feature – and I could see at once that the engine had been turning over.

'Speak, Jeeves,' I said.

'Very good, sir.'

'You have brooded?'

'Yes, sir.'

'With what success?'

'I have a plan, sir, which I fancy may produce satisfactory results.'

'Let's have it,' said Aunt Dahlia.

'In affairs of this description, madam, the first essential is to study the psychology of the individual.'

'The what of the individual?'

'The psychology, madam.'

'He means the psychology,' I said. 'And by psychology, Jeeves, you imply—?'

'The natures and dispositions of the principals in the matter, sir.'

'You mean, what they're like?'

'Precisely, sir.'

'Does he talk like this to you when you're alone, Bertie?' asked Aunt Dahlia.

'Sometimes. Occasionally. And, on the other hand, sometimes not. Proceed, Jeeves.'

'Well, sir, if I may say so, the thing that struck me most forcibly about Miss Bellinger when she was under my observation was that hers was a somewhat hard and intolerant nature. I could envisage Miss Bellinger applauding success. I could not so easily see her pitying and sympathizing with failure. Possibly you will recall, sir, her attitude when Mr Glossop endeavoured to light her cigarette with his automatic lighter? I thought I detected a certain impatience at his inability to produce the necessary flame.'

'True, Jeeves. She ticked him off.'

'Precisely, sir.'

'Let me get this straight,' said Aunt Dahlia, looking a bit fogged. 'You think that, if he goes on trying to light her cigarettes with his automatic lighter long enough, she will eventually get fed up and hand him the mitten? Is that the idea?'

'I merely mentioned the episode, madam, as an indication of Miss Bellinger's somewhat ruthless nature.'

'Ruthless,' I said, 'is right. The Bellinger is hard-boiled. Those eyes. That chin. I could read them. A woman of blood and iron, if ever there was one.'

'Precisely, sir. I think, therefore, that, should Miss Bellinger be a witness of Mr Glossop appearing to disadvantage in public, she would cease to entertain affection for him. In the event, for instance, of his failing to please the audience on Tuesday with his singing—'

I saw daylight.

'By Jove, Jeeves! You mean if he gets the bird, all will be off?'

'I shall be greatly surprised if such is not the case, sir.'

I shook my head.

'We cannot leave this thing to chance, Jeeves. Young Tuppy, singing "Sonny Boy", is the likeliest prospect for the bird that I can think of — but, no — you must see for yourself that we can't simply trust to luck.'

'We need not trust to luck, sir. I would suggest that you approach your friend, Mr Bingham, and volunteer your services as a performer at his forthcoming entertainment. It could readily be arranged that you sang immediately before Mr Glossop. I fancy, sir, that, if Mr Glossop were to sing "Sonny Boy" directly after you, too, had sung "Sonny Boy", the audience would respond satisfactorily. By the time Mr Glossop began to sing, they would have lost their taste for that particular song and would express their feelings warmly.'

'Jeeves,' said Aunt Dahlia, 'you're a marvel!'

'Thank you, madam.'

'Jeeves,' I said, 'you're an ass!'

'What do you mean, he's an ass?' said Aunt Dahlia hotly. 'I think it's the greatest scheme I ever heard.'

'Me sing "Sonny Boy" at Beefy Bingham's clean, bright entertainment? I can see myself!'

'You sing it daily in your bath, sir. Mr Wooster,' said Jeeves, turning to Aunt Dahlia, 'has a pleasant, light baritone—'

'I bet he has,' said Aunt Dahlia.

I froze the man with a look.

'Between singing "Sonny Boy" in one's bath, Jeeves, and singing it before a hall full of assorted blood-orange merchants and their young, there is a substantial difference.'

'Bertie,' said Aunt Dahlia, 'you'll sing, and like it!'

'I will not.'

'Bertie!'

'Nothing will induce—'

'Bertie,' said Aunt Dahlia firmly, 'you will sing "Sonny Boy" on Tuesday, the third *prox.*, and sing it like a lark at sunrise, or may an aunt's curse—'

'I won't!'

'Think of Angela!'

'Dash Angela!'

'Bertie!'

'No, I mean, hang it all!'

'You won't?'

'No, I won't.'

'That is your last word, is it?'

'It is. Once and for all, Aunt Dahlia, nothing will induce me to let out so much as a single note.'

And so that afternoon I sent a pre-paid wire to Beefy Bingham, offering my services in the cause, and by nightfall the thing was fixed up. I was billed to perform next but one after the intermission. Following me, came Tuppy. And, immediately after him, Miss Cora Bellinger, the well-known operatic soprano.

'Jeeves,' I said that evening – and I said it coldly – 'I shall be obliged if you will pop round to the nearest music-shop and procure me a copy of "Sonny Boy". It will now be necessary for me to learn both verse and refrain. Of the trouble and nervous strain which this will involve, I say nothing.'

'Very good, sir.'

'But this I do say—'

'I had better be starting immediately, sir, or the shop will be closed.'

'Ha!' I said.

And I meant it to sting.

Although I had steeled myself to the ordeal before me and had set out full of the calm, quiet courage which makes men do desperate deeds with careless smiles, I must admit that there was a moment, just after I had entered the Oddfellows' Hall at Bermondsey East and run an eye over the assembled pleasure-seekers, when it needed all the bull-dog pluck of the Woosters to keep me from calling it a day and taking a cab back to civilization. The clean, bright entertainment was in full swing when I arrived, and somebody who looked as if he might be the local undertaker was reciting 'Gunga Din'. And the audience, though not actually chi-yiking in the full technical sense of the term, had a grim look which I didn't like at all. The mere sight of them gave me the sort of feeling Shadrach, Meshach and Abednego must have had when preparing to enter the burning, fiery furnace.

Scanning the multitude, it seemed to me that they were for the nonce suspending judgement. Did you ever tap on the door of one of those New York speakeasy places and see the grille snap back and a Face appear? There is one long, silent moment when its eyes are fixed on yours and all your past life seems to rise up before you. Then you say that you are a friend of Mr Zinzinheimer and he told you they would treat you right if you mentioned his name, and the strain relaxes. Well, these costermongers and whelk-stallers appeared to me to be looking just like that Face. Start something, they seemed to say, and they would know what to do about it. And I couldn't help feeling that my singing 'Sonny Boy' would come, in their opinion, under the head of starting something.

'A nice, full house, sir,' said a voice at my elbow. It was Jeeves, watching the proceedings with an indulgent eye.

'You here, Jeeves?' I said, coldly.

'Yes, sir. I have been present since the commencement.'

'Oh?' I said. 'Any casualties yet?'

'Sir?'

'You know what I mean, Jeeves,' I said sternly, 'and don't pretend you don't. Anybody got the bird yet?'

'Oh, no, sir.'

'I shall be the first, you think?'

'No, sir. I see no reason to expect such a misfortune. I anticipate that you will be well received.'

A sudden thought struck me.

'And you think everything will go according to plan?'

'Yes, sir.'

'Well, I don't,' I said. 'And I'll tell you why I don't. I've spotted a flaw in your beastly scheme.'

'A flaw, sir?'

'Yes. Do you suppose for a moment that, if when Mr Glossop hears me singing that dashed song, he'll come calmly on a minute after me and sing it too? Use your intelligence, Jeeves. He will perceive the chasm in his path and pause in time. He will back out and refuse to go on at all.'

'Mr Glossop will not hear you sing, sir. At my advice, he has stepped across the road to the Jug and Bottle, an establishment immediately opposite the hall, and he intends to remain there until it is time for him to appear on the platform.'

'Oh?' I said.

'If I might suggest it, sir, there is another house named the Goat and Grapes only a short distance down the street. I think it might be a judicious move—'

'If I were to put a bit of custom in their way?'

'It would ease the nervous strain of waiting, sir.'

I had not been feeling any too pleased with the man for having let me in for this ghastly binge, but at these words, I'm bound to say, my austerity softened a trifle. He was undoubtedly right. He had studied the psychology of the individual, and it had not led him astray. A quiet ten minutes at the Goat and Grapes was exactly what my system required. To buzz off there and inhale a couple of swift whisky-and-sodas was with Bertram Wooster the work of a moment.

The treatment worked like magic. What they had put into the stuff, besides vitriol, I could not have said; but it completely altered my outlook on life. That curious, gulpy feeling passed. I was no longer conscious of the sagging sensation at the knees. The limbs ceased to quiver gently, the tongue became loosened in its socket, and the backbone stiffened. Pausing merely to order and swallow another of the same, I bade the barmaid a cheery good night, nodded affably to one or two fellows in the bar whose faces I liked, and came prancing back to the hall, ready for anything.

And shortly afterwards I was on the platform with about a million bulging eyes goggling up at me. There was a rummy sort of buzzing in my ears, and then through the buzzing I heard the sound of a piano starting to tinkle: and, commending my soul to God, I took a good, long breath and charged in.

Well, it was a close thing. The whole incident is a bit blurred, but I seem to recollect a kind of murmur as I hit the refrain. I thought at the time it was an attempt on the part of the many-headed to join in the chorus, and at the moment it rather encouraged me. I passed the thing over the larynx with all the vim at my disposal, hit the high note, and off gracefully into the wings. I didn't come on again to take a bow. I just receded and oiled round to where Jeeves awaited me among the standees at the back.

'Well, Jeeves,' I said, anchoring myself at his side and brushing the honest sweat from the brow, 'they didn't rush the platform.'

'No, sir.'

'But you can spread it about that that's the last time I perform outside my bath. My swan-song, Jeeves. Anybody who wants to hear me in future must present himself at the bathroom door and shove his ear against the keyhole. I may be wrong, but it seemed to me that towards the end they were hotting up a trifle. The bird was hovering in the air. I could hear the beating of its wings.'

'I did detect a certain restlessness, sir, in the audience. I fancy they had lost their taste for that particular melody.'

'Eh?'

'I should have informed you earlier, sir, that the song had already been sung twice before you arrived.'

'What!'

'Yes, sir. Once by a lady and once by a gentleman. It is a very popular song, sir.'

I gaped at the man. That, with this knowledge, he could calmly have allowed the young master to step straight into the jaws of death, so to speak, paralysed me. It seemed to show that the old feudal spirit had passed away altogether. I was about to give him my views on the matter in no uncertain fashion, when I was stopped by the spectacle of young Tuppy lurching on to the platform.

Young Tuppy had the unmistakable air of a man who has recently been round to the Jug and Bottle. A few cheery cries of welcome, presumably from some of his backgammon-playing pals who felt that blood was thicker than water, had the effect of causing the genial smile on his face to widen till it nearly met at the back. He was plainly feeling about as good as a man can feel and still remain on his feet. He waved a kindly hand to his supporters, and bowed in a regal sort of manner, rather like an Eastern monarch acknowledging the plaudits of the mob.

Then the female at the piano struck up the opening bars of 'Sonny Boy', and Tuppy swelled like a balloon, clasped his hands together, rolled his eyes up at the ceiling in a manner denoting Soul, and began.

I think the populace was too stunned for the moment to take immediate steps. It may seem incredible, but I give you my word that young Tuppy got right through the verse without so much as a murmur. Then they all seemed to pull themselves together.

A costermonger, roused, is a terrible thing. I had never seen the proletariat really stirred before, and I'm bound to say it rather awed me. I mean, it gave you some idea of what it must have been like during the French Revolution. From every corner of the hall there proceeded simultaneously the sort of noise which you hear, they tell me, at one of those East End boxing places when the referee disqualifies the popular favourite and makes the quick dash for life. And then they passed beyond mere words and began to introduce the vegetable motive.

I don't know why, but somehow I had got it into my head that the first thing thrown at Tuppy would be a potato. One gets these fancies. It was, however, as a matter of fact, a banana, and I saw in an instant that the choice had been made by wiser heads than mine. These blokes who have grown up from childhood in the knowledge of how to treat a dramatic entertainment that doesn't please them are aware by a sort of instinct just what to do for the best, and the moment I saw that banana splash on Tuppy's shirt-front I realized how infinitely more effective and artistic it was than any potato could have been.

Not that the potato school of thought had not also its supporters. As the proceedings warmed up, I noticed several intelligent-looking fellows who threw nothing else.

The effect on young Tuppy was rather remarkable. His eyes bulged and his hair seemed to stand up, and yet his mouth went on opening and shutting, and you could see that in a dazed, automatic way he was still singing 'Sonny Boy'. Then, coming out of his trance, he began to pull for the shore with some rapidity. The last seen of him, he was beating a tomato to the exit by a short head.

Presently the tumult and the shouting died. I turned to Jeeves.

'Painful, Jeeves,' I said. 'But what would you?'

'Yes, sir.'

'The surgeon's knife, what?'

'Precisely, sir.'

'Well, with this happening beneath her eyes, I think we may definitely consider the Glossop–Bellinger romance off.'

'Yes, sir.'

At this point old Beefy Bingham came out on to the platform.

'Ladies and gentlemen,' said old Beefy.

I supposed that he was about to rebuke his flock for the recent expression of feeling. But such was not the case. No doubt he was accustomed by now to the wholesome give-and-take of these clean, bright entertainments and had ceased to think it worth while to make any comment when there was a certain liveliness.

'Ladies and gentlemen,' said old Beefy, 'the next item on the programme was to have been Songs by Miss Cora Bellinger, the well-known operatic soprano. I have just received a telephone-message from Miss Bellinger, saying that her car has broken down. She is, however, on her way here in a cab and will arrive shortly. Meanwhile, our friend Mr Enoch Simpson will recite "Dangerous Dan McGrew".'

I clutched at Jeeves.

'Jeeves! You heard?'

'Yes, sir.'

'She wasn't there!'

'No, sir.'

'She saw nothing of Tuppy's Waterloo.'

'No, sir.'

'The whole bally scheme has blown a fuse.'

'Yes, sir.'

'Come, Jeeves,' I said, and those standing by wondered, no doubt, what had caused that clean-cut face to grow so pale and set. 'I have been subjected to a nervous strain unparalleled since the days of the early Martyrs. I have lost pounds in weight and permanently injured my entire system. I have gone through an ordeal, the recollection of which will make me wake up scream-ing in the night for months to come. And all for nothing. Let us go.'

'If you have no objection, sir, I would like to witness the remainder of the entertainment.'

'Suit yourself, Jeeves,' I said moodily. 'Personally, my heart is dead and I am going to look in at the Goat and Grapes for another of their cyanide specials and then home.'

It must have been about half-past ten, and I was in the

old sitting-room sombrely sucking down a more or less final restorative, when the front-door bell rang, and there on the mat was young Tuppy. He looked like a man who has passed through some great experience and stood face to face with his soul. He had the beginnings of a black eye.

'Oh, hullo, Bertie,' said young Tuppy.

He came in, and hovered about the mantelpiece as if he were looking for things to fiddle with and break.

'I've just been singing at Beefy Bingham's entertainment,' he said after a pause.

'Oh?' I said. 'How did you go?'

'Like a breeze,' said young Tuppy. 'Held them spellbound.'

'Knocked 'em, eh?'

'Cold,' said young Tuppy. 'Not a dry eye.'

And this, mark you, a man who had had a good upbringing and had, no doubt, spent years at his mother's knee being taught to tell the truth.

'I suppose Miss Bellinger is pleased?'

'Oh, yes. Delighted.'

'So now everything's all right?'

'Oh, quite.'

Tuppy paused.

'On the other hand, Bertie—'

'Yes?'

'Well, I've been thinking things over. Somehow I don't believe Miss Bellinger is the mate for me, after all.'

'You don't?'

'No, I don't.'

'Why don't you?'

'Oh, I don't know. These things sort of flash on you. I respect Miss Bellinger, Bertie. I admire her. But – er – well, I can't help feeling now that a sweet, gentle girl – er – like your cousin Angela, for instance, Bertie, would – er – in fact— well, what I came round for was to ask if you would 'phone Angela and find out how she reacts to the idea of coming out with me to-night to the Berkeley for a segment of supper and a spot of dancing.'

'Go ahead. There's the 'phone.'

'No, I'd rather you asked her, Bertie. What with one thing and another, if you paved the way— You see, there's just a chance that she may be— I mean, you know how misunderstandings occur— and— well, what I'm driving at, Bertie, old man, is that I'd rather you surged round and did a bit of paving, if you don't mind.'

I went to the 'phone and called up Aunt Dahlia's.

'She says come right along,' I said.

'Tell her,' said Tuppy in a devout sort of voice, 'that I will be with her in something under a couple of ticks.'

He had barely biffed, when I heard a click in the keyhole and a soft padding in the passage without.

'Jeeves,' I called.

'Sir?' said Jeeves, manifesting himself.

'Jeeves, a remarkably rummy thing has happened. Mr Glossop has just been here. He tells me that it is all off between him and Miss Bellinger.'

'Yes, sir.'

'You don't seem surprised.'

'No, sir. I confess I had anticipated some such eventuality.'

'Eh? What gave you that idea?'

'It came to me, sir, when I observed Miss Bellinger strike Mr Glossop in the eye.'

'Strike him!'

'Yes, sir.'

'In the eye?'

'The right eye, sir.'

I clutched the brow.

'What on earth made her do that?'

'I fancy she was a little upset, sir, at the reception accorded to her singing.'

'Great Scott! Don't tell me she got the bird, too?'

'Yes, sir.'

'But why? She's got a red-hot voice.'

'Yes, sir. But I think the audience resented her choice of a song.'

'Jeeves!' Reason was beginning to do a bit of tottering on its throne. 'You aren't going to stand there and tell me that Miss Bellinger sang "Sonny Boy", too!'

'Yes, sir. And – rashly, in my opinion – brought a large doll on to the platform to sing it to. The audience affected to mistake it for a ventriloquist's dummy, and there was some little disturbance.'

'But, Jeeves, what a coincidence!'

'Not altogether, sir. I ventured to take the liberty of accosting Miss Bellinger on her arrival at the hall and recalling myself to her recollection. I then said that Mr Glossop had asked me to request her that as a particular favour to him – the song being a favourite of his – she would sing "Sonny Boy". And when she found that you and Mr Glossop had also sung the song immediately before her, I rather fancy that she supposed that she had been made the victim of a practical pleasantry by Mr Glossop. Will there be anything further, sir?'

'No, thanks.'

'Good night, sir.'

'Good night, Jeeves,' I said reverently.

I was jerked from the dreamless by a sound like the rolling of distant thunder; and, the mists of sleep clearing away, was enabled to diagnose this and trace it to its source. It was my Aunt Agatha's dog, McIntosh, scratching at the door. The above, an Aberdeen terrier of weak intellect, had been left in my charge by the old relative while she went off to Aix-les-Bains to take the cure, and I had never been able to make it see eye to eye with me on the subject of early rising. Although a glance at my watch informed me that it was barely ten, here was the animal absolutely up and about.

I pressed the bell, and presently in shimmered Jeeves, complete with tea-tray and preceded by dog, which leaped upon the bed, licked me smartly in the right eye, and immediately curled up and fell into a deep slumber. And where the sense is in getting up at some ungodly hour of the morning and coming scratching at people's doors, when you intend at the first opportunity to go to sleep again, beats me. Nevertheless, every day for the last five weeks this loony hound had pursued the same policy, and I confess I was getting a bit fed.

There were one or two letters on the tray; and, having slipped a refreshing half-cupful into the abyss, I felt equal to dealing with them. The one on top was from my Aunt Agatha.

'Ha!' I said.

'Sir?'

'I said "Ha!" Jeeves. And I meant "Ha!" I was registering relief. My Aunt Agatha returns this evening. She will be at her town residence between the hours of six and seven, and she expects to find McIntosh waiting for her on the mat.'

'Indeed, sir? I shall miss the little fellow.'

'I, too, Jeeves. Despite his habit of rising with the milk and being hearty before breakfast, there is sterling stuff in McIntosh. Nevertheless, I cannot but feel relieved at the prospect of shooting him back to the old home. It has been a guardianship fraught with anxiety. You know what my Aunt Agatha is. She lavishes on that dog a love which might better be bestowed on a nephew: and if the slightest thing had gone wrong with him while I was *in loco parentis*; if, while in my charge, he had developed rabies or staggers or the botts, I should have been blamed.'

'Very true, sir.'

'And, as you are aware, London is not big enough to hold Aunt Agatha and anybody she happens to be blaming.'

I had opened the second letter, and was giving it the eye.

'Ha!' I said.

'Sir?'

'Once again "Ha!" Jeeves, but this time signifying mild surprise. This letter is from Miss Wickham.'

'Indeed, sir?'

I sensed – if that is the word I want – the note of concern in the man's voice, and I knew he was saying to himself 'Is the young master about to slip?' You see, there was a time when the Wooster heart was to some extent what you might call ensnared by this Roberta Wickham, and Jeeves had never approved of her. He considered her volatile and frivolous and more or less of a menace to man and beast. And events, I'm bound to say, had rather borne out his view.

'She wants me to give her lunch to-day.'

'Indeed, sir?'

'And two friends of hers.'

'Indeed, sir?'

'Here. At one-thirty.'

'Indeed, sir?'

I was piqued.

'Correct this parrot-complex, Jeeves,' I said, waving a slice of bread-and-butter rather sternly at the man. 'There is no need for you to stand there saying "Indeed, sir?" I know what you're thinking, and you're wrong. As far as Miss Wickham is concerned, Bertram Wooster is chilled steel. I see no earthly reason why I should not comply with this request. A Wooster may have ceased to love, but he can still be civil.'

'Very good, sir.'

'Employ the rest of the morning, then, in buzzing to and fro and collecting provender. The old King Wenceslas touch, Jeeves. You remember? Bring me fish and bring me fowl—'

'Bring me flesh and bring me wine, sir.'

'Just as you say. You know best. Oh, and roly-poly pudding, Jeeves.'

'Sir?'

'Roly-poly pudding with lots of jam in it. Miss Wickham specifically mentions this. Mysterious, what?'

'Extremely, sir.'

'Also oysters, ice-cream, and plenty of chocolates with that goo-ey, slithery stuff in the middle. Makes you sick to think of it, eh?'

'Yes, sir.'

'Me, too. But that's what she says. I think she must be on some kind of diet. Well, be that as it may, see to it, Jeeves, will you?'

'Yes, sir.'

'At one-thirty of the clock.'

'Very good, sir.'

'Very good, Jeeves.'

At half-past twelve I took the dog McIntosh for his morning saunter in the Park; and, returning at about one-ten, found young Bobbie Wickham in the sitting-room, smoking a cigarette and chatting to Jeeves, who seemed a bit distant, I thought.

I have an idea I've told you about this Bobbie Wickham. She was the red-haired girl who let me down so disgracefully in the sinister affair of Tuppy Glossop and the hot-water bottle, that Christmas when I went to stay at Skeldings Hall, her mother's place in Hertfordshire. Her mother is Lady Wickham, who writes novels which, I believe, command a ready sale among those who like their literature pretty sloppy. A formidable old bird, rather like my Aunt Agatha in appearance. Bobbie does not resemble her, being constructed more on the lines of Clara Bow. She greeted me cordially as I entered – in fact, so cordially that I saw Jeeves pause at the door before buffing off to mix the cocktails and shoot me the sort of grave, warning look a wise old father might pass out to the effervescent son on seeing him going fairly strong with the local vamp. I nodded back, as much as to say 'Chilled steel!' and he oozed out, leaving me to play the sparkling host.

'It was awfully sporting of you to give us this lunch, Bertie,' said Bobbie.

'Don't mention it, my dear old thing,' I said. 'Always a pleasure.'

'You got all the stuff I told you about?'

'The garbage, as specified, is in the kitchen. But since when have you become a roly-poly pudding addict?'

'That isn't for me. There's a small boy coming.'

'What!'

'I'm awfully sorry,' she said, noting my agitation. 'I know just how you feel, and I'm not going to pretend that this child isn't pretty near the edge. In fact, he has to be seen to be believed. But it's simply vital that he be cosseted and sucked up to and generally treated as the guest of honour, because everything depends on him.'

'How do you mean?'

'I'll tell you. You know mother?'

'Whose mother?'

'My mother.'

'Oh, yes. I thought you meant the kid's mother.'

'He hasn't got a mother. Only a father, who is a big theatrical manager in America. I met him at a party the other night.'

'The father?'

'Yes, the father.'

'Not the kid?'

'No, not the kid.'

'Right. All clear so far. Proceed.'

'Well, mother – my mother – has dramatized one of her novels, and when I met this father, this theatrical manager father, and, between ourselves, made rather a hit with him, I said to myself, "Why not?" '

'Why not what?'

'Why not plant mother's play on him.'

'Your mother's play?'

'Yes, not his mother's play. He is like his son, he hasn't got a mother, either.'

'These things run in families, don't they?'

'You see, Bertie, what with one thing and another, my stock isn't very high with mother just now. There was that matter of my smashing up the car – oh, and several things. So I thought, here is where I get a chance to put myself right. I cooed to old Blumenfeld—'

'Name sounds familiar.'

'Oh, yes, he's a big man over in America. He has come to London to see if there's anything in the play line worth buying. So I cooed to him a goodish bit and then asked him if he would listen to mother's play. He said he would, so I asked him to come to lunch and I'd read it to him.'

'You're going to read your mother's play – here?' I said, paling.

'Yes.'

'My God!'

'I know what you mean,' she said. 'I admit it's pretty sticky stuff. But I have an idea that I shall put it over. It all depends on how the kid likes it. You see, old Blumenfeld, for some reason, always banks on his verdict. I suppose he thinks the child's intelligence is exactly the same as an average audience's and—'

I uttered a slight yelp, causing Jeeves, who had entered with cocktails, to look at me in a pained sort of way. I had remembered.

'Jeeves!'

'Sir?'

'Do you recollect, when we were in New York, a dish-faced kid of the name of Blumenfeld who on a memorable occasion snootered Cyril Bassington-Bassington when the latter tried to go on the stage?'

'Very vividly, sir.'

'Well, prepare yourself for a shock. He's coming to lunch.'

'Indeed, sir?'

'I'm glad you can speak in that light, careless way. I only met the young stoup of arsenic for a few brief minutes, but I don't mind telling you the prospect of hobnobbing with him again makes me tremble like a leaf.'

'Indeed, sir?'

'Don't keep saying "Indeed, sir?" You have seen this kid in action and you know what he's like. He told Cyril Bassington-Bassington, a fellow to whom he had never been formally introduced, that he had a face like a fish. And this not thirty seconds after their initial meeting. I give you fair warning that, if he tells me I have a face like a fish, I shall clump his head.'

'Bertie!' cried the Wickham, contorted with anguish and apprehension and what not.

'Yes, I shall.'

'Then you'll simply ruin the whole thing.'

'I don't care. We Woosters have our pride.'

'Perhaps the young gentleman will not notice that you have a face like a fish, sir,' suggested Jeeves.

'Ah! There's that, of course.'

'But we can't just trust to luck,' said Bobbie. 'It's probably the first thing he will notice.'

'In that case, miss,' said Jeeves, 'it might be the best plan if Mr Wooster did not attend the luncheon.'

I beamed on the man. As always, he had found the way.

'But Mr Blumenfeld will think it so odd.'

'Well, tell him I'm eccentric. Tell him I have these moods,

which come upon me quite suddenly, when I can't stand the sight of people. Tell him what you like.'

'He'll be offended.'

'Not half so offended as if I socked his son on the upper maxillary bone.'

'I really think it would be the best plan, miss.'

'Oh, all right,' said Bobbie. 'Push off, then. But I wanted you to be here to listen to the play and laugh in the proper places.'

'I don't suppose there are any proper places,' I said. And with these words I reached the hall in two bounds, grabbed a hat, and made for the street. A cab was just pulling up at the door as I reached it, and inside it were Pop Blumenfeld and his foul son. With a slight sinking of the old heart, I saw that the kid had recognized me.

'Hullo!' he said.

'Hullo!' I said.

'Where are you off to?' said the kid.

'Ha, ha!' I said, and legged it for the great open spaces.

I lunched at the Drones, doing myself fairly well and lingering pretty considerably over the coffee and cigarettes. At four o'clock I thought it would be safe to think about getting back; but, not wishing to take any chances, I went to the 'phone and rang up the flat.

'All clear, Jeeves?'

'Yes, sir.'

'Blumenfeld junior nowhere about?'

'No, sir.'

'Not hiding in any nook or cranny, what?'

'No, sir.'

'How did everything go off?'

'Quite satisfactorily, I fancy, sir.'

'Was I missed?'

'I think Mr Blumenfeld and young Master Blumenfeld were somewhat surprised at your absence, sir. Apparently they encountered you as you were leaving the building.'

'They did. An awkward moment, Jeeves. The kid appeared to desire speech with me, but I laughed hollowly and passed on. Did they comment on this at all?'

'Yes, sir. Indeed, young Master Blumenfeld was somewhat outspoken.'

'What did he say?'

'I cannot recall his exact words, sir, but he drew a comparison between your mentality and that of a cuckoo.'

'A cuckoo, eh?'

'Yes, sir. To the bird's advantage.'

'He did, did he? Now you see how right I was to come away. Just one crack like that out of him face to face, and I should infallibly have done his upper maxillary a bit of no good. It was wise of you to suggest that I should lunch out.'

'Thank you, sir.'

'Well, the coast being clear, I will now return home.'

'Before you start, sir, perhaps you would ring Miss Wickham up. She instructed me to desire you to do so.'

'You mean she asked you to ask me?'

'Precisely, sir.'

'Right-ho. And the number?'

'Sloane 8090. I fancy it is the residence of Miss Wickham's aunt, in Eaton Square.'

I got the number. And presently young Bobbie's voice came floating over the wire. From the *timbre* I gathered that she was extremely bucked.

'Hullo? Is that you, Bertie?'

'In person. What's the news?'

'Wonderful. Everything went off splendidly. The lunch was just right. The child stuffed himself to the eyebrows and got more and more amiable, till by the time he had had his third go of ice-cream he was ready to say that any play – even one of mother's – was the goods. I fired it at him before he could come out from under the influence, and he sat there absorbing it in a sort of gorged way, and at the end old Blumenfeld said "Well, sonny, how about it?" and the child gave a sort of faint smile, as if he was thinking about roly-poly pudding, and said "O.K., pop," and that's all there was to it. Old Blumenfeld has taken him off to the movies, and I'm to look in at the Savoy at five-thirty to sign the contract. I've just been talking to mother on the 'phone, and she's quite consumedly braced.'

'Terrific!'

'I knew you'd be pleased. Oh, Bertie, there's just one other thing. You remember saying to me once that there wasn't any-thing in the world you wouldn't do for me?'

I paused a trifle warily. It is true that I had expressed myself in some such terms as she had indicated, but that was before the affair of Tuppy and the hot-water bottle, and in the calmer frame of mind induced by that episode I wasn't feeling quite so spacious. You know how it is. Love's flame flickers and dies, Reason returns to her throne, and you aren't nearly as ready to hop about and jump through hoops as in the first pristine glow of the divine passion.

'What do you want me to do?'

'Well, it's nothing I actually want you to do. It's something I've done that I hope you won't be sticky about. Just before I began reading the play, that dog of yours, the Aberdeen terrier, came into the room. The child Blumenfeld was very much taken with it and said he wished he had a dog like that, looking at me in a meaning sort of way. So naturally, I had to say "Oh, I'll give you this one!"'

I swayed somewhat.

'You . . . You . . . What was that?'

'I gave him the dog. I knew you wouldn't mind. You see, it was vital to keep cosseting him. If I'd refused, he would have cut up rough and all that roly-poly pudding and stuff would have been thrown away. You see—'

I hung up. The jaw had fallen, the eyes were protruding. I tottered from the booth and, reeling out of the club, hailed a taxi. I got to the flat and yelled for Jeeves.

'Jeeves!'

'Sir?'

'Do you know what?'

'No, sir.'

'The dog . . . my Aunt Agatha's dog . . . McIntosh . . .'

'I have not seen him for some little while, sir. He left me after the conclusion of luncheon. Possibly he is in your bedroom.'

'Yes, and possibly he jolly dashed well isn't. If you want to know where he is, he's in a suite at the Savoy.'

'Sir?'

'Miss Wickham has just told me she gave him to Blumenfeld junior.'

'Sir?'

'Gave him to Jumenfeld blunior, I tell you. As a present. As a gift. With warm personal regards.'

'What was her motive in doing that, sir?'

I explained the circs. Jeeves did a bit of respectful tongue-clicking.

'I have always maintained, if you will remember, sir,' he said, when I had finished, 'that Miss Wickham, though a charming young lady—'

'Yes, yes, never mind about that. What are we going to do? That's the point. Aunt Agatha is due back between the hours of six and seven. She will find herself short one Aberdeen terrier. And, as she will probably have been considerably sea-sick all the way over, you will readily perceive, Jeeves, that, when I break the news that her dog has been given away to a total stranger, I shall find her in no mood of gentle charity.'

'I see, sir. Most disturbing.'

'What did you say it was?'

'Most disturbing, sir.'

I snorted a trifle.

'Oh?' I said. 'And I suppose, if you had been in San Francisco when the earthquake started, you would just have lifted up your finger and said "Tweet, tweet! Shush, shush! Now, now! Come, come!" The English language, they used to tell me at school, is the richest in the world, crammed full from end to end with about a million red-hot adjectives. Yet the only one you can find to describe this ghastly business is the adjective "disturbing". It is not disturbing, Jeeves. It is . . . what's the word I want?'

'Cataclysmal, sir?'

'I shouldn't wonder. Well, what's to be done?'

'I will bring you a whisky-and-soda, sir.'

'What's the good of that?'

'It will refresh you, sir. And in the meantime, if it is your wish, I will give the matter consideration.'

'Carry on.'

'Very good, sir. I assume that it is not your desire to do anything that may in any way jeopardize the cordial relations which now exist between Miss Wickham and Mr and Master Blumenfeld?'

'Eh?'

'You would not, for example, contemplate proceeding to the Savoy Hotel and demanding the return of the dog?'

It was a tempting thought, but I shook the old onion firmly. There are things which a Wooster can do and things which, if you follow me, a Wooster cannot do. The procedure which he had indicated would undoubtedly have brought home the bacon, but the thwarted kid would have been bound to turn nasty and change his mind about the play. And, while I didn't think that any drama written by Bobbie's mother was likely to do the theatre-going public much good, I couldn't dash the cup of happiness, so to speak, from the blighted girl's lips, as it were. *Noblesse oblige* about sums the thing up.

'No, Jeeves,' I said. 'But if you can think of some way by which I can oil privily into the suite and sneak the animal out of it without causing any hard feelings, spill it.'

'I will endeavour to do so, sir.'

'Snap into it, then, without delay. They say fish are good for the brain. Have a go at the sardines and come back and report.'

'Very good, sir.'

It was about ten minutes later that he entered the presence once more.

'I fancy, sir—'

'Yes, Jeeves?'

'I rather fancy, sir, that I have discovered a plan of action.'

'Or scheme.'

'Or scheme, sir. A plan of action or scheme which will meet the situation. If I understood you rightly, sir, Mr and Master Blumenfeld have attended a motion-picture performance?'

'Correct.'

'In which case, they should not return to the hotel before five-fifteen?'

'Correct once more. Miss Wickham is scheduled in at five-thirty to sign the contract.'

'The suite, therefore, is at present unoccupied.'

'Except for McIntosh.'

'Except for McIntosh, sir. Everything, accordingly, must depend on whether Mr Blumenfeld left instructions that, in the event of her arriving before he did, Miss Wickham was to be shown straight up to the suite, to await his return.'

'Why does everything depend on that?'

'Should he have done so, the matter becomes quite simple. All that is necessary is that Miss Wickham shall present herself at the hotel at five o'clock. She will go up to the suite. You will also have arrived at the hotel at five, sir, and will have made your way to the corridor outside the suite. If Mr and Master Blumenfeld have not returned, Miss Wickham will open the door and come out and you will go in, secure the dog, and take your departure.'

I stared at the man.

'How many tins of sardines did you eat, Jeeves?'

'None, sir. I am not fond of sardines.'

'You mean, you thought of this great, this ripe, this amazing scheme entirely without the impetus given to the brain by fish?'

'Yes, sir.'

'You stand alone, Jeeves.'

'Thank you, sir.'

'But I say!'

'Sir?'

'Suppose the dog won't come away with me? You know how meagre his intelligence is. By this time, especially when he's got used to a new place, he may have forgotten me completely and will look on me as a perfect stranger.'

'I had thought of that, sir. The most judicious move will be for you to sprinkle your trousers with aniseed.'

'Aniseed?'

'Yes, sir. It is extensively used in the dog-stealing industry.'

'But, Jeeves . . . dash it . . . aniseed?'

'I consider it essential, sir.'

'But where do you get the stuff?'

'At any chemist's, sir. If you will go out now and procure a small bottle, I will be telephoning to Miss Wickham to apprise her of the contemplated arrangements and ascertain whether she is to be admitted to the suite.'

I don't know what the record is for popping out and buying aniseed, but I should think I hold it. The thought of Aunt Agatha getting nearer and nearer to the Metropolis every minute induced a rare burst of speed. I was back at the flat so quick that I nearly met myself coming out.

Jeeves had good news.

'Everything is perfectly satisfactory, sir. Mr Blumenfeld did leave instructions that Miss Wickham was to be admitted to his suite. The young lady is now on her way to the hotel. By the time you reach it, you will find her there.'

You know, whatever you may say against old Jeeves – and I, for one, have never wavered in my opinion that his views on shirts for evening wear are hidebound and reactionary to a degree – you've got to admit that the man can plan a campaign. Napoleon could have taken his correspondence course. When he sketches out a scheme, all you have to do is to follow it in detail, and there you are.

On the present occasion everything went absolutely according to plan. I had never realized before that dog-stealing could be so simple, having always regarded it rather as something that called for the ice-cool brain and the nerve of steel. I see now that a child can do it, if directed by Jeeves. I got to the hotel, sneaked up the stairs, hung about in the corridor trying to look like a potted palm in case anybody came along, and presently the door of the suite opened and Bobbie appeared, and suddenly, as I approached, out shot McIntosh, sniffing passionately, and the next moment his nose was up against my Spring trouserings and he was drinking me in with every evidence of enjoyment. If I had been a bird that had been dead about five days, he could not have nuzzled me more heartily. Aniseed isn't a scent that I care for particularly myself, but it seemed to speak straight to the deeps in McIntosh's soul.

The connection, as it were, having been established in this manner, the rest was simple. I merely withdrew, followed by the animal in the order named. We passed down the stairs in good shape, self reeking to heaven and animal inhaling the bouquet, and after a few anxious moments were safe in a cab, homeward bound. As smooth a bit of work as London had seen that day.

Arrived at the flat, I handed McIntosh to Jeeves and instructed him to shut him up in the bathroom or somewhere where the spell cast by my trousers would cease to operate. This done, I again paid the man a marked tribute.

'Jeeves,' I said, 'I have had occasion to express the view before, and I now express it again fearlessly – you stand in a class of your own.'

'Thank you very much, sir. I am glad that everything proceeded satisfactorily.'

'The festivities went like a breeze from start to finish. Tell me, were you always like this, or did it come on suddenly?'

'Sir?'

'The brain. The grey matter. Were you an outstandingly brilliant boy?'

'My mother thought me intelligent, sir.'

'You can't go by that. My mother thought *me* intelligent. Anyway, setting that aside for the moment, would a fiver be any use to you?'

'Thank you very much, sir.'

'Not that a fiver begins to cover it. Figure to yourself, Jeeves – try to envisage, if you follow what I mean, the probable behaviour of my Aunt Agatha if I had gone to her between the hours of six and seven and told her that McIntosh had passed out of the picture. I should have had to leave London and grow a beard.'

'I can readily imagine, sir, that she would have been somewhat perturbed.'

'She would. And on the occasions when my Aunt Agatha is perturbed heroes dive down drain-pipes to get out of her way. However, as it is, all has ended happily... Oh, great Scott!'

'Sir?'

I hesitated. It seemed a shame to cast a damper on the man just when he had extended himself so notably in the cause, but it had to be done.

'You've overlooked something, Jeeves.'

'Surely not, sir?'

'Yes, Jeeves, I regret to say that the late scheme or plan of

action, while gilt-edged as far as I am concerned, has rather
landed Miss Wickham in the cart.'

'In what way, sir?'

'Why, don't you see that, if they know that she was in the
suite at the time of the outrage, the Blumenfelds, father and
son, will instantly assume that she was mixed up in McIntosh's
disappearance, with the result that in their pique and chagrin
they will call off the deal about the play? I'm surprised at you
not spotting that, Jeeves. You'd have done much better to eat
those sardines, as I advised.'

I waggled the head rather sadly, and at this moment there
was a ring at the front-door bell. And not an ordinary ring,
mind you, but one of those resounding peals that suggest that
somebody with a high blood-pressure and a grievance stands
without. I leaped in my tracks. My busy afternoon had left the
old nervous system not quite in mid-season form.

'Good Lord, Jeeves!'

'Somebody at the door, sir.'

'Yes.'

'Probably Mr Blumenfeld, senior, sir.'

'What!'

'He rang up on the telephone, sir, shortly before you returned,
to say that he was about to pay you a call.'

'You don't mean that?'

'Yes, sir.'

'Advise me, Jeeves.'

'I fancy the most judicious procedure would be for you to
conceal yourself behind the settee, sir.'

I saw that his advice was good. I had never met this Blumenfeld socially, but I had seen him from afar on the occasion when
he and Cyril Bassington-Bassington had had their falling out,

and he hadn't struck me then as a bloke with whom, if in one of his emotional moods, it would be at all agreeable to be shut up in a small room. A large, round, fat, overflowing bird, who might quite easily, if stirred, fall on a fellow and flatten him to the carpet.

So I nestled behind the settee, and in about five seconds there was a sound like a mighty, rushing wind and something extraordinarily substantial bounded into the sitting-room.

'This guy Wooster,' bellowed a voice that had been strengthened by a lifetime of ticking actors off at dress-rehearsals from the back of the theatre. 'Where is he?'

Jeeves continued suave.

'I could not say, sir.'

'He's sneaked my son's dog.'

'Indeed, sir?'

'Walked into my suite as cool as dammit and took the animal away.'

'Most disturbing, sir.'

'And you don't know where he is?'

'Mr Wooster may be anywhere, sir. He is uncertain in his movements.'

The bloke Blumenfeld gave a loud sniff.

'Odd smell here!'

'Yes, sir?'

'What is it?'

'Aniseed, sir.'

'Aniseed?'

'Yes, sir. Mr Wooster sprinkles it on his trousers.'

'Sprinkles it on his trousers?'

'Yes, sir.'

'What on earth does he do that for?'

'I could not say, sir. Mr Wooster's motives are always some-what hard to follow. He is eccentric.'

'Eccentric? He must be a loony.'

'Yes, sir.'

'You mean he is?'

'Yes, sir!'

There was a pause. A long one.

'Oh?' said old Blumenfeld, and it seemed to me that a good deal of what you might call the vim had gone out of his voice.

He paused again.

'Not *dangerous*?'

'Yes, sir, when roused.'

'Er – what rouses him chiefly?'

'One of Mr Wooster's peculiarities is that he does not like the sight of gentlemen of full habit, sir. They seem to infuriate him.'

'You mean, fat men?'

'Yes, sir.'

'Why?'

'One cannot say, sir.'

There was another pause.

'*I'm* fat!' said old Blumenfeld in a rather pensive sort of voice.

'I would not have ventured to suggest it myself, sir, but as you say so ... You may recollect that, on being informed that you were to be a member of the luncheon party, Mr Wooster, doubting his power of self-control, refused to be present.'

'That's right. He went rushing out just as I arrived. I thought it odd at the time. My son thought it odd. We both thought it odd.'

'Yes, sir. Mr Wooster, I imagine, wished to avoid any possible unpleasantness, such as has occurred before ... With regard to the smell of aniseed, sir, I fancy I have now located it. Unless

I am mistaken it proceeds from behind the settee. No doubt Mr Wooster is sleeping there.'

'Doing what?'

'Sleeping, sir.'

'Does he often sleep on the floor?'

'Most afternoons, sir. Would you desire me to wake him?'

'No!'

'I thought you had something that you wished to say to Mr Wooster, sir.'

Old Blumenfeld drew a deep breath. 'So did I,' he said. 'But I find I haven't. Just get me alive out of here, that's all I ask.'

I heard the door close, and a little while later the front door banged. I crawled out. It hadn't been any too cosy behind the settee, and I was glad to be elsewhere. Jeeves came trickling back.

'Gone, Jeeves?'

'Yes, sir.'

I bestowed an approving look on him.

'One of your best efforts, Jeeves.'

'Thank you, sir.'

'But what beats me is why he ever came here. What made him think that I had sneaked McIntosh away?'

'I took the liberty of recommending Miss Wickham to tell Mr Blumenfeld that she had observed you removing the animal from his suite, sir. The point which you raised regarding the possibility of her being suspected of complicity in the affair, had not escaped me. It seemed to me that this would establish her solidly in Mr Blumenfeld's good opinion.'

'I see. Risky, of course, but possibly justified. Yes, on the whole, justified. What's that you've got there?'

'A five-pound note, sir.'

'Ah, the one I gave you?'

'No, sir. The one Mr Blumenfeld gave me.'

'Eh? Why did he give you a fiver?'

'He very kindly presented it to me on my handing him the dog, sir.'

I gaped at the man.

'You don't mean to say—?'

'Not McIntosh, sir. McIntosh is at present in my bedroom. This was another animal of the same species which I purchased at the shop in Bond Street during your absence. Except to the eye of love, one Aberdeen terrier looks very much like another Aberdeen terrier, sir. Mr Blumenfeld, I am happy to say, did not detect the innocent subterfuge.'

'Jeeves,' I said – and I am not ashamed to confess that there was a spot of chokiness in the voice – 'there is none like you, none.'

'Thank you very much, sir.'

'Owing solely to the fact that your head bulges in unexpected spots, thus enabling you to do about twice as much bright thinking in any given time as any other two men in existence, happiness, you might say, reigns supreme. Aunt Agatha is on velvet, I am on velvet, the Wickhams, mother and daughter, are on velvet, the Blumenfelds, father and son, are on velvet. As far as the eye can reach, a solid mass of humanity, owing to you, all on velvet. A fiver is not sufficient, Jeeves. If I thought the world thought that Bertram Wooster thought a measly five pounds an adequate reward for such services as yours, I should never hold my head up again. Have another?'

'Thank you, sir.'

'And one more?'

'Thank you very much, sir.'

'And a third for luck?'

'Really, sir, I am exceedingly obliged. Excuse me, sir, I fancy I heard the telephone.'

He pushed out into the hall, and I heard him doing a good deal of the 'Yes, madam,' 'Certainly, madam!' stuff. Then he came back.

'Mrs Spenser Gregson on the telephone, sir.'

'Aunt Agatha?'

'Yes, sir. Speaking from Victoria Station. She desires to communicate with you with reference to the dog McIntosh. I gather that she wishes to hear from your own lips that all is well with the little fellow, sir.'

I straightened the tie. I pulled down the waistcoat. I shot the cuffs. I felt absolutely all-righto.

'Lead me to her,' I said.

I was lunching at my Aunt Dahlia's, and despite the fact that Anatole, her outstanding cook, had rather excelled himself in the matter of the bill-of-fare, I'm bound to say the food was more or less turning to ashes in my mouth. You see, I had some bad news to break to her – always a prospect that takes the edge off the appetite. She wouldn't be pleased, I knew, and when not pleased Aunt Dahlia, having spent most of her youth in the hunting-field, has a crispish way of expressing herself.

However, I supposed I had better have a dash at it and get it over.

'Aunt Dahlia,' I said, facing the issue squarely.

'Hullo?'

'You know that cruise of yours?'

'Yes.'

'That yachting-cruise you are planning?'

'Yes.'

'That jolly cruise in your yacht in the Mediterranean to which you so kindly invited me and to which I have been looking forward with such keen anticipation?'

'Get on, fathead, what about it?'

I swallowed a chunk of *cotelette-suprême-aux-choux-fleurs* and slipped her the distressing info'.

'I'm frightfully sorry, Aunt Dahlia,' I said, 'but I shan't be able to come.'

As I had foreseen, she goggled.

'What!'

'I'm afraid not.'

'You poor, miserable hell-hound, what do you mean, you won't be able to come?'

'Well, I won't.'

'Why not?'

'Matters of the most extreme urgency render my presence in the Metropolis imperative.'

She sniffed.

'I suppose what you really mean is that you're hanging round some unfortunate girl again?'

I didn't like the way she put it, but I admit I was stunned by her penetration, if that's the word I want. I mean the sort of thing detectives have.

'Yes, Aunt Dahlia,' I said, 'you have guessed my secret. I do indeed love.'

'Who is she?'

'A Miss Pendlebury. Christian name, Gwladys. She spells it with a "w".'

'With a "g", you mean.'

'With a "w" *and* a "g".'

'Not Gwladys?'

'That's it.'

The relative uttered a yowl.

'You sit there and tell me you haven't enough sense to steer clear of a girl who calls herself Gwladys? Listen, Bertie,' said Aunt Dahlia earnestly, 'I'm an older woman than you are – well, you know what I mean – and I can tell you a thing or two. And one of them is that no good can come of association with anything labelled Gwladys or Ysobel or Ethyl or Mabelle or Kathryn. But particularly Gwladys. What sort of girl is she?'

'Slightly divine.'

'She isn't that female I saw driving you at sixty miles p.h. in the Park the other day. In a red two-seater?'

'She did drive me in the Park the other day. I thought it rather a hopeful sign. And her Widgeon Seven is red.'

Aunt Dahlia looked relieved.

'Oh well, then, she'll probably break your silly fat neck before she can get you to the altar. That's some consolation. Where did you meet her?'

'At a party in Chelsea. She's an artist.'

'Ye gods!'

'And swings a jolly fine brush, let me tell you. She's painted a portrait of me. Jeeves and I hung it up in the flat this morning. I have an idea Jeeves doesn't like it.'

'Well, if it's anything like you I don't see why he should. An artist! Calls herself Gwladys! And drives a car in the sort of way Segrave would if he were pressed for time.' She brooded awhile. 'Well, it's all very sad, but I can't see why you won't come on the yacht.'

I explained.

'It would be madness to leave the metrop. at this juncture,' I said. 'You know what girls are. They forget the absent face. And I'm not at all easy in my mind about a certain cove of the name of Lucius Pim. Apart from the fact that he's an artist, too, which forms a bond, his hair waves. One must never discount wavy hair, Aunt Dahlia. Moreover, this bloke is one of those strong, masterful men. He treats Gwladys as if she were less than the dust beneath his taxi wheels. He criticizes her hats and says nasty things about her chiaroscuro. For some reason, I've often noticed, this always seems to fascinate girls, and it has sometimes occurred to me that, being myself more the parfait gentle knight, if you know what I mean, I am in grave danger of getting the short end. Taking all these things into consideration, then, I cannot breeze off to the Mediterranean, leaving this Pim a clear field. You must see that?'

Aunt Dahlia laughed. Rather a nasty laugh. Scorn in its *timbre*, or so it seemed to me.

'I shouldn't worry,' she said. 'You don't suppose for a moment that Jeeves will sanction the match?'

I was stung.

'Do you imply, Aunt Dahlia,' I said – and I can't remember if I rapped the table with the handle of my fork or not, but I rather think I did – 'that I allow Jeeves to boss me to the extent of stopping me marrying somebody I want to marry?'

'Well, he stopped you wearing a moustache, didn't he? And purple socks. And soft-fronted shirts with dress-clothes.'

'That is a different matter altogether.'

'Well, I'm prepared to make a small bet with you, Bertie. Jeeves will stop this match.'

'What absolute rot!'

'And if he doesn't like that portrait, he will get rid of it.'

'I never heard such dashed nonsense in my life.'

'And, finally, you wretched, pie-faced wambler, he will present you on board my yacht at the appointed hour. I don't know how he will do it, but you will be there, all complete with yachting-cap and spare pair of socks.'

'Let us change the subject, Aunt Dahlia,' I said coldly.

* * *

Being a good deal stirred up by the attitude of the flesh-and-blood at the luncheon-table, I had to go for a bit of a walk in the Park after leaving, to soothe the nervous system. By about four-thirty the ganglions had ceased to vibrate, and I returned to the flat. Jeeves was in the sitting-room, looking at the portrait.

I felt a trifle embarrassed in the man's presence, because just before leaving I had informed him of my intention to scratch the yacht-trip, and he had taken it on the chin a bit. You see, he had been looking forward to it rather. From the moment I had accepted the invitation, there had been a sort of nautical glitter in his eye, and I'm not sure I hadn't heard him trolling Chanties in the kitchen. I think some ancestor of his must have been one of Nelson's tars or something, for he has always had the urge of the salt sea in his blood. I have noticed him on liners, when we were going to America, striding the deck with a sailorly roll and giving the distinct impression of being just about to heave the main-brace or splice the binnacle.

So, though I had explained my reasons, taking the man fully into my confidence and concealing nothing, I knew that he was distinctly peeved; and my first act, on entering, was to do the cheery a bit. I joined him in front of the portrait.

'Looks good, Jeeves, what?'

'Yes, sir.'

'Nothing like a spot of art for brightening the home.'

'No, sir.'

'Seems to lend the room a certain – what shall I say—'

'Yes, sir.'

The responses were all right, but his manner was far from hearty, and I decided to tackle him squarely. I mean, dash it. I mean, I don't know if you have ever had your portrait painted, but if you have you will understand my feelings. The spectacle of one's portrait hanging on the wall creates in one a sort of paternal fondness for the thing: and what you demand from the outside public is approval and enthusiasm – not the curling lip, the twitching nostril, and the kind of supercilious look which you see in the eye of a dead mackerel. Especially is this so when the artist is a girl for whom you have conceived sentiments deeper and warmer than those of ordinary friendship.

'Jeeves,' I said, 'you don't like this spot of art.'

'Oh, yes, sir.'

'No. Subterfuge is useless. I can read you like a book. For some reason this spot of art fails to appeal to you. What do you object to about it?'

'Is not the colour-scheme a trifle bright, sir?'

'I had not observed it, Jeeves. Anything else?'

'Well, in my opinion, sir, Miss Pendlebury has given you a somewhat too hungry expression.'

'Hungry?'

'A little like that of a dog regarding a distant bone, sir.'

I checked the fellow.

'There is no resemblance whatever, Jeeves, to a dog regarding a distant bone. The look to which you allude is wistful and denotes Soul.'

'I see, sir.'

I proceeded to another subject.

'Miss Pendlebury said she might look in this afternoon to inspect the portrait. Did she turn up?'

'Yes, sir.'

'But has left?'

'Yes, sir.'

'You mean she's gone, what?'

'Precisely, sir.'

'She didn't say anything about coming back, I suppose?'

'No, sir. I received the impression that it was not Miss Pendlebury's intention to return. She was a little upset, sir, and expressed a desire to go to her studio and rest.'

'Upset? What was she upset about?'

'The accident, sir.'

I didn't actually clutch the brow, but I did a bit of mental brow-clutching, as it were.

'Don't tell me she had an accident!'

'Yes, sir.'

'What sort of accident?'

'Automobile, sir.'

'Was she hurt?'

'No, sir. Only the gentleman.'

'What gentleman?'

'Miss Pendlebury had the misfortune to run over a gentleman in her car almost immediately opposite this building. He sustained a slight fracture of the leg.'

'Too bad! But Miss Pendlebury is all right?'

'Physically, sir, her condition appeared to be satisfactory. She was suffering a certain distress of mind.'

'Of course, with her beautiful, sympathetic nature. Naturally. It's a hard world for a girl, Jeeves, with fellows flinging themselves under the wheels of her car in one long, unending stream. It must have been a great shock to her. What became of the chump?'

'The gentleman, sir?'

'Yes.'

'He is in your spare bedroom, sir.'

'What!'

'Yes, sir.'

'In my spare bedroom?'

'Yes, sir. It was Miss Pendlebury's desire that he should be taken there. She instructed me to telegraph to the gentleman's sister, sir, who is in Paris, advising her of the accident. I also summoned a medical man, who gave it as his opinion that the patient should remain for the time being *in statu quo.*'

'You mean, the corpse is on the premises for an indefinite visit?'

'Yes, sir.'

'Jeeves, this is a bit thick!'

'Yes, sir.'

And I meant it, dash it. I mean to say, a girl can be pretty heftily divine and ensnare the heart and what not, but she's no right to turn a fellow's flat into a morgue. I'm bound to say that for a moment passion ebbed a trifle.

'Well, I suppose I'd better go and introduce myself to the blighter. After all, I am his host. Has he a name?'

'Mr Pim, sir.'

'Pim!'

'Yes, sir. And the young lady addressed him as Lucius. It was owing to the fact that he was on his way here to examine the portrait which she had painted that Mr Pim happened to be in the roadway at the moment when Miss Pendlebury turned the corner.'

I headed for the spare bedroom. I was perturbed to a degree. I don't know if you have ever loved and been handicapped in your wooing by a wavy-haired rival, but one of the things you don't want in such circs is the rival parking himself on the premises with a broken leg. Apart from anything else, the advantage the position gives him is obviously terrific. There he is, sitting up and toying with a grape and looking pale and interesting, the object of the girl's pity and concern, and where do you get off, bounding about the place in morning costume and spats and with the rude flush of health on the cheek? It seemed to me that things were beginning to look pretty mouldy.

I found Lucius Pim lying in bed, draped in a suit of my pyjamas, smoking one of my cigarettes, and reading a detective story. He waved the cigarette at me in what I considered a dashed patronizing manner.

'Ah, Wooster!' he said.

'Not so much of the "Ah, Wooster!"' I replied brusquely. 'How soon can you be moved?'

'In a week or so, I fancy.'

'In a week!'

'Or so. For the moment, the doctor insists on perfect quiet and repose. So forgive me, old man, for asking you not to raise your voice. A hushed whisper is the stuff to give the troops. And now, Wooster, about this accident. We must come to an understanding.'

'Are you sure you can't be moved?'

'Quite. The doctor said so.'

'I think we ought to get a second opinion.'

'Useless, my dear fellow. He was most emphatic, and evidently a man who knew his job. Don't worry about my not being comfortable here. I shall be quite all right. I like this bed. And now, to return to the subject of this accident. My sister will be arriving to-morrow. She will be greatly upset. I am her favourite brother.'

'You are?'

'I am.'

'How many of you are there?'

'Six.'

'And you're her favourite?'

'I am.'

It seemed to me that the other five must be pretty fairly sub-human, but I didn't say so. We Woosters can curb the tongue.

'She married a bird named Slingsby. Slingsby's Superb Soups. He rolls in money. But do you think I can get him to lend a trifle from time to time to a needy brother-in-law?' said Lucius Pim bitterly. 'No, sir! However, that is neither here nor there. The point is that my sister loves me devotedly: and, this being the case, she might try to prosecute and persecute and generally bite pieces out of poor little Gwladys if she knew that it was she who was driving the car that laid me out. She must never know, Wooster. I appeal to you as a man of honour to keep your mouth shut.'

'Naturally.'

'I'm glad you grasp the point so readily, Wooster. You are not the fool people take you for.'

'Who takes me for a fool?'

The Pim raised his eyebrows slightly.

'Don't people?' he said. 'Well, well. Anyway, that's settled. Unless I can think of something better I shall tell my sister that I was knocked down by a car which drove on without stopping and I didn't get its number. And now perhaps you had better leave me. The doctor made a point of quiet and repose. More-over, I want to go on with this story. The villain has just dropped a cobra down the heroine's chimney, and I must be at her side. It is impossible not to be thrilled by Edgar Wallace. I'll ring if I want anything.'

I headed for the sitting-room. I found Jeeves there, staring at the portrait in rather a marked manner, as if it hurt him.

'Jeeves,' I said, 'Mr Pim appears to be a fixture.'

'Yes, sir.'

'For the nonce, at any rate. And to-morrow we shall have his sister, Mrs Slingsby, of Slingsby's Superb Soups, in our midst.'

'Yes, sir. I telegraphed to Mrs Slingsby shortly before four. Assuming her to have been at her hotel in Paris at the moment of the telegram's delivery, she will no doubt take a boat early to-morrow afternoon, reaching Dover – or, should she prefer the alternative route, Folkestone – in time to begin the railway journey at an hour which will enable her to arrive in London at about seven. She will possibly proceed first to her London residence—'

'Yes, Jeeves,' I said, 'yes. A gripping story, full of action and human interest. You must have it set to music some time and sing it. Meanwhile, get this into your head. It is imperative that Mrs Slingsby does not learn that it was Miss Pendlebury who broke her brother in two places. I shall require you, therefore, to approach Mr Pim before she arrives, ascertain exactly what tale he intends to tell, and be prepared to back it up in every particular.'

'Very good, sir.'

'And now, Jeeves, what of Miss Pendlebury?'

'Sir?'

'She's sure to call to make enquiries.'

'Yes, sir.'

'Well, she mustn't find me here. You know all about women, Jeeves?'

'Yes, sir.'

'Then tell me this. Am I not right in supposing that if Miss Pendlebury is in a position to go into the sick-room, take a long look at the interesting invalid, and then pop out, with the memory of that look fresh in her mind, and get a square sight of me lounging about in sponge-bag trousers, she will draw damaging comparisons? You see what I mean? Look on this picture and on that – the one romantic, the other not ... Eh?'

'Very true, sir. It is a point which I had intended to bring to your attention. An invalid undoubtedly exercises a powerful appeal to the motherliness which exists in every woman's heart, sir. Invalids seem to stir their deepest feelings. The poet Scott has put the matter neatly in the lines – "Oh, Woman in our hours of ease uncertain, coy, and hard to please ... When pain and anguish rack the brow—"'

I held up a hand.

'At some other time, Jeeves,' I said, 'I shall be delighted to hear you say your piece, but just now I am not in the mood. The position being as I have outlined, I propose to clear out early to-morrow morning and not to reappear until nightfall. I shall take the car and dash down to Brighton for the day.'

'Very good, sir.'

'It is better so, is it not, Jeeves?'

'Indubitably, sir.'

'I think so, too. The sea breezes will tone up my system, which sadly needs a dollop of toning. I leave you in charge of the old home.'

'Very good, sir.'

'Convey my regrets and sympathy to Miss Pendlebury and tell her I have been called away on business.'

'Yes, sir.'

'Should the Slingsby require refreshment, feed her in moderation.'

'Very good, sir.'

'And, in poisoning Mr Pim's soup, don't use arsenic, which

is readily detected. Go to a good chemist and get something that leaves no traces.'

I sighed, and cocked an eye at the portrait.

'All this is very wonky, Jeeves.'

'Yes, sir.'

'When that portrait was painted, I was a happy man.'

'Yes, sir.'

'Ah, well, Jeeves!'

'Very true, sir.'

And we left it at that.

It was lateish when I got back on the following evening. What with a bit of ozone-sniffing, a good dinner, and a nice run home in the moonlight with the old car going as sweet as a nut, I was feeling in pretty good shape once more. In fact, coming through Purley, I went so far as to sing a trifle. The spirit of the Woosters is a buoyant spirit, and optimism had begun to reign again in the W. bosom.

The way I looked at it was, I saw I had been mistaken in assuming that a girl must necessarily love a fellow just because he has broken a leg. At first, no doubt, Gwladys Pendlebury would feel strangely drawn to the Pim when she saw him lying there a more or less total loss. But it would not be long before other reflections crept in. She would ask herself if she were wise in trusting her life's happiness to a man who hadn't enough sense to leap out of the way when he saw a car coming. She would tell herself that, if this sort of thing had happened once, who knew that it might not go on happening again and again all down the long years. And she would recoil from a married life which consisted entirely of going to hospitals and taking her husband fruit. She would realize how much better off she would be, teamed up with a fellow like Bertram Wooster, who, whatever his faults, at least walked on the pavement and looked up and down a street before he crossed it.

It was in excellent spirits, accordingly, that I put the car in the garage, and it was with a merry Tra-la on my lips that I let myself into the flat as Big Ben began to strike eleven. I rang the bell and presently, as if he had divined my wishes, Jeeves came in with siphon and decanter.

'Home again, Jeeves,' I said, mixing a spot.

'Yes, sir.'

'What has been happening in my absence? Did Miss Pendlebury call?'

'Yes, sir. At about two o'clock.'

'And left?'

'At about six, sir.'

I didn't like this so much. A four-hour visit struck me as a bit sinister. However, there was nothing to be done about it.

'And Mrs Slingsby?'

'She arrived shortly after eight and left at ten, sir.'

'Ah? Agitated?'

'Yes, sir. Particularly when she left. She was very desirous of seeing you, sir.'

'Seeing me?'

'Yes, sir.'

'Wanted to thank me brokenly, I suppose, for so courteously allowing her favourite brother a place to have his game legs in. Eh?'

'Possibly, sir. On the other hand, she alluded to you in terms suggestive of disapprobation, sir.'

'She – what?'

'"Feckless idiot" was one of the expressions she employed, sir.'

'Feckless idiot?'

'Yes, sir.'

I couldn't make it out. I simply couldn't see what the woman had based her judgement on. My Aunt Agatha has frequently said that sort of thing about me, but she has known me from a boy.

'I must look into this, Jeeves. Is Mr Pim asleep?'

'No, sir. He rang the bell a moment ago to enquire if we had not a better brand of cigarette in the flat.'

'He did, did he?'

'Yes, sir.'

'The accident doesn't seem to have affected his nerve.'

'No, sir.'

I found Lucius Pim sitting propped up among the pillows, reading his detective story.

'Ah, Wooster,' he said. 'Welcome home. I say, in case you were worrying, it's all right about that cobra. The hero had got at it without the villain's knowledge and extracted its poison-fangs. With the result that when it fell down the chimney and started trying to bite the heroine its efforts were null and void. I doubt if a cobra has ever felt so silly.'

'Never mind about cobras.'

'It's no good saying "Never mind about cobras",' said Lucius Pim in a gentle, rebuking sort of voice. 'You've jolly well *got* to mind about cobras, if they haven't had their poison-fangs extracted. Ask anyone. By the way, my sister looked in. She wants to have a word with you.'

'And I want to have a word with her.'

' "Two minds with but a single thought". What she wants to talk to you about is this accident of mine. You remember that story I was to tell her? About the car driving on? Well the understanding was, if you recollect, that I was only to tell it if I couldn't think of something better. Fortunately, I thought of something much better. It came to me in a flash as I lay in bed looking at the ceiling. You see, that driving-on story was thin. People don't knock fellows down and break their legs and go driving on. The thing wouldn't have held water for a minute. So I told her you did it.'

'What!'

'I said it was you who did it in your car. Much more likely. Makes the whole thing neat and well-rounded. I knew you would approve. At all costs we have got to keep it from her that I was outed by Gwladys. I made it as easy for you as I could, saying that you were a bit pickled at the time and so not to be blamed for what you did. Some fellows wouldn't have thought of that. Still,' said Lucius Pim with a sigh, 'I'm afraid she's not any too pleased with you.'

'She isn't, isn't she?'

'No, she is not. And I strongly recommend you, if you want anything like a pleasant interview to-morrow, to sweeten her a bit overnight.'

'How do you mean, sweeten her?'

'I'd suggest you sent her some flowers. It would be a graceful gesture. Roses are her favourites. Shoot her in a few roses – Number Three, Hill Street is the address – and it may make all the difference. I think it my duty to inform you, old man, that my sister Beatrice is rather a tough egg, when roused. My brother-in-law is due back from New York at any moment, and the danger, as I see it, is that Beatrice, unless sweetened, will get at him and make him bring actions against you for torts and malfeasances and what not and get thumping damages. He isn't over-fond of me and, left to himself, would rather approve than otherwise of people who broke my legs: but he's crazy about Beatrice and will do anything she asks him to. So my advice is, Gather ye rose-buds, while ye may and bung them in to Number Three, Hill Street. Otherwise, the case of Slingsby *v.* Wooster will be on the calendar before you can say "What-ho".'

I gave the fellow a look. Lost on him, of course.

'It's a pity you didn't think of all that before,' I said. And it wasn't so much the actual words, if you know what I mean, as the way I said it.

'I thought of it all right,' said Lucius Pim. 'But, as we were both agreed that at all costs—'

'Oh, all right,' I said. 'All right, all right.'

'You aren't annoyed?' said Lucius Pim, looking at me with a touch of surprise.

'Oh, no!'

'Splendid,' said Lucius Pim, relieved. 'I knew you would feel that I had done the only possible thing. It would have been awful if Beatrice had found out about Gwladys. I daresay you have noticed, Wooster, that when women find themselves in a position to take a running kick at one of their own sex they are twice as rough on her as they would be on a man. Now, you, being of the male persuasion, will find everything made nice and smooth for you. A quart of assorted roses, a few smiles, a tactful word or two, and she'll have melted before you know where you are. Play your cards properly, and you and Beatrice will be laughing merrily and having a game of Round and Round the Mulberry Bush together in about five minutes. Better not let Slingsby's Soups catch you at it, however. He's very jealous where Beatrice is concerned. And now you'll forgive me, old chap, if I send you away. The doctor says I ought not to talk too much for a day or two. Besides, it's time for bye-bye.'

The more I thought it over, the better that idea of sending those roses looked. Lucius Pim was not a man I was fond of – in fact, if I had had to choose between him and a cockroach as a companion for a walking-tour, the cockroach would have had it by a short head – but there was no doubt that he had outlined the right policy. His advice was good, and I decided to follow it. Rising next morning at ten-fifteen, I swallowed a strengthening breakfast and legged it off to that flower-shop in Piccadilly. I couldn't leave the thing to Jeeves. It was essentially a mission that demanded the personal touch. I laid out a couple of quid on a sizeable bouquet, sent it with my card to Hill Street, and then looked in at the Drones for a brief refresher. It is a thing I don't often do in the morning, but this threatened to be rather a special morning.

It was about noon when I got back to the flat. I went into the sitting-room and tried to adjust the mind to the coming interview. It had to be faced, of course, but it wasn't any good my telling myself that it was going to be one of those jolly scenes the memory of which cheer you up as you sit toasting your toes at the fire in your old age. I stood or fell by the roses. If they sweetened the Slingsby, all would be well. If they failed to sweeten her, Bertram was undoubtedly for it.

The clock ticked on, but she did not come. A late riser, I took it, and was slightly encouraged by the reflection. My experience of women has been that the earlier they leave the hay the more vicious specimens they are apt to be. My Aunt Agatha, for instance, is always up with the lark, and look at her.

Still, you couldn't be sure that this rule always worked, and after a while the suspense began to get in amongst me a bit. To divert the mind, I fetched the old putter out of its bag and began to practise putts into a glass. After all, even if the Slingsby turned out to be all that I had pictured her in my gloomier moments, I should have improved my close-to-the-hole work on the green and be that much up, at any rate.

It was while I was shaping for a rather tricky shot that the front-door bell went.

I picked up the glass and shoved the putter behind the settee. It struck me that if the woman found me engaged on what you might call a frivolous pursuit she might take it to indicate lack of remorse and proper feeling. I straightened the collar, pulled down the waistcoat, and managed to fasten on the face a sort of sad half-smile which was welcoming without being actually jovial. It looked all right in the mirror, and I held it as the door opened.

'Mr Slingsby,' announced Jeeves.

And, having spoken these words, he closed the door and left us alone together.

For quite a time there wasn't anything in the way of chit-chat. The shock of expecting Mrs Slingsby and finding myself confronted by something entirely different – in fact, not the same thing at all – seemed to have affected the vocal cords. And the visitor didn't appear to be disposed to make light conversation himself. He stood there looking strong and silent. I suppose you have to be like that if you want to manufacture anything in the nature of a really convincing soup.

Slingsby's Superb Soups was a Roman Emperor-looking sort of bird, with keen, penetrating eyes and one of those jutting chins. The eyes seemed to be fixed on me in a dashed unpleasant stare and, unless I was mistaken, he was grinding his teeth a trifle. For some reason he appeared to have taken a strong dislike to me at sight, and I'm bound to say this rather puzzled me.

I don't pretend to have one of those Fascinating Personalities which you get from studying the booklets advertised in the back pages of the magazines, but I couldn't recall another case in the whole of my career where a single glimpse of the old map had been enough to make anyone look as if he wanted to foam at the mouth. Usually, when people meet me for the first time, they don't seem to know I'm there.

However, I exerted myself to play the host.

'Mr Slingsby?'

'That is my name.'

'Just got back from America?'

'I landed this morning.'

'Sooner than you were expected, what?'

'So I imagine.'

'Very glad to see you.'

'You will not be long.'

I took time off to do a bit of gulping. I saw now what had happened. This bloke had been home, seen his wife, heard the story of the accident, and had hastened round to the flat to slip it across me. Evidently those roses had not sweetened the female of the species. The only thing to do now seemed to be to take a stab at sweetening the male.

'Have a drink?' I said.

'No!'

'A cigarette?'

'No!'

'A chair?'

'No!'

I went into the silence once more. These non-drinking, non-smoking non-sitters are hard birds to handle.

'Don't grin at me, sir!'

I shot a glance at myself in the mirror, and saw what he meant. The sad half-smile *had* slopped over a bit. I adjusted it, and there was another pause.

'Now, sir,' said the Superb Souper. 'To business. I think I need scarcely tell you why I am here.'

'No. Of course. Absolutely. It's about that little matter—'

He gave a snort which nearly upset a vase on the mantelpiece.

'Little matter? So you consider it a little matter, do you?'

'Well—'

'Let me tell you, sir, that when I find that during my absence from the country a man has been annoying my wife with his importunities I regard it as anything but a little matter. And I shall endeavour,' said the Souper, the eyes gleaming a trifle brighter as he rubbed his hands together in a hideous, menacing way, 'to make you see the thing in the same light.'

I couldn't make head or tail of this. I simply couldn't follow him. The lemon began to swim.

'Eh?' I said. 'Your wife?'

'You heard me.'

'There must be some mistake.'

'There is. You made it.'

'But I don't know your wife.'

'Ha!'

'I've never even met her.'

'Tchah!'

'Honestly, I haven't.'

'Bah!'

He drank me in for a moment.

'Do you deny you sent her flowers?'

I felt the heart turn a double somersault. I began to catch his drift.

'Flowers!' he proceeded. 'Roses, sir. Great, fat, beastly roses. Enough of them to sink a ship. Your card was attached to them by a small pin—'

His voice died away in a sort of gurgle, and I saw that he was staring at something behind me. I spun round, and there, in the doorway – I hadn't seen it open, because during the last spasm of dialogue I had been backing cautiously towards it – there in the doorway stood a female. One glance was enough to tell me who she was. No woman could look so like Lucius Pim who hadn't the misfortune to be related to him. It was Sister Beatrice, the tough egg. I saw all. She had left home before the flowers had arrived: she had sneaked, unsweetened, into the flat, while I was fortifying the system at the Drones: and here she was.

'Er—' I said.

'Alexander!' said the female.

'Goo!' said the Souper. Or it may have been 'Coo'.

Whatever it was, it was in the nature of a battle-cry or slogan of war. The Souper's worst suspicions had obviously been confirmed. His eyes shone with a strange light. His chin pushed itself out another couple of inches. He clenched and unclenched his fingers once or twice, as if to make sure that they were working properly and could be relied on to do a good, clean job of strangling. Then, once more observing 'Coo!' (or 'Goo!'), he sprang forward, trod on the golf-ball I had been practising putting with, and took one of the finest tosses I have ever witnessed. The purler of a lifetime. For a moment the air seemed to be full of arms and legs, and then, with a thud that nearly dislocated the flat, he made a forced landing against the wall.

And, feeling I had had about all I wanted, I oiled from the room and was in the act of grabbing my hat from the rack in the hall, when Jeeves appeared.

'I fancied I heard a noise, sir,' said Jeeves.

'Quite possibly,' I said. 'It was Mr Slingsby.'

'Sir?'

'Mr Slingsby practising Russian dances,' I explained. 'I rather think he has fractured an assortment of limbs. Better go in and see.'

'Very good, sir.'

'If he is the wreck I imagine, put him in my room and send for the doctor. The flat is filling up nicely with the various units of the Pim family and its connections, eh, Jeeves?'

'Yes, sir.'

'I think the supply is about exhausted, but should any aunts or uncles by marriage come along and break their limbs, bed them out on the Chesterfield.'

'Very good, sir.'

'I, personally, Jeeves,' I said, opening the front door and pausing on the threshold, 'am off to Paris. I will wire you the address. Notify me in due course when the place is free from Pims and completely purged of Slingsbys, and I will return. Oh, and Jeeves.'

'Sir?'

'Spare no effort to mollify these birds. They think – at least, Slingsby (female) thinks, and what she thinks to-day he will think to-morrow – that it was I who ran over Mr Pim in my car. Endeavour during my absence to sweeten them.'

'Very good, sir.'

'And now perhaps you had better be going in and viewing

the body. I shall proceed to the Drones, where I shall lunch, subsequently catching the two o'clock train at Charing Cross. Meet me there with an assortment of luggage.'

It was a matter of three weeks or so before Jeeves sent me the 'All clear' signal. I spent the time pottering pretty perturbedly about Paris and environs. It is a city I am fairly fond of, but I was glad to be able to return to the old home. I hopped on to a passing aeroplane and a couple of hours later was bowling through Croydon on my way to the centre of things. It was somewhere down in the Sloane Square neighbourhood that I first caught sight of the posters.

A traffic block had occurred, and I was glancing idly this way and that, when suddenly my eye was caught by something that looked familiar. And then I saw what it was.

Pasted on a blank wall and measuring about a hundred feet each way was an enormous poster, mostly red and blue. At the top of it were the words:

SLINGSBY'S SUPERB SOUPS

and at the bottom:

SUCCULENT AND STRENGTHENING

And, in between, me. Yes, dash it, Bertram Wooster in person. A reproduction of the Pendlebury portrait, perfect in every detail.

It was the sort of thing to make a fellow's eyes flicker, and mine flickered. You might say a mist seemed to roll before them. Then it lifted, and I was able to get a good long look before the traffic moved on.

Of all the absolutely foul sights I have ever seen, this took the biscuit with ridiculous ease. The thing was a bally libel on the Wooster face, and yet it was as unmistakable as if it had had my name under it. I saw now what Jeeves had meant when he said that the portrait had given me a hungry look. In the poster this look had become one of bestial greed. There I sat absolutely slavering through a monocle about six inches in circumference at a plateful of soup, looking as if I hadn't had a meal for weeks. The whole thing seemed to take one straight away into a different and a dreadful world.

I woke from a species of trance or coma to find myself at the door of the block of flats. To buzz upstairs and charge into the home was with me the work of a moment.

Jeeves came shimmering down the hall, the respectful beam of welcome on his face.

'I am glad to see you back, sir.'

'Never mind about that,' I yipped. 'What about—?'

'The posters, sir? I was wondering if you might have observed them.'

'I observed them!'

'Striking, sir?'

'Very striking. Now, perhaps you'll kindly explain—'

'You instructed me, if you recollect, sir, to spare no effort to mollify Mr Slingsby.'

'Yes, but—'

'It proved a somewhat difficult task, sir. For some time Mr Slingsby, on the advice and owing to the persuasion of Mrs Slingsby, appeared to be resolved to institute an action in law against you – a procedure which I knew you would find most distasteful.'

'Yes, but—'

'And then, the first day he was able to leave his bed, he

observed the portrait, and it seemed to me judicious to point out to him its possibilities as an advertising medium. He readily fell in with the suggestion and, on my assurance that, should he abandon the projected action in law, you would willingly permit the use of the portrait, he entered into negotiations with Miss Pendlebury for the purchase of the copyright.'

'Oh? Well, I hope she's got something out of it, at any rate?'

'Yes, sir. Mr Pim, acting as Miss Pendlebury's agent, drove, I understand, an extremely satisfactory bargain.'

'He acted as her agent, eh?'

'Yes, sir. In his capacity as fiancé to the young lady, sir.'

'Fiancé!'

'Yes, sir.'

It shows how the sight of that poster had got into my ribs when I state that, instead of being laid out cold by this announcement, I merely said 'Ha!' or 'Ho!' or it may have been 'H'm'. After the poster, nothing seemed to matter.

'After that poster, Jeeves,' I said, 'nothing seems to matter.'

'No, sir?'

'No, Jeeves. A woman has tossed my heart lightly away, but what of it?'

'Exactly, sir.'

'The voice of Love seemed to call to me, but it was a wrong number. Is that going to crush me?'

'No, sir.'

'No, Jeeves. It is not. But what does matter is this ghastly business of my face being spread from end to end of the Metropolis with the eyes fixed on a plate of Slingsby's Superb Soup. I must leave London. The lads at the Drones will kid me without ceasing.'

'Yes, sir. And Mrs Spenser Gregson—'

I paled visibly. I hadn't thought of Aunt Agatha and what she might have to say about letting down the family prestige.

'You don't mean to say she has been ringing up?'

'Several times daily, sir.'

'Jeeves, flight is the only resource.'

'Yes, sir.'

'Back to Paris, what?'

'I should not recommend the move, sir. The posters are, I understand, shortly to appear in that city also, advertising the *Bouillon Suprême*. Mr Slingsby's products command a large sale in France. The sight would be painful for you, sir.'

'Then where?'

'If I might make a suggestion, sir, why not adhere to your original intention of cruising in Mrs Travers' yacht in the Mediterranean? On the yacht you would be free from the annoyance of these advertising displays.'

The man seemed to me to be drivelling.

'But the yacht started weeks ago. It may be anywhere by now.'

'No, sir. The cruise was postponed for a month owing to the illness of Mr Travers' chef, Anatole, who contracted influenza. Mr Travers refused to sail without him.'

'You mean they haven't started?'

'Not yet, sir. The yacht sails from Southampton on Tuesday next.'

'Why, then, dash it, nothing could be sweeter.'

'No, sir.'

'Ring up Aunt Dahlia and tell her we'll be there.'

'I ventured to take the liberty of doing so a few moments before you arrived, sir.'

'You did?'

'Yes, sir. I thought it probable that the plan would meet with your approval.'

'It does! I've wished all along I was going on that cruise.'

'I, too, sir. It should be extremely pleasant.'

'The tang of the salt breezes, Jeeves!'

'Yes, sir.'

'The moonlight on the water!'

'Precisely, sir.'

'The gentle heaving of the waves!'

'Exactly, sir.'

I felt absolutely in the pink. Gwladys – pah! The posters – bah! That was the way I looked at it.

'Yo-ho-ho, Jeeves!' I said, giving the trousers a bit of a hitch.

'Yes, sir.'

'In fact, I will go further. Yo-ho-ho and a bottle of rum!'

'Very good, sir. I will bring it immediately.'

It has been well said of Bertram Wooster by those who know him best that, whatever other sporting functions he may see fit to oil out of, you will always find him battling to his sixteen handicap at the annual Golf tournament of the Drones Club. Nevertheless, when I heard that this year they were holding it at Bingley-on-Sea, I confess I hesitated. As I stood gazing out of the window of my suite at the Splendide on the morning of the opening day, I was not exactly a-twitter, if you understand me, but I couldn't help feeling I might have been rather rash.

'Jeeves,' I said, 'now that we have actually arrived, I find myself wondering if it was quite prudent to come here.'

'It is a pleasant spot, sir.'

'Where every prospect pleases,' I agreed. 'But though the spicy breezes blow fair o'er Bingley-on-Sea, we must never forget that this is where my Aunt Agatha's old friend, Miss Mapleton, runs a girls' school. If the relative knew I was here, she would expect me to call on Miss Mapleton.'

'Very true, sir.'

I shivered somewhat.

'I met her once, Jeeves. 'Twas on a summer's evening in my

tent, the day I overcame the Nervii. Or, rather, at lunch at Aunt
Agatha's a year ago come Lammas Eve. It is not an experience
I would willingly undergo again.'

'Indeed, sir?'

'Besides, you remember what happened last time I got into
a girls' school?'

'Yes, sir.'

'Secrecy and silence, then. My visit here must be strictly
incog. If Aunt Agatha happens to ask you where I spent this
week, tell her I went to Harrogate for the cure.'

'Very good, sir. Pardon me, sir, are you proposing to appear
in those garments in public?'

Up to this point our conversation had been friendly and
cordial, but I now perceived that the jarring note had been
struck. I had been wondering when my new plus-fours would
come under discussion, and I was prepared to battle for them
like a tigress for her young.

'Certainly, Jeeves,' I said. 'Why? Don't you like them?'

'No, sir.'

'You think them on the bright side?'

'Yes, sir.'

'A little vivid, they strike you as?'

'Yes, sir.'

'Well, I think highly of them, Jeeves,' I said firmly.

There already being a certain amount of chilliness in the
air, it seemed to me a suitable moment for springing another
item of information which I had been keeping from him for
some time.

'Er – Jeeves,' I said.

'Sir?'

'I ran into Miss Wickham the other day. After chatting of

this and that, she invited me to join a party she is getting up to go to Antibes this summer.'

'Indeed, sir?'

He now looked definitely squiggle-eyed. Jeeves, as I think I have mentioned before, does not approve of Bobbie Wickham.

There was what you might call a tense silence. I braced myself for an exhibition of the good old Wooster determination. I mean to say, one has got to take a firm stand from time to time. The trouble with Jeeves is that he tends occasionally to get above himself. Just because he has surged round and – I admit it freely – done the young master a bit of good in one or two crises, he has a nasty way of conveying the impression that he looks on Bertram Wooster as a sort of idiot child who, but for him, would conk in the first chukka. I resent this.

'I have accepted, Jeeves,' I said in a quiet, level voice, lighting a cigarette with a careless flick of the wrist.

'Indeed, sir?'

'You will like Antibes.'

'Yes, sir?'

'So shall I.'

'Yes, sir?'

'That's settled, then.'

'Yes, sir.'

I was pleased. The firm stand, I saw, had done its work. It was plain that the man was crushed beneath the iron heel – cowed, if you know what I mean.

'Right-ho, then, Jeeves.'

'Very good, sir.'

I had not expected to return from the arena until well on in the evening, but circumstances so arranged themselves that it was barely three o'clock when I found myself back again. I was wandering moodily to and fro on the pier, when I observed Jeeves shimmering towards me.

'Good afternoon, sir,' he said. 'I had not supposed that you would be returning quite so soon, or I would have remained at the hotel.'

'I had not supposed that I would be returning quite so soon myself, Jeeves,' I said, sighing somewhat. 'I was outed in the first round, I regret to say.'

'Indeed, sir? I am sorry to hear that.'

'And, to increase the mortification of defeat, Jeeves, by a blighter who had not spared himself at the luncheon-table and was quite noticeably sozzled. I couldn't seem to do anything right.'

'Possibly you omitted to keep your eye on the ball with sufficient assiduity, sir?'

'Something of that nature, no doubt. Anyway, here I am, a game and popular loser and . . .' I paused, and scanned the horizon with some interest. 'Great Scott, Jeeves! Look at that girl just coming on to the pier. I never saw anybody so extra-ordinarily like Miss Wickham. How do you account for these resemblances?'

'In the present instance, sir, I attribute the similarity to the fact that the young lady *is* Miss Wickham.'

'Eh?'

'Yes, sir. If you notice, she is waving to you now.'

'But what on earth is she doing down here?'

'I am unable to say, sir.'

His voice was chilly and seemed to suggest that, whatever had brought Bobbie Wickham to Bingley-on-Sea, it could not, in his opinion, be anything good. He dropped back into the offing, registering alarm and despondency, and I removed the old Homburg and waggled it genially.

'What-ho!' I said.

Bobbie came to anchor alongside.

'Hullo, Bertie,' she said. 'I didn't know you were here.'

'I am,' I assured her.

'In mourning?' she asked, eyeing the trouserings.

'Rather natty, aren't they?' I said, following her gaze. 'Jeeves doesn't like them, but then he's notoriously hidebound in the matter of leg-wear. What are you doing in Bingley?'

'My cousin Clementina is at school here. It's her birthday and I thought I would come down and see her. I'm just off there now. Are you staying here to-night?'

'Yes. At the Splendide.'

'You can give me dinner there if you like.'

Jeeves was behind me, and I couldn't see him, but at these words I felt his eye slap warningly against the back of my neck. I knew what it was that he was trying to broadcast – viz. that it would be tempting Providence to mix with Bobbie Wickham even to the extent of giving her a bite to eat. Dashed absurd, was my verdict. Get entangled with young Bobbie in the intricate life of a country-house, where almost anything can happen, and I'm not saying. But how any doom or disaster could lurk behind the simple pronging of a spot of dinner together, I failed to see. I ignored the man.

'Of course. Certainly. Rather. Absolutely,' I said.

'That'll be fine. I've got to get back to London to-night for revelry of sorts at the Berkeley, but it doesn't matter if I'm a bit late. We'll turn up at about seven-thirty, and you can take us to the movies afterwards.'

'We? Us?'

'Clementina and me.'

'You don't mean you intend to bring your ghastly cousin?'

'Of course I do. Don't you want the child to have a little pleasure on her birthday? And she isn't ghastly. She's a dear. She won't be any trouble. All you'll have to do is take her back to the school afterwards. You can manage that without straining a sinew, can't you?'

I eyed her keenly.

'What does it involve?'

'How do you mean, what does it involve?'

'The last time I was lured into a girls' school, a headmistress with an eye like a gimlet insisted on my addressing the chaingang on Ideals and the Life To Come. This will not happen to-night?'

'Of course not. You just go to the front door, ring the bell, and bung her in.'

I mused.

'That would appear to be well within our scope. Eh, Jeeves?'

'I should be disposed to imagine so, sir.'

The man's tone was cold and soupy: and, scanning his face, I observed on it an 'If-you-would-only-be-guided-by-me' expression which annoyed me intensely. There are moments when Jeeves looks just like an aunt.

'Right,' I said, ignoring him once more – and rather pointedly, at that. 'Then I'll expect you at seven-thirty. Don't be late. And see,' I added, just to show the girl that beneath the smiling exterior I was a man of iron, 'that the kid has her hands washed and does not sniff.'

I had not, I confess, looked forward with any great keenness to hobnobbing with Bobbie Wickham's cousin Clementina, but

I'm bound to admit that she might have been considerably worse. Small girls as a rule, I have noticed, are inclined, when confronted with me, to giggle a good deal. They snigger and they stare. I look up and find their eyes glued on me in an incredulous manner, as if they were reluctant to believe that I was really true. I suspect them of being in the process of memorizing any little peculiarities of deportment that I may possess, in order to reproduce them later for the entertainment of their fellow-inmates.

With the kid Clementina there was nothing of this description. She was a quiet, saintlike child of about thirteen – in fact, seeing that this was her birthday, exactly thirteen – and her gaze revealed only silent admiration. Her hands were spotless; she had not a cold in the head; and at dinner, during which her behaviour was unexceptionable, she proved a sympathetic listener, hanging on my lips, so to speak, when with the aid of a fork and two peas I explained to her how my opponent that afternoon had stymied me on the tenth.

She was equally above criticism at the movies, and at the conclusion of the proceedings thanked me for the treat with visible emotion. I was pleased with the child, and said as much to Bobbie while assisting her into her two-seater.

'Yes, I told you she was a dear,' said Bobbie, treading on the self-starter in preparation for the dash to London. 'I always insist that they misjudge her at that school. They're always misjudging people. They misjudged me when I was there.'

'Misjudge her? How?'

'Oh, in various ways. But, then, what can you expect of a dump like St Monica's?'

I started.

'St Monica's?'

'That's the name of the place.'

'You don't mean the kid is at Miss Mapleton's school?'

'Why shouldn't she be?'

'But Miss Mapleton is my Aunt Agatha's oldest friend.'

'I know. It was your Aunt Agatha who got mother to send me there when I was a kid.'

'I say,' I said earnestly, 'when you were there this afternoon you didn't mention having met me down here?'

'No.'

'That's all right.' I was relieved. 'You see, if Miss Mapleton knew I was in Bingley, she would expect me to call. I shall be leaving to-morrow morning, so all will be well. But, dash it,' I said, spotting the snag, 'how about to-night?'

'What about to-night?'

'Well, shan't I have to see her? I can't just ring the front-door bell, sling the kid in, and leg it. I should never hear the last of it from Aunt Agatha.'

Bobbie looked at me in an odd, meditative sort of way.

'As a matter of fact, Bertie,' she said, 'I had been meaning to touch on that point. I think, if I were you, I wouldn't ring the front-door bell.'

'Eh? Why not?'

'Well, it's like this, you see. Clementina is supposed to be in bed. They sent her there just as I was leaving this afternoon. Think of it! On her birthday – right plumb spang in the middle of her birthday – and all for putting sherbet in the ink to make it fizz!'

I reeled.

'You aren't telling me that this foul kid came out without leave?'

'Yes, I am. That's exactly it. She got up and sneaked out

when nobody was looking. She had set her heart on getting a square meal. I suppose I really ought to have told you right at the start, but I didn't want to spoil your evening.'

As a general rule, in my dealings with the delicately-nurtured, I am the soul of knightly chivalry – suave, genial and polished. But I can on occasion say the bitter, cutting thing, and I said it now.

'Oh?' I said.

'But it's all right.'

'Yes,' I said, speaking, if I recollect, between my clenched teeth, 'nothing could be sweeter, could it? The situation is one which it would be impossible to view with concern, what? I shall turn up with the kid, get looked at through steel-rimmed spectacles by the Mapleton, and after an agreeable five minutes shall back out, leaving the Mapleton to go to her escritoire and write a full account of the proceedings to my Aunt Agatha. And, contemplating what will happen after that, the imagination totters. I confidently expect my Aunt Agatha to beat all previous records.'

The girl clicked her tongue chidingly.

'Don't make such heavy weather, Bertie. You must learn not to fuss so.'

'I must, must I?'

'Everything's going to be all right. I'm not saying it won't be necessary to exercise a little strategy in getting Clem into the house, but it will be perfectly simple, if you'll only listen carefully to what I'm going to tell you. First, you will need a good long piece of string.'

'String?'

'String. Surely even you know what string is?'

I stiffened rather haughtily.

'Certainly,' I replied. 'You mean string.'

'That's right. String. You take this with you—'

'And soften the Mapleton's heart by doing tricks with it, I suppose?'

Bitter, I know. But I was deeply stirred.

'You take this string with you,' proceeded Bobbie patiently, 'and when you get into the garden you go through it till you come to a conservatory near the house. Inside it you will find a lot of flower-pots. How are you on recognizing a flower-pot when you see one, Bertie?'

'I am thoroughly familiar with flower-pots. If, as I suppose, you mean those sort of pot things they put flowers in.'

'That's exactly what I do mean. All right, then. Grab an armful of these flower-pots and go round the conservatory till you come to a tree. Climb this, tie a string to one of the pots, balance it on a handy branch which you will find overhangs the conservatory, and then, having stationed Clem near the front door, retire into the middle distance and jerk the string. The flower-pot will fall and smash the glass, someone in the house will hear the noise and come out to investigate, and while the door is open and nobody near Clem will sneak in and go up to bed.'

'But suppose no one comes out?'

'Then you repeat the process with another pot.'

It seemed sound enough.

'You're sure it will work?'

'It's never failed yet. That's the way I always used to get in after lock-up when I was at St Monica's. Now, you're sure you've got it clear, Bertie? Let's have a quick run-through to make certain, and then I really must be off. String.'

'String.'

'Conservatory.'

'Or greenhouse.'

'Flower-pot.'

'Flower-pot.'

'Tree. Climb. Branch. Climb down. Jerk. Smash. And then off to beddy-bye. Got it?'

'I've got it. But,' I said sternly, 'let me tell you just one thing—'

'I haven't time. I must rush. Write to me about it, using one side of the paper only. Good-bye.'

She rolled off, and after following her with burning eyes for a moment I returned to Jeeves, who was in the background showing the kid Clementina how to make a rabbit with a pocket handkerchief. I drew him aside. I was feeling a little better now, for I perceived that an admirable opportunity had presented itself for putting the man in his place and correcting his view that he is the only member of our establishment with brains and resource.

'Jeeves,' I said, 'you will doubtless be surprised to learn that something in the nature of a hitch has occurred.'

'Not at all, sir.'

'No?'

'No, sir. In matters where Miss Wickham is involved, I am, if I may take the liberty of saying so, always on the alert for hitches. If you recollect, sir, I have frequently observed that Miss Wickham, while a charming young lady, is apt—'

'Yes, yes, Jeeves. I know.'

'What would the precise nature of the trouble be this time, sir?'

I explained the circs.

'The kid is A.W.O.L. They sent her to bed for putting sherbet in the ink, and in bed they imagine her to have spent the evening. Instead of which, she was out with me, wolfing the eight-course table-d'hôte dinner at seven and six, and then going on to the Marine Plaza to enjoy an entertainment on the silver screen. It is our task to get her back into the house without anyone knowing. I may mention, Jeeves, that the school in which this young excrescence is serving her sentence is the one run by my Aunt Agatha's old friend, Miss Mapleton.'

'Indeed, sir?'

'A problem, Jeeves, what?'

'Yes, sir.'

'In fact, one might say a pretty problem?'

'Undoubtedly, sir. If I might suggest—'

I was expecting this. I raised a hand.

'I do not require any suggestions, Jeeves. I can handle this matter myself.'

'I was merely about to propose—'

I raised the hand again.

'Peace, Jeeves. I have the situation well under control. I have had one of my ideas. It may interest you to hear how my brain worked. It occurred to me, thinking the thing over, that a house like St Monica's would be likely to have near it a conservatory containing flower-pots. Then, like a flash, the whole thing came to me. I propose to procure some string, to tie it to a flower-pot, to balance the pot on a branch – there will, no doubt, be a tree near the conservatory with a branch overhanging it – and to retire to a distance, holding the string. You will station yourself with the kid near the front door, taking care to keep carefully concealed. I shall then jerk the string, the pot will smash the glass, the noise will bring someone out, and while the front door is open you will shoot the kid in and leave the rest to her personal judgement. Your share in the proceedings, you will notice, is simplicity itself – mere routine-work – and should not tax you unduly. How about it?'

'Well, sir—'

'Jeeves, I have had occasion before to comment on this habit of yours of saying "Well, sir" whenever I suggest anything in the nature of a ruse or piece of strategy. I dislike it more every time you do it. But I shall be glad to hear what possible criticism you can find to make.'

'I was merely about to express the opinion, sir, that the plan seems a trifle elaborate.'

'In a place as tight as this you have got to be elaborate.'

'Not necessarily, sir. The alternative scheme which I was about to propose—'

I shushed the man.

'There will be no need for alternative schemes, Jeeves. We will carry on along the lines I have indicated. I will give you ten minutes' start. That will enable you to take up your position near the front door and self to collect the string. At the conclusion of that period I will come along and do all the difficult part. So no more discussion. Snap into it, Jeeves.'

'Very good, sir.'

I felt pretty bucked as I tooled up the hill to St Monica's and equally bucked as I pushed open the front gate and stepped into the dark garden. But, just as I started to cross the lawn, there suddenly came upon me a rummy sensation as if all my bones had been removed and spaghetti substituted, and I paused.

I don't know if you have ever had the experience of starting off on a binge filled with a sort of glow of exhilaration, if that's the word I want, and then, without a moment's warning, having it disappear as if somebody had pressed a switch. That is what happened to me at this juncture, and a most unpleasant feeling it was – rather like when you take one of those express elevators in New York at the top of the building and discover, on reaching the twenty-seventh floor, that you have carelessly left all your insides up on the thirty-second, and too late now to stop and fetch them back.

The truth came to me like a bit of ice down the neck. I perceived that I had been a dashed sight too impulsive. Purely in order to score off Jeeves, I had gone and let myself in for what promised to be the mouldiest ordeal of a lifetime. And the nearer I got to the house, the more I wished that I had been a bit less haughty with the man when he had tried to outline that alternative scheme of his. An alternative scheme was just what I felt I could have done with, and the more alternative it was the better I would have liked it.

At this point I found myself at the conservatory door, and a few moments later I was inside, scooping up the pots.

Then ho, for the tree, bearing 'mid snow and ice the banner with the strange device 'Excelsior!'

I will say for that tree that it might have been placed there for the purpose. My views on the broad, general principle of leaping from branch to branch in a garden belonging to Aunt Agatha's closest friend remained unaltered; but I had to admit that, if it was to be done, this was undoubtedly the tree to do it on. It was a cedar of sorts; and almost before I knew where I was, I was sitting on top of the world with the conservatory roof gleaming below me. I balanced the flower-pot on my knee and began to tie the string round it.

And, as I tied, my thoughts turned in a moody sort of way to the subject of Woman.

I was suffering from a considerable strain of the old nerves at the moment, of course, and, looking back, it may be that I was too harsh; but the way I felt in that dark, roosting hour was that you can say what you like, but the more a thoughtful man has to do with women, the more extraordinary it seems to him that such a sex should be allowed to clutter up the earth.

Women, the way I looked at it, simply wouldn't do. Take the females who were mixed up in this present business. Aunt Agatha, to start with, better known as the Pest of Pont Street, the human snapping-turtle. Aunt Agatha's closest friend, Miss Mapleton, of whom I can only say that on the single occasion on which I had met her she had struck me as just the sort of person who would be Aunt Agatha's closest friend. Bobbie Wickham, a girl who went about the place letting the pure in heart in for the sort of thing I was doing now. And Bobbie Wickham's cousin Clementina, who, instead of sticking sedulously to her studies and learning to be a good wife and mother, spent the springtime of her life filling inkpots with sherbet—

What a crew! What a crew!

I mean to say, what a *crew*!

I had just worked myself up into rather an impressive state of moral indignation, and was preparing to go even further, when a sudden bright light shone upon me from below and a voice spoke.

'Ho!' it said.

It was a policeman. Apart from the fact of his having a lantern, I knew it was a policeman because he had said 'Ho!' I don't know if you recollect my telling you of the time I broke into Bingo Little's house to pinch the dictaphone record of the mushy article his wife had written about him and sailed out of the study window right into the arms of the Force? On that occasion the guardian of the Law had said 'Ho!' and kept on saying it, so evidently policemen are taught this as part of their training. And after all, it's not a bad way of opening conversation in the sort of circs in which they generally have to chat with people.

'You come on down out of that,' he said.

I came on down. I had just got the flower-pot balanced on its branch, and I left it there, feeling rather as if I had touched off the time-fuse of a bomb. Much seemed to me to depend on its stability and poise, as it were. If it continued to balance, an easy nonchalance might still get me out of this delicate position. If it fell, I saw things being a bit hard to explain. In fact, even as it was, I couldn't see my way to any explanation which would be really convincing.

However, I had a stab at it.

'Ah, officer,' I said.

It sounded weak. I said it again, this time with the emphasis on the 'Ah!' It sounded weaker than ever. I saw that Bertram would have to do better than this.

'It's all right, officer,' I said.

'All right, is it?'

'Oh, yes. Oh, yes.'

'What you doing up there?'

'Me, officer?'

'Yes, you.'

'Nothing, sergeant.'

'Ho!'

We eased into the silence, but it wasn't one of those restful silences that occur in talks between old friends. Embarrassing. Awkward.

'You'd better come along with me,' said the gendarme.

The last time I had heard those words from a similar source

had been in Leicester Square one Boat Race night when, on my advice, my old pal Oliver Randolph Sipperley had endeavoured to steal a policeman's helmet at a moment when the policeman was inside it. On that occasion they had been addressed to young Sippy, and they hadn't sounded any too good, even so. Addressed to me, they more or less froze the marrow.

'No, I say, dash it!' I said.

And it was at this crisis, when Bertram had frankly shot his bolt and could only have been described as nonplussed, that a soft step sounded beside us and a soft voice broke the silence.

'Have you got them, officer? No, I see. It is Mr Wooster.'

The policeman switched the lantern round.

'Who are you?'

'I am Mr Wooster's personal gentleman's gentleman.'

'Whose?'

'Mr Wooster's.'

'Is this man's name Wooster?'

'This gentleman's name is Mr Wooster. I am in his employment as gentleman's personal gentleman.'

I think the cop was awed by the man's majesty of demeanour, but he came back strongly.

'Ho!' he said. 'Not in Miss Mapleton's employment?'

'Miss Mapleton does not employ a gentleman's personal gentleman.'

'Then what are you doing in her garden?'

'I was in conference with Miss Mapleton inside the house, and she desired me to step out and ascertain whether Mr Wooster had been successful in apprehending the intruders.'

'What intruders?'

'The suspicious characters whom Mr Wooster and I had observed passing through the garden as we entered it.'

'And what were you doing entering it?'

'Mr Wooster had come to pay a call on Miss Mapleton, who is a close friend of his family. We noticed suspicious characters crossing the lawn. On perceiving these suspicious characters, Mr Wooster despatched me to warn and reassure Miss Mapleton, he himself remaining to investigate.'

'I found him up a tree.'

'If Mr Wooster was up a tree, I have no doubt he was actuated by excellent motives and had only Miss Mapleton's best interests at heart.'

The policeman brooded.

'Ho!' he said. 'Well, if you want to know, I don't believe a word of it. We had a telephone call at the station saying there was somebody in Miss Mapleton's garden, and I found this fellow up a tree. It's my belief you're both in this, and I'm going to take you in to the lady for identification.'

Jeeves inclined his head gracefully.

'I shall be delighted to accompany you, officer, if such is your wish. And I feel sure that in this connection I may speak for Mr Wooster also. He too, I am confident, will interpose no obstacle in the way of your plans. If you consider that circumstances have placed Mr Wooster in a position that may be termed equivocal, or even compromising, it will naturally be his wish to exculpate himself at the earliest possible—'

'Here!' said the policeman, slightly rattled.

'Officer?'

'Less of it.'

'Just as you say, officer.'

'Switch it off and come along.'

'Very good, officer.'

I must say that I have enjoyed functions more than that walk to the front door. It seemed to me that the doom had come upon me, so to speak, and I thought it hard that a gallant effort like Jeeves's, well reasoned and nicely planned, should have failed to click. Even to me his story had rung almost true in spots, and it was a great blow that the man behind the lantern had not sucked it in without question. There's no doubt about it, being a policeman warps a man's mind and ruins that sunny faith in his fellow human beings which is the foundation of a lovable character. There seems no way of avoiding this.

I could see no gleam of light in the situation. True, the Mapleton would identify me as the nephew of her old friend, thus putting the stopper on the stroll to the police station and the night in the prison cell, but, when you came right down to it, a fat lot of use that was. The kid Clementina was presumably still out in the night somewhere, and she would be lugged in and the full facts revealed, and then the burning glance, the few cold words and the long letter to Aunt Agatha. I wasn't sure that a good straight term of penal servitude wouldn't have been a happier ending.

So, what with one consideration and another, the heart, as I toddled in through the front door, was more or less bowed down with weight of woe. We went along the passage and into the study, and there, standing behind a desk with the steel-rimmed spectacles glittering as nastily as on the day when I had seen them across Aunt Agatha's luncheon-table, was the boss in person. I gave her one swift look, then shut my eyes.

'Ah!' said Miss Mapleton.

Now, uttered in a certain way – dragged out, if you know what I mean, and starting high up and going down into the lower register, the word 'Ah!' can be as sinister and devastating as the word 'Ho!' In fact, it is a very moot question which is the scalier. But what stunned me was that this wasn't the way she had said it. It had been, or my ears deceived me, a genial 'Ah!'. A matey 'Ah!'. The 'Ah!' of one old buddy to another. And this startled me so much that, forgetting the dictates of prudence, I actually ventured to look at her again. And a stifled exclamation burst from Bertram's lips.

The breath-taking exhibit before me was in person a bit on the short side. I mean to say, she didn't tower above one, or anything like that. But, to compensate for this lack of inches, she possessed to a remarkable degree that sort of quiet air of being unwilling to stand any rannygazoo which females who run schools always have. I had noticed the same thing when in *statu pupillari*, in my old head master, one glance from whose eye had invariably been sufficient to make me confess all. Sergeant-majors are like that, too. Also traffic-cops and some post office girls. It's something in the way they purse up their lips and look through you.

In short, through years of disciplining the young – ticking off Isabel and speaking with quiet severity to Gertrude and that sort of thing – Miss Mapleton had acquired in the process of time rather the air of a female lion-tamer; and it was this air which had caused me after the first swift look to shut my eyes and utter a short prayer. But now, though she still resembled a lion-tamer, her bearing had most surprisingly become that of a chummy lion-tamer – a tamer who, after tucking the lions in for the night, relaxes in the society of the boys.

'So you did not find them, Mr Wooster?' she said. 'I am sorry. But I am none the less grateful for the trouble you have taken, nor lacking in appreciation of your courage. I consider that you have behaved splendidly.'

I felt the mouth opening feebly and the vocal cords twitching, but I couldn't manage to say anything. I was simply unable to follow her train of thought. I was astonished. Amazed. In fact, dumbfounded about sums it up.

The hell-hound of the Law gave a sort of yelp, rather like a wolf that sees its Russian peasant getting away.

'You identify this man, ma'am?'

'Identify him? In what way identify him?'

Jeeves joined the symposium.

'I fancy the officer is under the impression, madam, that Mr Wooster was in your garden for some unlawful purpose. I informed him that Mr Wooster was the nephew of your friend, Mrs Spenser Gregson, but he refused to credit me.'

There was a pause. Miss Mapleton eyed the constable for an instant as if she had caught him sucking acid-drops during the Scripture lesson.

'Do you mean to tell me, officer,' she said, in a voice that hit him just under the third button of the tunic and went straight through to the spinal column, 'that you have had the imbecility to bungle this whole affair by mistaking Mr Wooster for a burglar?'

'He was up a tree, ma'am.'

'And why should he not be up a tree? No doubt you had climbed the tree in order to watch the better, Mr Wooster?'

I could answer that. The first shock over, the old sang-froid was beginning to return.

'Yes. Rather. That's it. Of course. Certainly. Absolutely,' I said. 'Watch the better. That's it in a nutshell.'

'I took the liberty of suggesting that to the officer, madam, but he declined to accept the theory as tenable.'

'The officer is a fool,' said Miss Mapleton. It seemed a close thing for a moment whether or not she would rap him on the knuckles with a ruler. 'By this time, no doubt, owing to his idiocy, the miscreants have made good their escape. And it is for this,' said Miss Mapleton, 'that we pay rates and taxes!'

'Awful!' I said.

'Iniquitous.'

'A bally shame.'

'A crying scandal,' said Miss Mapleton.

'A grim show,' I agreed.

In fact, we were just becoming more like a couple of love-birds than anything, when through the open window there suddenly breezed a noise.

I'm never at my best at describing things. At school, when we used to do essays and English composition, my report gener-ally read 'Has little or no ability, but does his best,' or words to that effect. True, in the course of years I have picked up a vocabulary of sorts from Jeeves, but even so I'm not nearly hot enough to draw a word-picture that would do justice to that extraordinarily hefty crash. Try to imagine the Albert Hall fall-ing on the Crystal Palace, and you will have got the rough idea.

All four of us, even Jeeves, sprang several inches from the floor. The policeman uttered a startled 'Ho!'

Miss Mapleton was her calm masterful self again in a second.

'One of the men appears to have fallen through the conserva-tory roof,' she said. 'Perhaps you will endeavour at the eleventh hour to justify your existence, officer, by proceeding there and making investigations.'

'Yes, ma'am.'

'And try not to bungle matters this time.'

'No, ma'am.'

'Please hurry, then. Do you intend to stand there gaping all night?'

'Yes, ma'am. No, ma'am. Yes, ma'am.'

It was pretty to hear him.

'It is an odd coincidence, Mr Wooster,' said Miss Mapleton, becoming instantly matey once more as the outcast removed himself. 'I had just finished writing a letter to your aunt when you arrived. I shall certainly reopen it to tell her how gallantly you have behaved to-night. I have not in the past entertained a very high opinion of the modern young man, but you have caused me to alter it. To track these men unarmed through a dark garden argues courage of a high order. And it was most courteous of you to think of calling upon me. I appreciate it. Are you making a long stay in Bingley?'

This was another one I could answer.

'No,' I said. 'Afraid not. Must be in London to-morrow.'

'Perhaps you could lunch before your departure?'

'Afraid not. Thanks most awfully. Very important engagement that I can't get out of. Eh, Jeeves?'

'Yes, sir.'

'Have to catch the ten-thirty train, what?'

'Without fail, sir.'

'I am sorry,' said Miss Mapleton. 'I had hoped that you would be able to say a few words to my girls. Some other time perhaps?'

'Absolutely.'

'You must let me know when you are coming to Bingley again.'

'When I come to Bingley again,' I said, 'I will certainly let you know.'

'If I remember your plans correctly, sir, you are not likely to be in Bingley for some little time, sir.'

'Not for some considerable time, Jeeves,' I said.

* * *

The front door closed. I passed a hand across the brow.

'Tell me all, Jeeves,' I said.

'Sir?'

'I say, tell me all. I am fogged.'

'It is quite simple, sir. I ventured to take the liberty, on my own responsibility, of putting into operation the alternative scheme which, if you remember, I wished to outline to you.'

'What was it?'

'It occurred to me, sir, that it would be most judicious for me to call at the back door and desire an interview with Miss Mapleton. This, I fancied, would enable me, while the maid had gone to convey my request to Miss Mapleton, to introduce the young lady into the house unobserved.'

'And did you?'

'Yes, sir. She proceeded up the back stairs and is now safely in bed.'

I frowned. The thought of the kid Clementina jarred upon me.

'She is, is she?' I said. 'A murrain on her, Jeeves, and may she be stood in the corner next Sunday for not knowing her Collect. And then you saw Miss Mapleton?'

'Yes, sir.'

'And told her that I was out in the garden, chivvying burglars with my bare hands?'

'Yes, sir.'

'And had been on my way to call upon her?'

'Yes, sir.'

'And now she's busy adding a postscript to her letter to Aunt Agatha, speaking of me in terms of unstinted praise.'

'Yes, sir.'

I drew a deep breath. It was too dark for me to see the

superhuman intelligence which must have been sloshing about all over the surface of the man's features. I tried to, but couldn't make it.

'Jeeves,' I said, 'I should have been guided by you from the first.'

'It might have spared you some temporary unpleasantness, sir.'

'Unpleasantness is right. When that lantern shone up at me in the silent night, Jeeves, just as I had finished poising the pot, I thought I had unshipped a rib. Jeeves!'

'Sir?'

'That Antibes expedition is off.'

'I am glad to hear it, sir.'

'If young Bobbie Wickham can get me into a mess like this in a quiet spot like Bingley-on-Sea, what might she not be able to accomplish at a really lively resort like Antibes?'

'Precisely, sir. Miss Wickham, as I have sometimes said, though a charming—'

'Yes, yes, Jeeves. There is no necessity to stress the point. The Wooster eyes are definitely opened.'

I hesitated.

'Jeeves.'

'Sir?'

'Those plus-fours.'

'Yes, sir?'

'You may give them to the poor.'

'Thank you very much, sir.'

I sighed.

'It is my heart's blood, Jeeves.'

'I appreciate the sacrifice, sir. But, once the first pang of separation is over, you will feel much easier without them.'

'You think so?'

'I am convinced of it, sir.'

'So be it, then, Jeeves,' I said, 'so be it.'

There is a ghastly moment in the year, generally about the beginning of August, when Jeeves insists on taking a holiday, the slacker, and legs it off to some seaside resort for a couple of weeks, leaving me stranded. This moment had now arrived, and we were discussing what was to be done with the young master.

'I had gathered the impression, sir,' said Jeeves, 'that you were proposing to accept Mr Sipperley's invitation to join him at his Hampshire residence.'

I laughed. One of those bitter, rasping ones.

'Correct, Jeeves. I was. But mercifully I was enabled to discover young Sippy's foul plot in time. Do you know what?'

'No, sir.'

'My spies informed me that Sippy's fiancée, Miss Moon, was to be there. Also his fiancée's mother, Mrs Moon, and his fiancée's small brother, Master Moon. You see the hideous treachery lurking behind the invitation? You see the man's loathsome design? Obviously my job was to be the task of keeping Mrs Moon and little Sebastian Moon interested and amused while Sippy and his blighted girl went off for the day, roaming the pleasant woodlands and talking of this and that. I doubt if anyone has ever had a narrower escape. You remember little Sebastian?'

'Yes, sir.'

'His goggle eyes? His golden curls?'

'Yes, sir.'

'I don't know why it is, but I've never been able to bear with fortitude anything in the shape of a kid with golden curls. Confronted with one, I feel the urge to step on him or drop things on him from a height.'

'Many strong natures are affected in the same way, sir.'

'So no *chez* Sippy for me. Was that the front-door bell ringing?'

'Yes, sir.'

'Somebody stands without.'

'Yes, sir.'

'Better go and see who it is.'

'Yes, sir.'

He oozed off, to return a moment later bearing a telegram. I opened it, and a soft smile played about the lips.

'Amazing how often things happen as if on a cue, Jeeves. This is from my Aunt Dahlia, inviting me down to her place in Worcestershire.'

'Most satisfactory, sir.'

'Yes. How I came to overlook her when searching for a haven, I can't think. The ideal home from home. Picturesque surroundings. Company's own water, and the best cook in England. You have not forgotten Anatole?'

'No, sir.'

'And above all, Jeeves, at Aunt Dahlia's there should be an almost total shortage of blasted kids. True, there is her son Bonzo, who, I take it, will be home for the holidays, but I don't mind Bonzo. Buzz off and send a wire, accepting.'

'Yes, sir.'

'And then shove a few necessaries together, including golf-clubs and tennis racquet.'

'Very good, sir. I am glad that matters have been so happily adjusted.'

I think I have mentioned before that my Aunt Dahlia stands alone in the grim regiment of my aunts as a real good sort and a chirpy sportsman. She is the one, if you remember, who married old Tom Travers and, with the assistance of Jeeves, lured Mrs Bingo Little's French cook, Anatole, away from Mrs B. L. and into her own employment. To visit her is always a pleasure. She generally has some cheery birds staying with her, and there is none of that rot about getting up for breakfast which one is sadly apt to find at country-houses.

It was, accordingly, with unalloyed lightness of heart that I edged the two-seater into the garage at Brinkley Court, Worc., and strolled round to the house by way of the shrubbery and the tennis-lawn, to report arrival. I had just got across the lawn when a head poked itself out of the smoking-room window and beamed at me in an amiable sort of way.

'Ah, Mr Wooster,' it said. 'Ha, ha!'

'Ho, ho!' I replied, not to be outdone in the courtesies.

It had taken me a couple of seconds to place this head. I now perceived that it belonged to a rather moth-eaten septuagenarian of the name of Anstruther, an old friend of Aunt Dahlia's late father. I had met him at her house in London once or twice. An agreeable cove, but somewhat given to nervous breakdowns.

'Just arrived?' he asked, beaming as before.

'This minute,' I said, also beaming.

'I fancy you will find our good hostess in the drawing-room.'

'Right,' I said, and after a bit more beaming to and fro I pushed on.

Aunt Dahlia was in the drawing-room, and welcomed me with gratifying enthusiasm. She beamed, too. It was one of those big days for beamers.

'Hullo, ugly,' she said. 'So here you are. Thank heaven you were able to come.'

It was the right tone, and one I should be glad to hear in others of the family circle, notably my Aunt Agatha.

'Always a pleasure to enjoy your hosp., Aunt Dahlia,' I said cordially. 'I anticipate a delightful and restful visit. I see you've got Mr Anstruther staying here. Anybody else?'

'Do you know Lord Snettisham?'

'I've met him, racing.'

'He's here, and Lady Snettisham.'

'And Bonzo, of course?'

'Yes. And Thomas.'

'Uncle Thomas?'

'No, he's in Scotland. Your cousin Thomas.'

'You don't mean Aunt Agatha's loathly son?'

'Of course I do. How many cousin Thomases do you think you've got, fathead? Agatha has gone to Homburg and planted the child on me.'

I was visibly agitated.

'But, Aunt Dahlia! Do you realize what you've taken on? Have you an inkling of the sort of scourge you've introduced into your home? In the society of young Thos., strong men quail. He is England's premier fiend in human shape. There is no devilry beyond his scope.'

'That's what I have always gathered from the form book,' agreed the relative. 'But just now, curse him, he's behaving like something out of a Sunday School story. You see, poor old Mr Anstruther is very frail these days, and when he found he was in a house containing two small boys he acted promptly. He offered a prize of five pounds to whichever behaved best during his stay. The consequence is that, ever since, Thomas has had large white wings sprouting out of his shoulders.' A shadow seemed to pass across her face. She appeared embittered. 'Mercenary little brute!' she said. 'I never saw such a sickeningly well-behaved kid in my life. It's enough to make one despair of human nature.'

I couldn't follow her.

'But isn't that all to the good?'

'No, it's not.'

'I can't see why. Surely a smug, oily Thos. about the house is better than a Thos., raging hither and thither and being a menace to society? Stands to reason.'

'It doesn't stand to anything of the kind. You see, Bertie, this Good Conduct prize has made matters a bit complex. There are wheels within wheels. The thing stirred Jane Snettisham's sporting blood to such an extent that she insisted on having a bet on the result.'

A great light shone upon me. I got what she was driving at.

'Ah!' I said. 'Now I follow. Now I see. Now I comprehend. She's betting on Thos., is she?'

'Yes. And naturally, knowing him, I thought the thing was in the bag.'

'Of course.'

'I couldn't see myself losing. Heaven knows I have no illusions about my darling Bonzo. Bonzo is, and has been from the cradle, a pest. But to back him to win a Good Conduct contest with Thomas seemed to me simply money for jam.'

'Absolutely.'

'When it comes to devilry, Bonzo is just a good, ordinary selling-plater. Whereas Thomas is a classic yearling.'

'Exactly. I don't see that you have any cause to worry, Aunt Dahlia. Thos. can't last. He's bound to crack.'

'Yes. But before that the mischief may be done.'

'Mischief?'

'Yes. There is dirty work afoot, Bertie,' said Aunt Dahlia gravely. 'When I booked this bet, I reckoned without the hideous blackness of the Snettishams' souls. Only yesterday it came to my knowledge that Jack Snettisham had been urging Bonzo to climb on the roof and boo down Mr Anstruther's chimney.'

'No!'

'Yes. Mr Anstruther is very frail, poor old fellow, and it would have frightened him into a fit. On coming out of which, his first action would have been to disqualify Bonzo and declare Thomas the winner by default.'

'But Bonzo did not boo?'

'No,' said Aunt Dahlia, and a mother's pride rang in her voice. 'He firmly refused to boo. Mercifully, he is in love at the moment, and it has quite altered his nature. He scorned the tempter.'

'In love? Who with?'

'Lilian Gish. We had an old film of hers at the Bijou Dream in the village a week ago, and Bonzo saw her for the first time. He came out with a pale, set face, and ever since has been trying to lead a finer, better life. So the peril was averted.'

'That's good.'

'Yes. But now it's my turn. You don't suppose I am going to take a thing like that lying down, do you? Treat me right, and I am fairness itself: but try any of this nobbling of starters, and I can play that game, too. If this Good Conduct contest is to be run on rough lines, I can do my bit as well as anyone. Far too much hangs on the issue for me to handicap myself by remembering the lessons I learned at my mother's knee.'

'Lot of money involved?'

'Much more than mere money. I've betted Anatole against Jane Snettisham's kitchen-maid.'

'Great Scott! Uncle Thomas will have something to say if he comes back and finds Anatole gone.'

'And won't he say it!'

'Pretty long odds you gave her, didn't you? I mean, Anatole is famed far and wide as a hash-slinger without peer.'

'Well, Jane Snettisham's kitchen-maid is not to be sneezed at. She is very hot stuff, they tell me, and good kitchen-maids nowadays are about as rare as original Holbeins. Besides, I had to give her a shade the best of the odds. She stood out for it. Well, anyway, to get back to what I was saying, if the opposition are going to place temptations in Bonzo's path, they shall jolly well be placed in Thomas's path, too, and plenty of them. So ring for Jeeves and let him get his brain working.'

'But I haven't brought Jeeves.'

'You haven't brought Jeeves?'

'No. He always takes his holiday at this time of year. He's down at Bognor for the shrimping.'

Aunt Dahlia registered deep concern.

'Then send for him at once! What earthly use do you suppose you are without Jeeves, you poor ditherer?'

I drew myself up a trifle – in fact, to my full height. Nobody has a greater respect for Jeeves than I have, but the Wooster pride was stung.

'Jeeves isn't the only one with brains,' I said coldly. 'Leave this thing to me, Aunt Dahlia. By dinner-time to-night I shall hope to have a fully matured scheme to submit for your approval. If I can't thoroughly encompass this Thos., I'll eat my hat.'

'About all you'll get to eat if Anatole leaves,' said Aunt Dahlia in a pessimistic manner which I did not like to see.

I was brooding pretty tensely as I left the presence. I have always had a suspicion that Aunt Dahlia, while invariably matey and bonhomous and seeming to take pleasure in my society, has a lower opinion of my intelligence than I quite like. Too often it is her practice to address me as 'fathead', and if I put forward any little thought or idea or fancy in her hearing it is apt to be greeted with the affectionate but jarring guffaw. In our recent interview she had hinted quite plainly that she considered me negligible in a crisis which, like the present one, called for initiative and resource. It was my intention to show her how greatly she had underestimated me.

To let you see the sort of fellow I really am, I got a ripe, excellent idea before I had gone half-way down the corridor. I examined it for the space of one and a half cigarettes, and could see no flaw in it, provided – I say, provided old Mr Anstruther's notion of what constituted bad conduct squared with mine.

The great thing on these occasions, as Jeeves will tell you, is to get a toe-hold on the psychology of the individual. Study the individual, and you will bring home the bacon. Now, I had been studying young Thos. for years, and I knew his psychology from caviare to nuts. He is one of those kids who never let the sun go down on their wrath, if you know what I mean. I mean to say, do something to annoy or offend or upset this juvenile thug, and he will proceed at the earliest possible opp. to wreak a hideous vengeance upon you. Only the previous summer, for instance, it having been drawn to his attention that the latter had reported him for smoking, he had marooned a Cabinet Minister on an island in the lake, at Aunt Agatha's place in Hertfordshire – in the rain, mark you, and with no company but that of one of the nastiest-minded swans I have ever encountered. Well, I mean!

So now it seemed to me that a few well-chosen taunts, or jibes, directed at his more sensitive points, must infallibly induce in this Thos. a frame of mind which would lead to his working some sensational violence upon me. And, if you wonder that I was willing to sacrifice myself to this frightful extent in order to do Aunt Dahlia a bit of good, I can only say that we Woosters are like that.

The one point that seemed to me to want a spot of clearing up was this: viz., would old Mr Anstruther consider an outrage perpetrated on the person of Bertram Wooster a crime sufficiently black to cause him to rule Thos. out of the race? Or would he just give a senile chuckle and mumble something about boys being boys? Because, if the latter, the thing was off. I decided to have a word with the old boy and make sure.

He was still in the smoking-room, looking very frail over the morning *Times*. I got to the point at once.

'Oh, Mr Anstruther,' I said. 'What-ho!'

'I don't like the way the American market is shaping,' he said. 'I don't like this strong Bear movement.'

'No?' I said. 'Well, be that as it may, about this Good Conduct prize of yours?'

'Ah, you have heard of that, eh?'

'I don't quite understand how you are doing the judging.'

'No? It is very simple. I have a system of daily marks. At the beginning of each day I accord the two lads twenty marks apiece. These are subject to withdrawal either in small or large quantities according to the magnitude of the offence. To take a simple example, shouting outside my bedroom in the early morning would involve a loss of three marks, – whistling two. The penalty for a more serious lapse would be correspondingly greater. Before retiring to rest at night I record the day's marks in my little book. Simple, but, I think, ingenious, Mr Wooster?'

'Absolutely.'

'So far the result has been extremely gratifying. Neither of the little fellows has lost a single mark, and my nervous system is acquiring a tone which, when I learned that two lads of immature years would be staying in the house during my visit, I confess I had not dared to anticipate.'

'I see,' I said. 'Great work. And how do you react to what I might call general moral turpitude?'

'I beg your pardon?'

'Well, I mean when the thing doesn't affect you personally. Suppose one of them did something to me, for instance? Set a booby-trap or something? Or, shall we say, put a toad or so in my bed?'

He seemed shocked at the very idea.

'I would certainly in such circumstances deprive the culprit of a full ten marks.'

'Only ten?'

'Fifteen, then.'

'Twenty is a nice, round number.'

'Well, possibly even twenty. I have a peculiar horror of practical joking.'

'Me, too.'

'You will not fail to advise me, Mr Wooster, should such an outrage occur?'

'You shall have the news before anyone,' I assured him.

And so out into the garden, ranging to and fro in quest of young Thos. I knew where I was now. Bertram's feet were on solid ground.

I hadn't been hunting long before I found him in the summer-house, reading an improving book.

'Hullo,' he said, smiling a saintlike smile.

This scourge of humanity was a chunky kid whom a too indulgent public had allowed to infest the country for a matter of fourteen years. His nose was snub, his eyes green, his general aspect that of one studying to be a gangster. I had never liked his looks much, and with a saintlike smile added to them they became ghastly to a degree.

I ran over in my mind a few assorted taunts.

'Well, young Thos.,' I said. 'So there you are. You're getting as fat as a pig.'

It seemed as good an opening as any other. Experience had taught me that if there was a subject on which he was unlikely to accept persiflage in a spirit of amused geniality it was this matter of his bulging tum. On the last occasion when I made a remark of this nature, he had replied to me, child though he was, in terms which I would have been proud to have had in my own vocabulary. But now, though a sort of wistful gleam did flit for a moment into his eyes, he merely smiled in a more saintlike manner than ever.

'Yes, I think I have been putting on a little weight,' he said gently. 'I must try and exercise a lot while I'm here. Won't you sit down, Bertie?' he asked, rising. 'You must be tired after your journey. I'll get you a cushion. Have you cigarettes?

And matches? I could bring you some from the smoking-room. Would you like me to fetch you something to drink?'

It is not too much to say that I felt baffled. In spite of what Aunt Dahlia had told me, I don't think that until this moment I had really believed there could have been anything in the nature of a genuinely sensational change in this young plugugly's attitude towards his fellows. But now, hearing him talk as if he were a combination of Boy Scout and delivery wagon, I felt definitely baffled. However, I stuck at it in the old bull-dog way.

'Are you still at that rotten kids' school of yours?' I asked.

He might have been proof against jibes at his *embonpoint*, but it seemed to me incredible that he could have sold himself for gold so completely as to lie down under taunts directed at his school. I was wrong. The money-lust evidently held him in its grip. He merely shook his head.

'I left this term. I'm going to Pevenhurst next term.'

'They wear mortar-boards there, don't they?'

'Yes.'

'With pink tassels?'

'Yes.'

'What a priceless ass you'll look!' I said, but without much hope. And I laughed heartily.

'I expect I shall,' he said, and laughed still more heartily.

'Mortar-boards!'

'Ha, ha!'

'Pink tassels!'

'Ha, ha!'

I gave the thing up.

'Well, teuf-teuf,' I said moodily, and withdrew.

A couple of days later I realized that the virus had gone even deeper than I had thought. The kid was irredeemably sordid.

It was old Mr Anstruther who sprang the bad news.

'Oh, Mr Wooster,' he said, meeting me on the stairs as I came down after a refreshing breakfast. 'You were good enough to express an interest in this little prize for Good Conduct which I am offering.'

'Oh, ah?'

'I explained to you my system of marking, I believe. Well, this morning I was impelled to vary it somewhat. The circumstances seemed to me to demand it. I happened to encounter our hostess's nephew, the boy Thomas, returning to the house, his aspect somewhat weary, it appeared to me, and travel-stained. I inquired of him where he had been at that early hour – it was not yet breakfast-time – and he replied that he had heard you mention overnight a regret that you had omitted to order the *Sporting Times* to be sent to you before leaving London, and he had actually walked all the way to the railway-station, a distance of more than three miles, to procure it for you.'

The old boy swam before my eyes. He looked like two old Mr Anstruthers, both flickering at the edges.

'What!'

'I can understand your emotion, Mr Wooster. I can appreciate it. It is indeed rarely that one encounters such unselfish kindliness in a lad of his age. So genuinely touched was I by the goodness of heart which the episode showed that I have deviated from my original system and awarded the little fellow a bonus of fifteen marks.'

'Fifteen!'

'On second thoughts, I shall make it twenty. That, as you yourself suggested, is a nice, round number.'

He doddered away, and I bounded off to find Aunt Dahlia.

'Aunt Dahlia,' I said, 'matters have taken a sinister turn.'

'You bet your Sunday spats they have,' agreed Aunt Dahlia emphatically. 'Do you know what happened just now? That crook Snettisham, who ought to be warned off the turf and hounded out of his clubs, offered Bonzo ten shillings if he would burst a paper bag behind Mr Anstruther's chair at breakfast. Thank heaven the love of a good woman triumphed again. My sweet Bonzo merely looked at him and walked away in a marked manner. But it just shows you what we are up against.'

'We are up against worse than that, Aunt Dahlia,' I said. And I told her what had happened.

She was stunned. Aghast, you might call it.

'*Thomas* did that?'

'Thos. in person.'

'Walked six miles to get you a paper?'

'Six miles and a bit.'

'The young hound! Good heavens, Bertie, do you realize that he may go on doing these Acts of Kindness daily – perhaps twice a day? Is there no way of stopping him?'

'None that I can think of. No, Aunt Dahlia, I must confess it. I am baffled. There is only one thing to do. We must send for Jeeves.'

'And about time,' said the relative churlishly. 'He ought to have been here from the start. Wire him this morning.'

There is good stuff in Jeeves. His heart is in the right place. The acid test does not find him wanting. Many men in his position, summoned back by telegram in the middle of their annual vacation, might have cut up rough a bit. But not Jeeves. On the following afternoon in he blew, looking bronzed and fit, and I gave him the scenario without delay.

'So there you have it, Jeeves,' I said, having sketched out the facts. 'The problem is one that will exercise your intelligence to the utmost. Rest now, and to-night, after a light repast, withdraw to some solitary place and get down to it. Is there any particularly stimulating food or beverage you would like for dinner? Anything that you feel would give the old brain just that extra fillip? If so, name it.'

'Thank you very much, sir, but I have already hit upon a plan which should, I fancy, prove effective.'

I gazed at the man with some awe.

'Already?'

'Yes, sir.'

'Not *already*?'

'Yes, sir.'

'Something to do with the psychology of the individual?'

'Precisely, sir.'

I shook my head, a bit discouraged. Doubts had begun to creep in.

'Well, spring it, Jeeves,' I said. 'But I have not much hope. Having only just arrived, you cannot possibly be aware of the frightful change that has taken place in young Thos. You are probably building on your knowledge of him, when last seen. Useless, Jeeves. Stirred by the prospect of getting his hooks on five of the best, this blighted boy has become so dashed virtuous that his armour seems to contain no chink. I mocked at his waistline and sneered at his school and he merely smiled in a pale, dying-duck sort of way. Well, that'll show you. However, let us hear what you have to suggest.'

'It occurred to me, sir, that the most judicious plan in the circumstances would be for you to request Mrs Travers to invite Master Sebastian Moon here for a short visit.'

I shook the onion again. The scheme sounded to me like apple sauce, and Grade A apple sauce, at that.

'What earthly good would that do?' I asked, not without a touch of asperity. 'Why Sebastian Moon?'

'He has golden curls, sir.'

'What of it?'

'The strongest natures are sometimes not proof against long golden curls.'

Well, it was a thought, of course. But I can't say I was leaping about to any great extent. It might be that the sight of Sebastian Moon would break down Thos.'s iron self-control to the extent of causing him to inflict mayhem on the person, but I wasn't any too hopeful.

'It may be so, Jeeves.'

'I do not think I am too sanguine, sir. You must remember that Master Moon, apart from his curls, has a personality which is not uniformly pleasing. He is apt to express himself with a breezy candour which I fancy Master Thomas might feel inclined to resent in one some years his junior.'

I had had a feeling all along that there was a flaw somewhere, and now it seemed to me that I had spotted it.

'But, Jeeves. Granted that little Sebastian is the pot of poison you indicate, why won't he act just as forcibly on young Bonzo as on Thos.? Pretty silly we should look if our nominee started putting it across him. Never forget that already Bonzo is twenty marks down and falling back in the betting.'

'I do not anticipate any such contingency, sir. Master Travers is in love, and love is a very powerful restraining influence at the age of thirteen.'

'H'm.' I mused. 'Well, we can but try, Jeeves.'

'Yes, sir.'

'I'll get Aunt Dahlia to write to Sippy to-night.'

I'm bound to say that the spectacle of little Sebastian when he arrived two days later did much to remove pessimism from my outlook. If ever there was a kid whose whole appearance seemed to call aloud to any right-minded boy to lure him into a quiet spot and inflict violence upon him, that kid was undeniably Sebastian Moon. He reminded me strongly of Little Lord Fauntleroy. I marked young Thos.'s demeanour closely at the moment of their meeting and, unless I was much mistaken, there came into his eyes the sort of look which would come into those of an Indian chief – Chinchagook, let us say, or Sitting Bull – just before he started reaching for his scalping-knife. He had the air of one who is about ready to begin.

True, his manner as he shook hands was guarded. Only a keen observer could have detected that he was stirred to his depths. But I had seen, and I summoned Jeeves forthwith.

'Jeeves,' I said, 'if I appeared to think poorly of that scheme of yours, I now withdraw my remarks. I believe you have found the way. I was noticing Thos. at the moment of impact. His eyes had a strange gleam.'

'Indeed, sir?'

'He shifted uneasily on his feet and his ears wiggled. He had, in short, the appearance of a boy who was holding himself in with an effort almost too great for his frail body.'

'Yes, sir?'

'Yes, Jeeves. I received a distinct impression of something being on the point of exploding. To-morrow I shall ask Aunt Dahlia to take the two warts for a country ramble, to lose them in some sequestered spot, and to leave the rest to Nature.'

'It is a good idea, sir.'

'It is more than a good idea, Jeeves,' I said. 'It is a pip.'

You know, the older I get the more firmly do I become convinced that there is no such thing as a pip in existence. Again and again have I seen the apparently sure thing go phut, and now it is rarely indeed that I can be lured from my aloof scepticism. Fellows come sidling up to me at the Drones and elsewhere, urging me to invest on some horse that can't lose even if it gets struck by lightning at the starting-post, but Bertram Wooster shakes his head. He has seen too much of life to be certain of anything.

If anyone had told me that my Cousin Thos., left alone for an extended period of time with a kid of the superlative foulness of Sebastian Moon, would not only refrain from cutting off his curls with a pocket-knife and chasing him across country into a muddy pond but would actually return home carrying the gruesome kid on his back because he had got a blister on his foot, I would have laughed scornfully. I knew Thos. I knew his work. I had seen him in action. And I was convinced that not even the prospect of collecting five pounds would be enough to give him pause.

And yet what happened? In the quiet evenfall, when the little birds were singing their sweetest and all Nature seemed to whisper of hope and happiness, the blow fell. I was chatting with old Mr Anstruther on the terrace when suddenly round a bend in the drive the two kids hove in view. Sebastian, seated on Thos.'s back, his hat off and his golden curls floating on the breeze, was singing as much as he could remember of a comic song, and Thos., bowed down by the burden but carrying on gamely, was trudging along, smiling that bally saintlike smile of his. He parked the kid on the front steps and came across to us.

'Sebastian got a nail in his shoe,' he said in a low, virtuous voice. 'It hurt him to walk, so I gave him a piggy-back.'

I heard old Mr Anstruther draw in his breath sharply.

'All the way home?'

'Yes, sir.'

'In this hot sunshine?'

'Yes, sir.'

'But was he not very heavy?'

'He was a little, sir,' said Thos., uncorking the saintlike once more. 'But it would have hurt him awfully to walk.'

I pushed off. I had had enough. If ever a septuagenarian looked on the point of handing out another bonus, that septuagenarian was old Mr Anstruther. He had the unmistakable bonus glitter in his eye. I withdrew, and found Jeeves in my bedroom messing about with ties and things.

He pursed the lips a bit on hearing the news.

'Serious, sir.'

'Very serious, Jeeves.'

'I had feared this, sir.'

'Had you? I hadn't. I was convinced Thos. would have massacred young Sebastian. I banked on it. It just shows what the greed for money will do. This is a commercial age, Jeeves. When I was a boy, I would cheerfully have forfeited five quid in order to deal faithfully with a kid like Sebastian. I would have considered it money well spent.'

'You are mistaken, sir, in your estimate of the motives actuating Master Thomas. It was not a mere desire to win five pounds that caused him to curb his natural impulses.'

'Eh?'

'I have ascertained the true reason for his change of heart, sir.'

I felt fogged.

'Religion, Jeeves?'

'No, sir. Love.'

'Love?'

'Yes, sir. The young gentleman confided in me during a brief conversation in the hall shortly after luncheon. We had been speaking for a while on neutral subjects, when he suddenly turned a deeper shade of pink and after some slight hesitation inquired of me if I did not think Miss Greta Garbo the most beautiful woman at present in existence.'

I clutched the brow.

'Jeeves! Don't tell me Thos. is in love with Greta Garbo?'

'Yes, sir. Unfortunately such is the case. He gave me to understand that it had been coming on for some time, and her last picture settled the issue. His voice shook with an emotion which it was impossible to misread. I gathered from his observations, sir, that he proposes to spend the remainder of his life trying to make himself worthy of her.'

It was a knock-out. This was the end.

'This is the end, Jeeves,' I said. 'Bonzo must be a good forty marks behind by now. Only some sensational and spectacular outrage upon the public weal on the part of young Thos. could have enabled him to wipe out the lead. And of that there is now, apparently, no chance.'

'The eventuality does appear remote, sir.'

I brooded.

'Uncle Thomas will have a fit when he comes back and finds Anatole gone.'

'Yes, sir.'

'Aunt Dahlia will drain the bitter cup to the dregs.'

'Yes, sir.'

'And, speaking from a purely selfish point of view, the finest cooking I have ever bitten will pass out of my life for ever, unless the Snettishams invite me in some night to take pot luck. And that eventuality is also remote.'

'Yes, sir.'

'Then the only thing I can do is square the shoulders and face the inevitable.'

'Yes, sir.'

'Like some aristocrat of the French Revolution popping into the tumbril, what? The brave smile. The stiff upper lip.'

'Yes, sir.'

'Right-ho, then. Is the shirt studded?'

'Yes, sir.'

'The tie chosen?'

'Yes, sir.'

'The collar and evening underwear all in order?'

'Yes, sir.'

'Then I'll have a bath and be with you in two ticks.'

It is all very well to talk about the brave smile and the stiff upper lip, but my experience – and I daresay others have found the same – is that they are a dashed sight easier to talk about than actually to fix on the face. For the next few days, I'm bound to admit, I found myself, in spite of every effort, registering gloom pretty consistently. For, as if to make things tougher than they might have been, Anatole at this juncture suddenly developed a cooking streak which put all his previous efforts in the shade.

Night after night we sat at the dinner-table, the food melting in our mouths, and Aunt Dahlia would look at me and I would look at Aunt Dahlia, and the male Snettisham would ask the female Snettisham in a ghastly, gloating sort of way if she had ever tasted such cooking and the female Snettisham would smirk at the male Snettisham and say she never had in all her puff, and I would look at Aunt Dahlia and Aunt Dahlia would look at me and our eyes would be full of unshed tears, if you know what I mean.

And all the time old Mr Anstruther's visit drawing to a close. The sands running out, so to speak.

And then, on the very last afternoon of his stay, the thing happened.

It was one of those warm, drowsy, peaceful afternoons. I was up in my bedroom, getting off a spot of correspondence which I had neglected of late, and from where I sat I looked down on the shady lawn, fringed with its gay flower-beds. There was a bird or two hopping about, a butterfly or so fluttering to and fro, and an assortment of bees buzzing hither and thither. In a garden-chair sat old Mr Anstruther, getting his eight hours. It was a sight which, had I had less on my mind, would no doubt have soothed the old soul a bit. The only blot on the landscape was Lady Snettisham, walking among the flower-beds and probably sketching out future menus, curse her.

And so for a time everything carried on. The birds hopped, the butterflies fluttered, the bees buzzed, and old Mr Anstruther snored – all in accordance with the programme. And I worked through a letter to my tailor to the point where I proposed to say something pretty strong about the way the right sleeve of my last coat bagged.

There was a tap on the door, and Jeeves entered, bringing the second post. I laid the letters listlessly on the table beside me.

'Well, Jeeves,' I said sombrely.

'Sir?'

'Mr Anstruther leaves to-morrow.'

'Yes, sir.'

I gazed down at the sleeping septuagenarian.

'In my young days, Jeeves,' I said, 'however much I might have been in love, I could never have resisted the spectacle of an old gentleman asleep like that in a deck-chair. I would have done *something* to him, no matter what the cost.'

'Indeed, sir?'

'Yes. Probably with a pea-shooter. But the modern boy is degenerate. He has lost his vim. I suppose Thos. is indoors on this lovely afternoon, showing Sebastian his stamp-album or something. Ha!' I said, and I said it rather nastily.

'I fancy Master Thomas and Master Sebastian are playing in the stable-yard, sir. I encountered Master Sebastian not long back and he informed me he was on his way thither.'

'The motion-pictures, Jeeves,' I said, 'are the curse of the age. But for them, if Thos. had found himself alone in a stable-yard with a kid like Sebastian—'

I broke off. From some point to the south-west, out of my line of vision, there had proceeded a piercing squeal.

It cut through the air like a knife, and old Mr Anstruther leaped up as if it had run into the fleshy part of his leg. And the next moment little Sebastian appeared, going well and followed at a short interval by Thos., who was going even better. In spite of the fact that he was hampered in his movements by a large stable-bucket which he bore in his right hand, Thos. was running a great race. He had almost come up with Sebastian, when the latter, with great presence of mind, dodged behind Mr Anstruther, and there for a moment the matter rested.

But only for a moment. Thos., for some reason plainly stirred to the depths of his being, moved adroitly to one side and, poising the bucket for an instant, discharged its contents. And Mr Anstruther, who had just moved to the same side, received, as far as I could gather from a distance, the entire consignment. In one second, without any previous training or upbringing, he had become the wettest man in Worcestershire.

'Jeeves!' I cried.

'Yes, indeed, sir,' said Jeeves, and seemed to me to put the whole thing in a nutshell.

Down below, things were hotting up nicely. Old Mr Anstruther may have been frail, but he undoubtedly had his moments. I have rarely seen a man of his years conduct himself with such a lissom abandon. There was a stick lying beside the chair, and with this in hand he went into action like a two-year-old. A moment later, he and Thos. had passed out of the picture round the side of the house, Thos. cutting out a rare pace but, judging from the sounds of anguish, not quite good enough to distance the field.

The tumult and the shouting died; and, after gazing for a while with considerable satisfaction at the Snettisham, who was standing there with a sand-bagged look watching her nominee pass right out of the betting, I turned to Jeeves. I felt quietly triumphant. It is not often that I score off him, but now I had scored in no uncertain manner.

'You see, Jeeves,' I said, 'I was right and you were wrong. Blood will tell. Once a Thos., always a Thos. Can the leopard change his spots or the Ethiopian his what-not? What was that thing they used to teach us at school about expelling Nature?'

'You may expel Nature with a pitchfork, sir, but she will always return? In the original Latin—'

'Never mind about the original Latin. The point is that I

told you Thos. could not resist those curls, and he couldn't. You would have it that he could.'

'I do not fancy it was the curls that caused the upheaval, sir.'

'Must have been.'

'No, sir. I think Master Sebastian had been speaking disparagingly of Miss Garbo.'

'Eh? Why would he do that?'

'I suggested that he should do so, sir, not long ago when I encountered him on his way to the stable-yard. It was a move which he was very willing to take, as he informed me that in his opinion Miss Garbo was definitely inferior both in beauty and talent to Miss Clara Bow, for whom he has long nourished a deep regard. From what we have just witnessed, sir, I imagine that Master Sebastian must have introduced the topic into the conversation at an early point.'

I sank into a chair. The Wooster system can stand just so much.

'Jeeves!'

'Sir?'

'You tell me that Sebastian Moon, a stripling of such tender years that he can go about the place with long curls without causing mob violence, is in love with Clara Bow?'

'And has been for some little time, he gave me to understand, sir.'

'Jeeves, this Younger Generation is hot stuff.'

'Yes, sir.'

'Were you like that in your day?'

'No, sir.'

'Nor I, Jeeves. At the age of fourteen I once wrote to Marie Lloyd for her autograph, but apart from that my private life could bear the strictest investigation. However, that is not the point. The point is, Jeeves, that once more I must pay you a marked tribute.'

'Thank you very much, sir.'

'Once more you have stepped forward like the great man you are and spread sweetness and light in no uncertain measure.'

'I am glad to have given satisfaction, sir. Would you be requiring my services any further?'

'You mean you wish to return to Bognor and its shrimps? Do so, Jeeves, and stay there another fortnight, if you wish. And may success attend your net.'

'Thank you very much, sir.'

I eyed the man fixedly. His head stuck out at the back, and his eyes sparkled with the light of pure intelligence.

'I am sorry for the shrimp that tries to pit its feeble cunning against you, Jeeves,' I said.

And I meant it.

In the autumn of the year in which Yorkshire Pudding won the Manchester November Handicap, the fortunes of my old pal Richard ('Bingo') Little seemed to have reached their – what's the word I want? He was, to all appearances, absolutely on plush. He ate well, slept well, was happily married; and, his Uncle Wilberforce having at last handed in his dinner-pail, respected by all, had come into possession of a large income and a fine old place in the country about thirty miles from Norwich. Buzzing down there for a brief visit, I came away convinced that, if ever a bird was sitting on top of the world, that bird was Bingo.

I had to come away because the family were shooting me off to Harrogate to chaperone my Uncle George, whose liver had been giving him the elbow again. But, as we sat pushing down the morning meal on the day of my departure, I readily agreed to play a return date as soon as ever I could fight my way back to civilization.

'Come in time for the Lakenham races,' urged young Bingo. He took aboard a second cargo of sausages and bacon, for he had always been a good trencherman and the country air seemed to improve his appetite. 'We're going to motor over with a luncheon basket, and more or less revel.'

I was just about to say that I would make a point of it, when Mrs Bingo, who was opening letters behind the coffee-apparatus, suddenly uttered a pleased yowl.

'Oh, sweetie-lambkin!' she cried.

Mrs B., if you remember, before her marriage, was the celebrated female novelist, Rosie M. Banks, and it is in some such ghastly fashion that she habitually addresses the other half of the sketch. She has got that way, I take it, from a lifetime of writing heart-throb fiction for the masses. Bingo doesn't seem to mind. I suppose, seeing that the little woman is the author of such outstanding bilge as *Mervyn Keene, Clubman*, and *Only A Factory Girl*, he is thankful it isn't anything worse.

'Oh, sweetie-lambkin, isn't that lovely?'

'What?'

'Laura Pyke wants to come here.'

'Who?'

'You must have heard me speak of Laura Pyke. She was my dearest friend at school. I simply worshipped her. She always had such a wonderful mind. She wants us to put her up for a week or two.'

'Right-ho. Bung her in.'

'You're sure you don't mind?'

'Of course not. Any pal of yours—'

'Darling!' said Mrs Bingo, blowing him a kiss.

'Angel!' said Bingo, going on with the sausages. All very charming, in fact. Pleasant domestic scene, I mean. Cheery give-and-take in the home and all that. I said as much to Jeeves as we drove off.

'In these days of unrest, Jeeves,' I said, 'with wives yearning to fulfil themselves and husbands slipping round the corner to do what they shouldn't, and the home, generally speaking, in the melting-pot, as it were, it is nice to find a thoroughly united couple.'

'Decidedly agreeable, sir.'

'I allude to the Bingos – Mr and Mrs.'

'Exactly, sir.'

'What was it the poet said of couples like the Bingeese?'

'"Two minds with but a single thought, two hearts that beat as one," sir.'

'A dashed good description, Jeeves.'

'It has, I believe, given uniform satisfaction, sir.'

And yet, if I had only known, what I had been listening to that a.m. was the first faint rumble of the coming storm. Unseen, in the background, Fate was quietly slipping the lead into the boxing-glove.

I managed to give Uncle George a miss at a fairly early date and, leaving him wallowing in the waters, sent a wire to the Bingos, announcing my return. It was a longish drive and I fetched up at my destination only just in time to dress for dinner. I had done a quick dash into the soup and fish and was feeling pretty good at the prospect of a cocktail and the well-cooked, when the door opened and Bingo appeared.

'Hello, Bertie,' he said. 'Ah, Jeeves.'

He spoke in one of those toneless voices: and, catching Jeeves's eye as I adjusted the old cravat, I exchanged a questioning glance with it. From its expression I gathered that the same thing had struck him that had struck me – viz., that our host, the young Squire, was none too chirpy. The brow was furrowed, the eye lacked that hearty sparkle, and the general bearing and demeanour were those of a body discovered after being several days in the water.

'Anything up, Bingo?' I asked, with the natural anxiety of a boyhood friend. 'You have a mouldy look. Are you sickening for some sort of plague?'

'I've got it.'

'Got what?'

'The plague.'

'How do you mean?'

'She's on the premises now,' said Bingo, and laughed in an unpleasant, hacking manner, as if he were missing on one tonsil.

I couldn't follow him. The old egg seemed to me to speak in riddles.

'You seem to me, old egg,' I said, 'to speak in riddles. Don't you think he speaks in riddles, Jeeves?'

'Yes, sir.'

'I'm talking about the Pyke,' said Bingo.

'What pike?'

'Laura Pyke. Don't you remember—?'

'Oh, ah. Of course. The school chum. The seminary crony. Is she still here?'

'Yes, and looks like staying for ever. Rosie's absolutely potty about her. Hangs on her lips.'

'The glamour of the old days still persists, eh?'

'I should say it does,' said young Bingo. 'This business of schoolgirl friendships beats me. Hypnotic is the only word. I can't understand it. Men aren't like that. You and I were at school together, Bertie, but, my gosh, I don't look on you as a sort of mastermind.'

'You don't?'

'I don't treat your lightest utterance as a pearl of wisdom.'

'Why not?'

'Yet Rosie does with this Pyke. In the hands of the Pyke she is mere putty. If you want to see what was once a first-class Garden of Eden becoming utterly ruined as a desirable residence by the machinations of a Serpent, take a look round this place.'

'Why, what's the trouble?'

'Laura Pyke,' said young Bingo with intense bitterness, 'is a food crank, curse her. She says we all eat too much and eat it too quickly and, anyway, ought not to be eating it at all but living on parsnips and similar muck. And Rosie, instead of telling the woman not to be a fathead, gazes at her in wide-eyed admiration, taking it in through the pores. The result is that the cuisine of this house has been shot to pieces, and I am starving on my feet. Well, when I tell you that it's weeks since a beefsteak pudding raised its head in the home, you'll understand what I mean.'

At this point the gong went. Bingo listened with a moody frown.

'I don't know why they still bang that damned thing,' he said. 'There's nothing to bang it for. By the way, Bertie, would you like a cocktail?'

'I would.'

'Well, you won't get one. We don't have cocktails any more. The girl friend says they corrode the stomachic tissues.'

I was appalled. I had had no idea that the evil had spread as far as this.

'No cocktails!'

'No. And you'll be dashed lucky if it isn't a vegetarian dinner.'

'Bingo,' I cried, deeply moved, 'you must act. You must assert yourself. You must put your foot down. You must take a strong stand. You must be master in the home.'

He looked at me. A long, strange look.

'You aren't married, are you, Bertie?'

'You know I'm not.'

'I should have guessed it, anyway. Come on.'

Well, the dinner wasn't absolutely vegetarian, but when you had said that you had said everything. It was sparse, meagre, not at all the jolly, chunky repast for which the old tum was standing up and clamouring after its long motor ride. And what there was of it was turned to ashes in the mouth by the conversation of Miss Laura Pyke.

In happier circs, and if I had not been informed in advance of the warped nature of her soul, I might have been favourably impressed by this female at the moment of our meeting. She was really rather a good-looking girl, a bit strong in the face but nevertheless quite reasonably attractive. But had she been a thing of radiant beauty, she could never have clicked with Bertram Wooster. Her conversation was of a kind which would have queered Helen of Troy with any right-thinking man.

During dinner she talked all the time, and it did not take me long to see why the iron had entered into Bingo's soul. Practically all she said was about food and Bingo's tendency to shovel it down in excessive quantities, thereby handing the lemon to his stomachic tissues. She didn't seem particularly interested in my stomachic tissues, rather giving the impression that if Bertram burst it would be all right with her. It was on young Bingo that she concentrated as the brand to be saved from the burning. Gazing at him like a high priestess at the favourite, though erring, disciple, she told him all the things that were happening to his inside because he would insist on eating stuff lacking in fat-soluble vitamins. She spoke freely of proteins, carbohydrates, and the physiological requirements of the average individual. She was not a girl who believed in mincing her words, and a racy little anecdote she told about a man who refused to eat prunes had the effect of causing me to be a non-starter for the last two courses.

'Jeeves,' I said, on reaching the sleeping chamber that night, 'I don't like the look of things.'

'No, sir?'

'No, Jeeves, I do not. I view the situation with concern. Things are worse than I thought they were. Mr Little's remarks before dinner may have given you the impression that the Pyke merely lectured on food-reform in a general sort of way. Such, I now find, is not the case. By way of illustrating her theme, she points to Mr Little as the awful example. She criticizes him, Jeeves.'

'Indeed, sir?'

'Yes. Openly. Keeps telling him he eats too much, drinks too much, and gobbles his food. I wish you could have heard a comparison she drew between him and the late Mr Gladstone, considering them in the capacity of food chewers. It left young Bingo very much with the short end of the stick. And the sinister thing is that Mrs Bingo approves. Are wives often like that? Welcoming criticism of the lord and master, I mean?'

'They are generally open to suggestions from the outside public with regard to the improvement of their husbands, sir.'

'That is why married men are wan, what?'

'Yes, sir.'

I had had the foresight to send the man downstairs for a plate of biscuits. I bit a representative specimen thoughtfully.

'Do you know what I think, Jeeves?'

'No, sir.'

'I think Mr Little doesn't realize the full extent of the peril which threatens his domestic happiness. I'm beginning to understand this business of matrimony. I'm beginning to see how the thing works. Would you care to hear how I figure it out, Jeeves?'

'Extremely, sir.'

'Well, it's like this. Take a couple of birds. These birds get married, and for a while all is gas and gaiters. The female regards her mate as about the best thing that ever came a girl's way. He is her king, if you know what I mean. She looks up to him and respects him. Joy, as you might say, reigns supreme. Eh?'

'Very true, sir.'

'Then gradually, by degrees – little by little, if I may use the expression – disillusionment sets in. She sees him eating a poached egg, and the glamour starts to fade. She watches him mangling a chop, and it continues to fade. And so on and so on, if you follow me, and so forth.'

'I follow you perfectly, sir.'

'But mark this, Jeeves. This is the point. Here we approach the nub. Usually it is all right, because, as I say, the disillusionment comes gradually and the female has time to adjust herself. But in the case of young Bingo, owing to the indecent outspokenness of the Pyke, it's coming in a rush. Absolutely in a flash, without any previous preparation, Mrs Bingo is having Bingo presented to her as a sort of human boa-constrictor full of unpleasantly jumbled interior organs. The picture which the Pyke is building up for her in her mind is that of one of those men you see in restaurants with three chins, bulging eyes, and the veins starting out on the forehead. A little more of this, and love must wither.'

'You think so, sir?'

'I'm sure of it. No affection can stand the strain. Twice during dinner to-night the Pyke said things about young Bingo's intestinal canal which I shouldn't have thought would have been possible in mixed company even in this lax post-War era. Well, you see what I mean. You can't go on knocking a man's intestinal canal indefinitely without causing his wife to stop and ponder. The danger, as I see it, is that after a bit more of this Mrs Little will decide that tinkering is no use and that the only thing to do is to scrap Bingo and get a newer model.'

'Most disturbing, sir.'

'Something must be done, Jeeves. You must act. Unless you can find some way of getting this Pyke out of the woodwork, and that right speedily, the home's number is up. You see, what makes matters worse is that Mrs Bingo is romantic. Women like her, who consider the day ill-spent if they have not churned out five thousand words of superfatted fiction, are apt even at the best of times to yearn a trifle. The ink gets into their heads. I mean to say, I shouldn't wonder if right from the start Mrs Bingo hasn't had a sort of sneaking regret that Bingo isn't one of those strong, curt, Empire-building kind of Englishmen she puts into her books, with sad, unfathomable eyes, lean, sensitive hands, and riding-boots. You see what I mean?'

'Precisely, sir. You imply that Miss Pyke's criticisms will have been instrumental in moving the hitherto unformulated dissatisfaction from the subconscious to the conscious mind.'

'Once again, Jeeves?' I said, trying to grab it as it came off the bat, but missing it by several yards.

He repeated the dose.

'Well, I daresay you're right,' I said. 'Anyway, the point is, P.M.G. Pyke must go. How do you propose to set about it?'

'I fear I have nothing to suggest at the moment, sir.'

'Come, come, Jeeves.'

'I fear not, sir. Possibly after I have seen the lady—'

'You mean, you want to study the psychology of the individual and what not?'

'Precisely, sir.'

'Well, I don't know how you're going to do it. After all, I mean, you can hardly cluster round the dinner-table and drink in the Pyke's small talk.'

'There is that difficulty, sir.'

'Your best chance, it seems to me, will be when we go to the Lakenham races on Thursday. We shall feed out of a luncheon-basket in God's air, and there's nothing to stop you hanging about and passing the sandwiches. Prick the ears and be at your most observant then, is my advice.'

'Very good, sir.'

'Very good, Jeeves. Be there, then, with the eyes popping. And, meanwhile, dash downstairs and see if you can dig up another instalment of these biscuits. I need them sorely.'

The morning of the Lakenham races dawned bright and juicy. A casual observer would have said that God was in His Heaven and all right with the world. It was one of those days you sometimes get lateish in the autumn when the sun beams, the birds toot, and there is a bracing tang in the air that sends the blood beetling briskly through the veins.

Personally, however, I wasn't any too keen on the bracing tang. It made me feel so exceptionally fit that almost immediately after breakfast I found myself beginning to wonder what there would be for lunch. And the thought of what there probably would be for lunch, if the Pyke's influence made itself felt, lowered my spirits considerably.

'I fear the worst, Jeeves,' I said. 'Last night at dinner Miss Pyke threw out the remark that the carrot was the best of all vegetables, having an astonishing effect on the blood and beautifying the complexion. Now, I am all for anything that bucks up the Wooster blood. Also, I would like to give the natives a treat by letting them take a look at my rosy, glowing cheeks. But not at the expense of lunching on raw carrots. To avoid any rannygazoo, therefore, I think it will be best if you add a bit for the young master to your personal packet of sandwiches. I don't want to be caught short.'

'Very good, sir.'

At this point, young Bingo came up. I hadn't seen him look so jaunty for days.

'I've just been superintending the packing of the lunch-basket, Bertie,' he said. 'I stood over the butler and saw that there was no nonsense.'

'All pretty sound?' I asked, relieved.

'All indubitably sound.'

'No carrots?'

'No carrots,' said young Bingo. 'There's ham sandwiches,' he proceeded, a strange, soft light in his eyes, 'and tongue sandwiches and potted meat sandwiches and game sandwiches and hard-boiled eggs and lobster and a cold chicken and sardines and a cake and a couple of bottles of Bollinger and some old brandy—'

'It has the right ring,' I said. 'And if we want a bite to eat after that, of course we can go to the pub.'

'What pub?'

'Isn't there a pub on the course?'

'There's not a pub for miles. That's why I was so particularly careful that there should be no funny work about the basket. The common where these races are held is a desert without an oasis. Practically a death-trap. I met a fellow the other day who told me he got there last year and unpacked his basket and found that the champagne had burst and, together with the salad dressing, had soaked into the ham, which in its turn had got mixed up with the gorgonzola cheese, forming a sort of paste. He had had rather a bumpy bit of road to travel over.'

'What did he do?'

'Oh, he ate the mixture. It was the only course. But he said he could still taste it sometimes, even now.'

In ordinary circs I can't say I should have been any too braced at the news that we were going to split up for the journey in the following order – Bingo and Mrs Bingo in their car and the Pyke in mine, with Jeeves sitting behind in the dickey. But, things being as they were, the arrangement had its points. It meant that Jeeves would be able to study the back of her head and draw his deductions, while I could engage her in conversation and let him see for himself what manner of female she was.

I started, accordingly, directly we had rolled off and all through the journey until we fetched up at the course she gave of her best. It was with considerable satisfaction that I parked the car beside a tree and hopped out.

'You were listening, Jeeves?' I said gravely.

'Yes, sir.'

'A tough baby?'

'Undeniably, sir.'

Bingo and Mrs Bingo came up.

'The first race won't be for half an hour,' said Bingo. 'We'd better lunch now. Fish the basket out, Jeeves, would you mind?'

'Sir?'

'The luncheon-basket,' said Bingo in a devout sort of voice, licking his lips slightly.

'The basket is not in Mr Wooster's car, sir.'

'What!'

'I assumed that you were bringing it in your own, sir.'

I have never seen the sunshine fade out of anybody's face as quickly as it did out of Bingo's. He uttered a sharp, wailing cry.

'Rosie!'

'Yes, sweetie-pie?'

'The bunch! The lasket!'

'What, darling?'

'The luncheon-basket!'

'What about it, precious?'

'It's been left behind!'

'Oh, has it?' said Mrs Bingo.

I confess she had never fallen lower in my estimation. I had always known her as a woman with as healthy an appreciation of her meals as any of my acquaintance. A few years previously, when my Aunt Dahlia had stolen her French cook, Anatole, she had called Aunt Dahlia some names in my presence which had impressed me profoundly. Yet now, when informed that she was marooned on a bally prairie without bite or sup, all she could find to say was, 'Oh, has it?' I had never fully realized before the extent to which she had allowed herself to be dominated by the deleterious influence of the Pyke.

The Pyke, for her part, touched an even lower level.

'It is just as well,' she said, and her voice seemed to cut Bingo like a knife. 'Luncheon is a meal better omitted. If taken, it should consist merely of a few muscatels, bananas and grated carrots. It is a well-known fact—'

And she went on to speak at some length of the gastric juices in a vein far from suited to any gathering at which gentlemen were present.

'So, you see, darling,' said Mrs Bingo, 'you will really feel ever so much better and brighter for not having eaten a lot of indigestible food. It is much the best thing that could have happened.'

Bingo gave her a long, lingering look.

'I see,' he said. 'Well, if you will excuse me, I'll just go off somewhere where I can cheer a bit without exciting comment.'

I perceived Jeeves withdrawing in a meaning manner, and I followed him, hoping for the best. My trust was not misplaced. He had brought enough sandwiches for two. In fact, enough for three. I whistled to Bingo, and he came slinking up, and we restored the tissues in a makeshift sort of way behind a hedge. Then Bingo went off to interview bookies about the first race, and Jeeves gave a cough.

'Swallowed a crumb the wrong way?' I said.

'No, sir, I thank you. It is merely that I desired to express a hope that I had not been guilty of taking a liberty, sir.'

'How?'

'In removing the luncheon-basket from the car before we started, sir.'

I quivered like an aspen. I stared at the man. Aghast. Shocked to the core.

'You, Jeeves?' I said, and I should rather think Cæsar spoke in the same sort of voice on finding Brutus puncturing him with the sharp instrument. 'You mean to tell me it was you who deliberately, if that's the word I want—?'

'Yes, sir. It seemed to me the most judicious course to pursue. It would not have been prudent, in my opinion, to have allowed Mrs Little, in her present frame of mind, to witness Mr Little eating a meal on the scale which he outlined in his remarks this morning.'

I saw his point.

'True, Jeeves,' I said thoughtfully. 'I see what you mean. If young Bingo has a fault, it is that, when in the society of a sandwich, he is apt to get a bit rough. I've picnicked with him before, many a time and oft, and his method of approach to the ordinary tongue or ham sandwich rather resembles that of the lion, the king of beasts, tucking into an antelope. Add lobster and cold chicken, and I admit the spectacle might have been something of a jar for the consort . . . Still . . . all the same . . . nevertheless—'

'And there is another aspect of the matter, sir.'

'What's that?'

'A day spent without nourishment in the keen autumnal air may induce in Mrs Little a frame of mind not altogether in sympathy with Miss Pyke's views on diet.'

'You mean, hunger will gnaw and she'll be apt to bite at the Pyke when she talks about how jolly it is for the gastric juices to get a day off?'

'Exactly, sir.'

I shook the head. I hated to damp the man's pretty enthusiasm, but it had to be done.

'Abandon the idea, Jeeves,' I said. 'I fear you have not studied the sex as I have. Missing her lunch means little or nothing to the female of the species. The feminine attitude towards lunch is notoriously airy and casual. Where you have made your bloomer is in confusing lunch with tea. Hell, it is well known, has no fury like a woman who wants her tea and can't get it. At such times the most amiable of the sex become mere bombs which a spark may ignite. But lunch, Jeeves, no. I should have thought you would have known that – a bird of your established intelligence.'

'No doubt you are right, sir.'

'If you could somehow arrange for Mrs Little to miss her tea... but these are idle dreams, Jeeves. By tea-time she will be back at the old home, in the midst of plenty. It only takes an hour to do the trip. The last race is over shortly after four. By five o'clock Mrs Little will have her feet tucked under the table and will be revelling in buttered toast. I am sorry, Jeeves, but your scheme was a wash-out from the start. No earthly. A dud.'

'I appreciate the point you have raised, sir. What you say is extremely true.'

'Unfortunately. Well, there it is. The only thing to do seems to be to get back to the course and try to skin a bookie or two and forget.'

Well, the long day wore on, so to speak. I can't say I enjoyed myself much. I was distrait, if you know what I mean. Preoccupied. From time to time assorted clusters of spavined local horses clumped down the course with farmers on top of them, but I watched them with a languid eye. To get into the spirit of one of these rural meetings, it is essential that the subject have a good, fat lunch inside him. Subtract the lunch, and what ensues? Ennui. Not once but many times during the afternoon I found myself thinking hard thoughts about Jeeves. The man seemed to me to be losing his grip. A child could have told him that that footling scheme of his would not have got him anywhere.

I mean to say, when you reflect that the average woman considers she has lunched luxuriously if she swallows a couple of macaroons, half a chocolate éclair and a raspberry vinegar, is she going to be peevish because you do her out of a midday sandwich? Of course not. Perfectly ridiculous. Too silly for words. All that Jeeves had accomplished by his bally trying to be clever was to give me a feeling as if foxes were gnawing my vitals and a strong desire for home.

It was a relief, therefore, when, as the shades of evening were beginning to fall, Mrs Bingo announced her intention of calling it a day and shifting.

'Would you mind very much missing the last race, Mr Wooster?' she asked.

'I am all for it,' I replied cordially. 'The last race means little or nothing in my life. Besides, I am a shilling and sixpence ahead of the game, and the time to leave off is when you're winning.'

'Laura and I thought we would go home. I feel I should like an early cup of tea. Bingo says he will stay on. So I thought you could drive our car, and he would follow later in yours, with Jeeves.'

'Right-ho.'

'You know the way?'

'Oh yes. Main road as far as that turning by the pond, and then across country.'

'I can direct you from there.'

I sent Jeeves to fetch the car, and presently we were bowling off in good shape. The short afternoon had turned into a rather chilly, misty sort of evening, the kind of evening that sends a fellow's thoughts straying off in the direction of hot Scotch-and-water with a spot of lemon in it. I put the foot firmly on the accelerator, and we did the five or six miles of main road in quick time.

Turning eastward at the pond, I had to go a bit slower, for we had struck a wildish stretch of country where the going wasn't so good. I don't know any part of England where you feel so off the map as on the by-roads of Norfolk. Occasionally we would meet a cow or two, but otherwise we had the world pretty much to ourselves.

I began to think about that drink again, and the more I thought the better it looked. It's rummy how people differ in this matter of selecting the beverage that is to touch the spot. It's what Jeeves would call the psychology of the individual. Some fellows in my position might have voted for a tankard of ale, and the Pyke's idea of a refreshing snort was, as I knew from what she had told me on the journey out, a cupful of tepid pip-and-peel water or, failing that, what she called the fruit-liquor. You make this, apparently, by soaking raisins in cold water and adding the juice of a lemon. After which, I suppose, you invite a couple of old friends in and have an orgy, burying the bodies in the morning.

Personally, I had no doubts. I never wavered. Hot Scotch-and-water was the stuff for me – stressing the Scotch, if you know what I mean, and going fairly easy on the H_2O. I seemed to see the beaker smiling at me across the misty fields, beckoning me on, as it were, and saying 'Courage, Bertram! It will not be long now!' And with renewed energy I bunged the old foot down on the accelerator and tried to send the needle up to sixty.

Instead of which, if you follow my drift, the bally thing flickered for a moment to thirty-five and then gave the business up as a bad job. Quite suddenly and unexpectedly, no one more surprised than myself, the car let out a faint gurgle like a sick moose and stopped in its tracks. And there we were, somewhere in Norfolk, with darkness coming on and a cold wind that smelled of guano and dead mangold-wurzels playing searchingly about the spinal column.

The back-seat drivers gave tongue.

'What's the matter? What has happened? Why don't you go on? What are you stopping for?'

I explained.

'I'm not stopping. It's the car.'

'Why has the car stopped?'

'Ah!' I said, with a manly frankness that became me well. 'There you have me.'

You see, I'm one of those birds who drive a lot but don't know the first thing about the works. The policy I pursue is to get aboard, prod the self-starter, and leave the rest to Nature. If anything goes wrong, I scream for an A.A. scout. It's a system that answers admirably as a rule, but on the present occasion it blew a fuse owing to the fact that there wasn't an A.A. scout within miles. I explained as much to the fair cargo and received in return a 'Tchah!' from the Pyke that nearly lifted the top of my head off. What with having a covey of female relations who have regarded me from childhood as about ten degrees short of a half-wit, I have become rather a connoisseur of 'Tchahs', and the Pyke's seemed to me well up in Class A, possessing much of the *timbre* and *brio* of my Aunt Agatha's.

'Perhaps I can find out what the trouble is,' she said, becoming calmer. 'I understand cars.'

She got out and began peering into the thing's vitals. I thought for a moment of suggesting that its gastric juices might have taken a turn for the worse owing to lack of fat-soluble vitamins, but decided on the whole not. I'm a pretty close observer, and it didn't seem to me that she was in the mood.

And yet, as a matter of fact, I should have been about right, at that. For after fiddling with the engine for awhile in a discontented sort of way the female was suddenly struck with an idea.

She tested it, and it was proved correct. There was not a drop of petrol in the tank. No gas. In other words, a complete lack of fat-soluble vitamins. What it amounted to was that the job now before us was to get the old bus home purely by will-power.

Feeling that, from whatever angle they regarded the regrettable occurrence, they could hardly blame me, I braced up a trifle – in fact, to the extent of a hearty 'Well, well, well!'

'No petrol,' I said. 'Fancy that.'

'But Bingo told me he was going to fill the tank this morning,' said Mrs Bingo.

'I suppose he forgot,' said the Pyke. 'He would!'

'What do you mean by that?' said Mrs Bingo, and I noted in her voice a touch of what-is-it.

'I mean he is just the sort of man who would forget to fill the tank,' replied the Pyke, who also appeared somewhat moved.

'I should be very much obliged, Laura,' said Mrs Bingo, doing the heavy loyal-little-woman stuff, 'if you would refrain from criticizing my husband.'

'Tchah!' said the Pyke.

'And don't say "Tchah!"' said Mrs Bingo.

'I shall say whatever I please,' said the Pyke.

'Ladies, ladies!' I said. 'Ladies, ladies, ladies!'

It was rash. Looking back, I can see that. One of the first lessons life teaches us is that on these occasions of back-chat between the delicately-nurtured a man should retire into the offing, curl up in a ball, and imitate the prudent tactics of the opossum, which, when danger is in the air, pretends to be dead, frequently going to the length of hanging out crêpe and instructing its friends to stand round and say what a pity it all is. The only result of my dash at the soothing intervention was that the Pyke turned on me like a wounded leopardess.

'Well!' she said. 'Aren't you proposing to do anything, Mr Wooster?'

'What can I do?'

'There's a house over there. I should have thought it would be well within even your powers to go and borrow a tin of petrol.'

I looked. There was a house. And one of the lower windows was lighted, indicating to the trained mind the presence of a ratepayer.

'A very sound and brainy scheme,' I said ingratiatingly. 'I will first honk a little on the horn to show we're here, and then rapid action.'

I honked, with the most gratifying results. Almost immediately a human form appeared in the window. It seemed to be waving its arms in a matey and welcoming sort of way. Stimulated and encouraged, I hastened to the front door and gave it a breezy bang with the knocker. Things, I felt, were moving.

The first bang produced no result. I had just lifted the knocker for the encore, when it was wrenched out of my hand. The door flew open, and there was a bloke with spectacles on his face and all round the spectacles an expression of strained anguish. A bloke with a secret sorrow.

I was sorry he had troubles, of course, but, having some of my own, I came right down to the agenda without delay.

'I say...' I began.

The bloke's hair was standing up in a kind of tousled mass, and at this juncture, as if afraid it would not stay like that without assistance, he ran a hand through it. And for the first time I noted that the spectacles had a hostile gleam.

'Was that you making that infernal noise?' he asked.

'Er – yes,' I said. 'I did toot.'

'Toot once more – just once,' said the bloke, speaking in a low, strangled voice, 'and I'll shred you up into little bits with my bare hands. My wife's gone out for the evening and after hours of ceaseless toil I've at last managed to get the baby to sleep, and you come along making that hideous din with your damned horn. What do you mean by it, blast you?'

'Er—'

'Well, that's how matters stand,' said the bloke, summing up. 'One more toot – just one single, solitary suggestion of the faintest shadow or suspicion of anything remotely approaching a toot – and may the Lord have mercy on your soul.'

'What I want,' I said, 'is petrol.'

'What you'll get,' said the bloke, 'is a thick ear.'

And, closing the door with the delicate caution of one brushing flies off a sleeping Venus, he passed out of my life.

Women as a sex are always apt to be a trifle down on the defeated warrior. Returning to the car, I was not well received. The impression seemed to be that Bertram had not acquitted himself in a fashion worthy of his Crusading ancestors. I did my best to smooth matters over, but you know how it is. When you've broken down on a chilly autumn evening miles from anywhere and have missed lunch and look like missing tea as well, mere charm of manner can never be a really satisfactory substitute for a tinful of the juice.

Things got so noticeably unpleasant, in fact, that after a while, mumbling something about getting help, I sidled off down the road. And, by Jove, I hadn't gone half a mile before I saw lights in the distance and there, in the middle of this forsaken desert, was a car.

I stood in the road and whooped as I had never whooped before.

'Hi!' I shouted. 'I say! Hi! Half a minute! Hi! Ho! I say! Ho! Hi! Just a second if you don't mind.'

The car reached me and slowed up. A voice spoke.

'Is that you, Bertie?'

'Hullo, Bingo! Is that you? I say, Bingo, we've broken down.'

Bingo hopped out.

'Give us five minutes, Jeeves,' he said, 'and then drive slowly on.'

'Very good, sir.'

Bingo joined me.

'We aren't going to walk, are we?' I asked. 'Where's the sense?'

'Yes, walk, laddie,' said Bingo, 'and warily withal. I want to make sure of something. Bertie, how were things when you left? Hotting up?'

'A trifle.'

'You observed symptoms of a row, a quarrel, a parting of brass rags between Rosie and the Pyke?'

'There did seem a certain liveliness.'

'Tell me.'

I related what had occurred. He listened intently.

'Bertie,' he said as we walked along, 'you are present at a crisis in your old friend's life. It may be that this vigil in a broken-down car will cause Rosie to see what you'd have thought she ought to have seen years ago – viz.: that the Pyke is entirely unfit for human consumption and must be cast into outer darkness where there is wailing and gnashing of teeth. I am not betting on it, but stranger things have happened. Rosie is the sweetest girl in the world, but, like all women, she gets edgy towards tea-time. And to-day, having missed lunch...Hark!'

He grabbed my arm, and we paused. Tense. Agog. From down the road came the sound of voices, and a mere instant was enough to tell us that it was Mrs Bingo and the Pyke talking things over.

I had never listened in on a real, genuine female row before, and I'm bound to say it was pretty impressive. During my absence, matters appeared to have developed on rather a spacious scale. They had reached the stage now where the combatants had begun to dig into the past and rake up old scores. Mrs Bingo was saying that the Pyke would never have got into the hockey team at St Adela's if she hadn't flattered and fawned upon the captain in a way that it made Mrs Bingo, even after all these years, sick to think of. The Pyke replied that she had refrained from mentioning it until now, having always felt it better to let bygones be bygones, but that if Mrs Bingo supposed her to be unaware that Mrs Bingo had won the Scripture prize by taking a list of the Kings of Judah into the examination room, tucked into her middy-blouse, Mrs Bingo was vastly mistaken.

Furthermore, the Pyke proceeded, Mrs Bingo was also labouring under an error if she imagined that the Pyke proposed to remain a night longer under her roof. It had been in a moment of weakness, a moment of mistaken kindliness, supposing her to be lonely and in need of intellectual society, that the Pyke had decided to pay her a visit at all. Her intention now was, if ever Providence sent them aid and enabled her to get out of this beastly car and back to her trunks, to pack those trunks and leave by the next train, even if that train was a milk-train, stopping at every station. Indeed, rather than endure another night at Mrs Bingo's, the Pyke was quite willing to walk to London.

To this, Mrs Bingo's reply was long and eloquent and touched on the fact that in her last term at St Adela's a girl named

Simpson had told her (Mrs Bingo) that a girl named Waddesley had told her (the Simpson) that the Pyke, while pretending to be a friend of hers (the Bingo's), had told her (the Waddesley) that she (the Bingo) couldn't eat strawberries and cream without coming out in spots, and, in addition, had spoken in the most catty manner about the shape of her nose. It could all have been condensed, however, into the words 'Right-ho'.

It was when the Pyke had begun to say that she had never had such a hearty laugh in her life as when she read the scene in Mrs Bingo's last novel where the heroine's little boy dies of croup that we felt it best to call the meeting to order before bloodshed set in. Jeeves had come up in the car, and Bingo, removing a tin of petrol from the dickey, placed it in the shadows at the side of the road. Then we hopped on and made the spectacular entry.

'Hullo, hullo hullo,' said Bingo brightly. 'Bertie tells me you've had a breakdown.'

'Oh, Bingo!' cried Mrs Bingo, wifely love thrilling in every syllable. 'Thank goodness you've come.'

'Now, perhaps,' said the Pyke, 'I can get home and do my packing. If Mr Wooster will allow me to use his car, his man can drive me back to the house in time to catch the six-fifteen.'

'You aren't leaving us?' said Bingo.

'I am,' said the Pyke.

'Too bad,' said Bingo.

She climbed in beside Jeeves and they popped off. There was a short silence after they had gone. It was too dark to see her, but I could feel Mrs Bingo struggling between love of her mate and the natural urge to say something crisp about his forgetting to fill the petrol tank that morning. Eventually nature took its course.

'I must say, sweetie-pie,' she said, 'it was a little careless of you to leave the tank almost empty when we started to-day. You promised me you would fill it, darling.'

'But I did fill it, darling.'

'But, darling, it's empty.'

'It can't be, darling.'

'Laura said it was.'

'The woman's an ass,' said Bingo. 'There's plenty of petrol. What's wrong is probably that the sprockets aren't running true with the differential gear. It happens that way sometimes. I'll fix it in a second. But I don't want you to sit freezing out here while I'm doing it. Why not go to that house over there and ask them if you can't come in and sit down for ten minutes? They might give you a cup of tea, too.'

A soft moan escaped Mrs Bingo.

'Tea!' I heard her whisper.

I had to bust Bingo's daydream.

'I'm sorry, old man,' I said, 'but I fear the old English hospitality which you outline is off. That house is inhabited by a sort of bandit. As unfriendly a bird as I ever met. His wife's out and he's just got the baby to sleep, and this has darkened his outlook. Tap even lightly on his front door and you take your life into your hands.'

'Nonsense,' said Bingo. 'Come along.'

He banged the knocker, and produced an immediate reaction.

'Hell!' said the Bandit, appearing as if out of a trap.

'I say,' said young Bingo, 'I'm just fixing our car outside. Would you object to my wife coming in out of the cold for a few minutes?'

'Yes,' said the Bandit, 'I would.'

'And you might give her a cup of tea.'

'I might,' said the Bandit, 'but I won't.'

'You won't?'

'No. And for heaven's sake don't talk so loud. I know that baby. A whisper sometimes does it.'

'Let us get this straight,' said Bingo. 'You refuse to give my wife tea?'

'Yes.'

'You would see a woman starve?'

'Yes.'

'Well, you jolly well aren't going to,' said young Bingo. 'Unless you go straight to your kitchen, put the kettle on, and start slicing bread for the buttered toast, I'll yell and wake the baby.'

The Bandit turned ashen.

'You wouldn't do that?'

'I would.'

'Have you no heart?'

'No.'

'No human feeling?'

'No.'

The Bandit turned to Mrs Bingo. You could see his spirit was broken.

'Do your shoes squeak?' he asked humbly.

'No.'

'Then come on in.'

'Thank you,' said Mrs Bingo.

She turned for an instant to Bingo, and there was a look in her eyes that one of those damsels in distress might have given the knight as he shot his cuffs and turned away from the dead dragon. It was a look of adoration, of almost reverent respect. Just the sort of look, in fact, that a husband likes to see.

'Darling!' she said.

'Darling!' said Bingo.

'Angel!' said Mrs Bingo.

'Precious!' said Bingo. 'Come along, Bertie, let's get at that car.'

He was silent till he had fetched the tin of petrol and filled the tank and screwed the cap on again. Then he drew a deep breath.

'Bertie,' he said, 'I am ashamed to admit it, but occasionally in the course of a lengthy acquaintance there have been moments when I have temporarily lost faith in Jeeves.'

'My dear chap!' I said, shocked.

'Yes, Bertie, there have. Sometimes my belief in him has wobbled. I have said to myself, "Has he the old speed, the ancient vim?" I shall never say it again. From now on, childlike trust. It was his idea, Bertie, that if a couple of women headed for tea suddenly found the cup snatched from their lips, so to speak, they would turn and rend one another. Observe the result.'

'But, dash it, Jeeves couldn't have known that the car would break down.'

'On the contrary. He let all the petrol out of the tank when you sent him to fetch the machine – all except just enough to carry it well into the wilds beyond the reach of human aid. He foresaw what would happen. I tell you, Bertie, Jeeves stands alone.'

'Absolutely.'

'He's a marvel.'

'A wonder.'

'A wizard.'

'A stout fellow,' I agreed. 'Full of fat-soluble vitamins.'

'The exact expression,' said young Bingo. 'And now let's go

and tell Rosie the car is fixed, and then home to the tankard of ale.'

'Not the tankard of ale, old man,' I said firmly. 'The hot Scotch-and-water with a spot of lemon in it.'

'You're absolutely right,' said Bingo. 'What a flair you have in these matters, Bertie. Hot Scotch-and-water it is.'

Ask anyone at the Drones, and they will tell you that Bertram Wooster is a fellow whom it is dashed difficult to deceive. Old Lynx-Eye is about what it amounts to. I observe and deduce. I weigh the evidence and draw my conclusions. And that is why Uncle George had not been in my midst more than about two minutes before I, so to speak, saw all. To my trained eye the thing stuck out a mile.

And yet it seemed so dashed absurd. Consider the facts, if you know what I mean.

I mean to say, for years, right back to the time when I first went to school, this bulging relative had been one of the recognized eyesores of London. He was fat then, and day by day in every way has been getting fatter ever since, till now tailors measure him just for the sake of the exercise. He is what they call a prominent London clubman – one of those birds in tight morning-coats and grey toppers whom you see toddling along St James's Street on fine afternoons, puffing a bit as they make the grade. Slip a ferret into any good club between Piccadilly and Pall Mall, and you would start half a dozen Uncle Georges.

He spends his time lunching and dining at the Buffers and, between meals, sucking down spots in the smoking-room and talking to anyone who will listen about the lining of his stomach. About twice a year his liver lodges a formal protest and he goes off to Harrogate or Carlsbad to get planed down. Then back again and on with the programme. The last bloke in the world, in short, who you would think would ever fall a victim to the divine pash. And yet, if you will believe me, that was absolutely the strength of it.

This old pestilence blew in on me one morning at about the hour of the after-breakfast cigarette.

'Oh, Bertie,' he said.

'Hullo?'

'You know those ties you've been wearing. Where did you get them?'

'Blucher's, in the Burlington Arcade.'

'Thanks.'

He walked across to the mirror and stood in front of it, gazing at himself in an earnest manner.

'Smut on your nose?' I asked courteously.

Then I suddenly perceived that he was wearing a sort of horrible simper, and I confess it chilled the blood to no little extent. Uncle George, with face in repose, is hard enough on the eye. Simpering, he goes right above the odds.

'Ha!' he said.

He heaved a long sigh, and turned away. Not too soon, for the mirror was on the point of cracking

'I'm not so old,' he said, in a musing sort of voice.

'So old as what?'

'Properly considered, I'm in my prime. Besides, what a young and inexperienced girl needs is a man of weight and years to lean on. The sturdy oak, not the sapling.'

It was at this point that, as I said above, I saw all.

'Great Scott, Uncle George!' I said. 'You aren't thinking of getting married?'

'Who isn't?' he said.

'You aren't,' I said.

'Yes, I am. Why not?'

'Oh, well—'

'Marriage is an honourable state.'

'Oh, absolutely.'

'It might make you a better man, Bertie.'

'Who says so?'

'I say so. Marriage might turn you from a frivolous young scallywag into – er – a non-scallywag. Yes, confound you, I *am* thinking of getting married, and if Agatha comes sticking her oar in I'll – I'll – well, I shall know what to do about it.'

He exited on the big line, and I rang the bell for Jeeves. The situation seemed to me one that called for a cosy talk.

'Jeeves,' I said.

'Sir?'

'You know my Uncle George?'

'Yes, sir. His lordship has been familiar to me for some years.'

'I don't mean do you know my Uncle George. I mean do you know what my Uncle George is thinking of doing?'

'Contracting a matrimonial alliance, sir.'

'Good Lord! Did he tell you?'

'No, sir. Oddly enough, I chance to be acquainted with the other party in the matter.'

'The girl?'

'The young person, yes, sir. It was from her aunt, with whom she resides, that I received the information that his lordship was contemplating matrimony.'

'Who is she?'

'A Miss Platt, sir. Miss Rhoda Platt. Of Wistaria Lodge, Kitchener Road, East Dulwich.'

'Young?'

'Yes, sir.'

'The old fathead!'

'Yes, sir. The expression is one which I would, of course, not have ventured to employ myself, but I confess to thinking his lordship somewhat ill-advised. One must remember, however, that it is not unusual to find gentlemen of a certain age yielding to what might be described as a sentimental urge. They appear to experience what I may term a sort of Indian summer, a kind of temporarily renewed youth. The phenomenon is particularly noticeable, I am given to understand, in the United States of America among the wealthier inhabitants of the city of Pittsburgh. It is notorious, I am told, that sooner or later, unless restrained, they always endeavour to marry chorus-girls. Why this should be so, I am at a loss to say, but—'

I saw that this was going to take some time. I tuned out.

'From something in Uncle George's manner, Jeeves, as he referred to my Aunt Agatha's probable reception of the news, I gather that this Miss Platt is not of the *noblesse*.'

'No, sir. She is a waitress at his lordship's club.'

'My God! The proletariat!'

'The lower middle classes, sir.'

'Well, yes, by stretching it a bit, perhaps. Still, you know what I mean.'

'Yes, sir.'

'Rummy thing, Jeeves,' I said thoughtfully, 'this modern tendency to marry waitresses. If you remember, before he settled down, young Bingo Little was repeatedly trying to do it.'

'Yes, sir.'

'Odd!'

'Yes, sir.'

'Still, there it is, of course. The point to be considered now is, What will Aunt Agatha do about this? You know her, Jeeves. She is not like me. I'm broad-minded. If Uncle George wants to marry waitresses, let him, say I. I hold that the rank is but the penny stamp—'

'Guinea stamp, sir.'

'All right, guinea stamp. Though I don't believe there is such a thing. I shouldn't have thought they came higher than five bob. Well, as I was saying, I maintain that the rank is but the guinea stamp and a girl's a girl for all that.'

'"For *a*' that", sir. The poet Burns wrote in the North British dialect.'

'Well, "a' that", then, if you prefer it.'

'I have no preference in the matter, sir. It is simply that the poet Burns—'

'Never mind about the poet Burns.'

'No, sir.'

'Forget the poet Burns.'

'Very good, sir.'

'Expunge the poet Burns from your mind.'

'I will do so immediately, sir.'

'What we have to consider is not the poet Burns but the Aunt Agatha. She will kick, Jeeves.'

'Very probably, sir.'

'And, what's worse, she will lug me into the mess. There is only one thing to be done. Pack the toothbrush and let us escape while we may, leaving no address.'

'Very good, sir.'

At this moment the bell rang.

'Ha!' I said. 'Someone at the door.'

'Yes, sir.'

'Probably Uncle George back again. I'll answer it. You go and get ahead with the packing.'

'Very good, sir.'

I sauntered along the passage, whistling carelessly, and there on the mat was Aunt Agatha. Herself. Not a picture.

A nasty jar.

'Oh, hullo!' I said, it seeming but little good to tell her I was out of town and not expected back for some weeks.

'I wish to speak to you, Bertie,' said the Family Curse. 'I am greatly upset.'

She legged it into the sitting-room and volplaned into a chair. I followed, thinking wistfully of Jeeves packing in the bedroom. That suitcase would not be needed now. I knew what she must have come about.

'I've just seen Uncle George,' I said, giving her a lead.

'So have I,' said Aunt Agatha, shivering in a marked manner. 'He called on me while I was still in bed to inform me of his intention of marrying some impossible girl from South Norwood.'

'East Dulwich, the *cognoscenti* inform me.'

'Well, East Dulwich, then. It is the same thing. But who told you?'

'Jeeves.'

'And how, pray, does Jeeves come to know all about it?'

'There are very few things in this world, Aunt Agatha,' I said gravely, 'that Jeeves doesn't know all about. He's met the girl.'

'Who is she?'

'One of the waitresses at the Buffers.'

I had expected this to register, and it did. The relative let out a screech rather like the Cornish Express going through a junction.

'I take it from your manner, Aunt Agatha,' I said, 'that you want this thing stopped.'

'Of course it must be stopped.'

'Then there is but one policy to pursue. Let me ring for Jeeves and ask his advice.'

Aunt Agatha stiffened visibly. Very much the *grande dame* of the old *régime*.

'Are you seriously suggesting that we should discuss this intimate family matter with your manservant?'

'Absolutely. Jeeves will find the way.'

'I have always known that you were an imbecile, Bertie,' said the flesh-and-blood, now down at about three degrees Fahrenheit, 'but I did suppose that you had some proper feeling, some pride, some respect for your position.'

'Well, you know what the poet Burns says.'

She squelched me with a glance.

'Obviously the only thing to do,' she said, 'is to offer this girl money.'

'Money?'

'Certainly. It will not be the first time your uncle has made such a course necessary.'

We sat for a bit, brooding. The family always sits brooding when the subject of Uncle George's early romance comes up. I was too young to be actually in on it at the time, but I've had the details frequently from many sources, including Uncle George. Let him get even the slightest bit pickled, and he will tell you the whole story, sometimes twice in an evening. It was a barmaid at the Criterion, just before he came into the title. Her name was Maudie and he loved her dearly, but the family would have none of it. They dug down into the sock and paid her off. Just one of those human-interest stories, if you know what I mean.

I wasn't so sold on this money-offering scheme.

'Well, just as you like, of course,' I said, 'but you're taking an awful chance. I mean, whenever people do it in novels and plays, they always get the dickens of a welt. The girl gets the sympathy of the audience every time. She just draws herself up and looks at them with clear, steady eyes, causing them to feel not a little cheesey. If I were you, I would sit tight and let Nature take its course.'

'I don't understand you.'

'Well, consider for a moment what Uncle George looks like. No Greta Garbo, believe me. I should simply let the girl go on looking at him. Take it from me, Aunt Agatha, I've studied human nature and I don't believe there's a female in the world who could see Uncle George fairly often in those waistcoats he wears without feeling that it was due to her better self to give him the gate. Besides, this girl sees him at meal-times, and Uncle George with head down among the food-stuffs is a spectacle which—'

'If it is not troubling you too much, Bertie, I should be greatly obliged if you would stop drivelling.'

'Just as you say. All the same, I think you're going to find it dashed embarrassing, offering this girl money.'

'I am not proposing to do so. *You* will undertake the negotiations.'

'Me?'

'Certainly. I should think a hundred pounds would be ample. But I will give you a blank cheque, and you are at liberty to fill it in for a higher sum if it becomes necessary. The essential point is that, cost what it may, your uncle must be released from this entanglement.'

'So you're going to shove this off on me?'

'It is quite time you did something for the family.'

'And when she draws herself up and looks at me with clear, steady eyes, what do I do for an encore?'

'There is no need to discuss the matter any further. You can get down to East Dulwich in half an hour. There is a frequent service of trains. I will remain here to await your report.'

'But, listen!'

'Bertie, you will go and see this woman immediately.'

'Yes, but dash it!'

'Bertie!'

I threw in the towel.

'Oh, right-ho, if you say so.'

'I do say so.'

'Oh, well, in that case, right-ho.'

I don't know if you have ever tooled off to East Dulwich to offer a strange female a hundred smackers to release your Uncle George. In case you haven't, I may tell you that there are plenty of things that are lots better fun. I didn't feel any too good driving to the station. I didn't feel any too good in the train. And I didn't feel any too good as I walked to Kitchener Road. But the moment when I felt least good was when I had actually pressed the front-door bell and a rather grubby-looking maid had let me in and shown me down a passage and into a room with pink paper on the walls, a piano in the corner and a lot of photographs on the mantelpiece.

Barring a dentist's waiting-room, which it rather resembles, there isn't anything that quells the spirit much more than one of these suburban parlours. They are extremely apt to have stuffed birds in glass cases standing about on small tables, and if there is one thing which gives the man of sensibility that sinking feeling it is the cold, accusing eye of a ptarmigan or whatever it may be that has had its interior organs removed and sawdust substituted.

There were three of these cases in the parlour of Wistaria Lodge, so that, wherever you looked, you were sure to connect. Two were singletons, the third a family group, consisting of a father bullfinch, a mother bullfinch, and little Master Bullfinch, the last-named of whom wore an expression that was definitely that of a thug, and did more to damp my *joie de vivre* than all the rest of them put together.

I had moved to the window and was examining the aspidistra in order to avoid this creature's gaze, when I heard the door open and, turning, found myself confronted by something which, since it could hardly be the girl, I took to be the aunt.

'Oh, what-ho,' I said. 'Good morning.'

The words came out rather roopily, for I was feeling a bit on the stunned side. I mean to say, the room being so small and this exhibit so large, I had got that sensation of wanting air. There are some people who don't seem to be intended to be seen close to, and this aunt was one of them. Billowy curves, if you know what I mean. I should think that in her day she must have been a very handsome girl, though even then on the substantial side. By the time she came into my life, she had taken on a good deal of excess weight. She looked like a photograph of an opera singer of the 'eighties. Also the orange hair and the magenta dress.

However, she was a friendly soul. She seemed glad to see Bertram. She smiled broadly.

'So here you are at last!' she said.

I couldn't make anything of this.

'Eh?'

'But I don't think you had better see my niece just yet. She's just having a nap.'

'Oh, in that case—'

'Seems a pity to wake her, doesn't it?'

'Oh, absolutely,' I said, relieved.

'When you get the influenza, you don't sleep at night, and then if you doze off in the morning – well, it seems a pity to wake someone, doesn't it?'

'Miss Platt has influenza?'

'That's what we think it is. But, of course, you'll be able to say. But we needn't waste time. Since you're here, you can be taking a look at my knee.'

'Your knee?'

I am all for knees at their proper time and, as you might say, in their proper place, but somehow this didn't seem the moment. However, she carried on according to plan.

'What do you think of that knee?' she asked, lifting the seven veils.

Well, of course, one has to be polite.

'Terrific!' I said.

'You wouldn't believe how it hurts me sometimes.'

'Really?'

'A sort of shooting pain. It just comes and goes. And I'll tell you a funny thing.'

'What's that?' I said, feeling I could do with a good laugh.

'Lately I've been having the same pain just here, at the end of the spine.'

'You don't mean it!'

'I do. Like red-hot needles. I wish you'd have a look at it.'

'At your spine?'

'Yes.'

I shook my head. Nobody is fonder of a bit of fun than myself, and I am all for Bohemian camaraderie and making a party go, and all that. But there is a line, and we Woosters know when to draw it.

'It can't be done,' I said austerely. 'Not spines. Knees, yes. Spines, no,' I said.

She seemed surprised.

'Well,' she said, 'you're a funny sort of doctor, I must say.'

I'm pretty quick, as I said before, and I began to see that something in the nature of a misunderstanding must have arisen.

'Doctor?'

'Well, you call yourself a doctor, don't you?'

'Did you think I was a doctor?'

'Aren't you a doctor?'

'No. Not a doctor.'

We had got it straightened out. The scales had fallen from our eyes. We knew where we were.

I had suspected that she was a genial soul. She now endorsed this view. I don't think I have ever heard a woman laugh so heartily.

'Well, that's the best thing!' she said, borrowing my handkerchief to wipe her eyes. 'Did you ever! But, if you aren't the doctor, who are you?'

'Wooster's the name. I came to see Miss Platt.'

'What about?'

This was the moment, of course, when I should have come out with the cheque and sprung the big effort. But somehow I couldn't make it. You know how it is. Offering people money to release your uncle is a scaly enough job at best, and when the atmosphere's not right the shot simply isn't on the board.

'Oh, just came to see her, you know.' I had rather a bright idea. 'My uncle heard she was seedy, don't you know, and asked me to look in and make enquiries,' I said.

'Your uncle?'

'Lord Yaxley.'

'Oh! So you are Lord Yaxley's nephew?'

'That's right. I suppose he's always popping in and out here, what?'

'No. I've never met him.'

'You haven't?'

'No. Rhoda talks a lot about him, of course, but for some reason she's never so much as asked him to look in for a cup of tea.'

I began to see that this Rhoda knew her business. If I'd been a girl with someone wanting to marry me and knew that there was an exhibit like this aunt hanging around the home, I, too, should have thought twice about inviting him to call until the ceremony was over and he had actually signed on the dotted line. I mean to say, a thoroughly good soul – heart of gold beyond a doubt – but not the sort of thing you wanted to spring on Romeo before the time was ripe.

'I suppose you were all very surprised when you heard about it?' she said.

'Surprised is right.'

'Of course, nothing is definitely settled yet.'

'You don't mean that? I thought—'

'Oh, no. She's thinking it over.'

'I see.'

'Of course, she feels it's a great compliment. But then sometimes she wonders if he isn't too old.'

'My Aunt Agatha has rather the same idea.'

'Of course, a title *is* a title.'

'Yes, there's that. What do you think about it yourself?'

'Oh, it doesn't matter what I think. There's no doing anything with girls these days, is there?'

'Not much.'

'What I often say is, I wonder what girls are coming to. Still, there it is.'

'Absolutely.'

There didn't seem much reason why the conversation shouldn't go on for ever. She had the air of a woman who had settled down for the day. But at this point the maid came in and said the doctor had arrived.

I got up.

'I'll be tooling off, then.'

'If you must.'

'I think I'd better.'

'Well, pip pip.'

'Toodle-oo,' I said, and out into the fresh air.

Knowing what was waiting for me at home, I would have preferred to have gone to the club and spent the rest of the day there. But the thing had to be faced.

'Well?' said Aunt Agatha, as I trickled into the sitting-room.

'Well, yes and no,' I replied.

'What do you mean? Did she refuse the money?'

'Not exactly.'

'She accepted it?'

'Well, there, again, not precisely.'

I explained what had happened. I wasn't expecting her to be any too frightfully pleased, and it's as well that I wasn't, because she wasn't. In fact, as the story unfolded, her comments became fruitier and fruitier, and when I had finished she uttered an exclamation that nearly broke a window. It sounded something like 'Gor!' as if she had started to say 'Gorblimey!' and had remembered her ancient lineage just in time.

'I'm sorry,' I said. 'And can a man say more? I lost my nerve. The old *morale* suddenly turned blue on me. It's the sort of thing that might have happened to anyone.'

'I never heard of anything so spineless in my life.'

I shivered, like a warrior whose old wound hurts him.

'I'd be most awfully obliged, Aunt Agatha,' I said, 'if you would not use that word spine. It awakens memories.'

The door opened. Jeeves appeared.

'Sir?'

'Yes, Jeeves?'

'I thought you called, sir.'

'No, Jeeves.'

'Very good, sir.'

There are moments when, even under the eye of Aunt Agatha, I can take the firm line. And now, seeing Jeeves standing there with the light of intelligence simply fizzing in every feature, I suddenly felt how perfectly footling it was to give this pre-eminent source of balm and comfort the go-by simply because Aunt Agatha had prejudices against discussing family affairs with the staff. It might make her say 'Gor!' again, but I decided to do as we ought to have done right from the start – put the case in his hands.

'Jeeves,' I said, 'this matter of Uncle George.'

'Yes, sir.'

'You know the circs?'

'Yes, sir.'

'You know what we want.'

'Yes, sir.'

'Then advise us. And make it snappy. Think on your feet.'

I heard Aunt Agatha rumble like a volcano just before it starts to set about the neighbours, but I did not wilt. I had seen the sparkle in Jeeves's eye which indicated that an idea was on the way.

'I understand that you have been visiting the young person's home, sir?'

'Just got back.'

'Then you no doubt encountered the young person's aunt?'

'Jeeves, I encountered nothing else but.'

'Then the suggestion which I am about to make will, I feel sure, appeal to you, sir. I would recommend that you confronted his lordship with this woman. It has always been her intention to continue residing with her niece after the latter's marriage. Should he meet her, this reflection might give his lordship pause. As you are aware, sir, she is a kind-hearted woman, but definitely of the people.'

'Jeeves, you are right! Apart from anything else, that orange hair!'

'Exactly, sir.'

'Not to mention the magenta dress.'

'Precisely, sir.'

'I'll ask her to lunch to-morrow, to meet him. You see,' I said to Aunt Agatha, who was still fermenting in the background, 'a ripe suggestion first crack out of the box. Did I or did I not tell you—'

'That will do, Jeeves,' said Aunt Agatha.

'Very good, madam.'

For some minutes after he had gone, Aunt Agatha strayed from the point a bit, confining her remarks to what she thought of a Wooster who could lower the prestige of the clan by allowing menials to get above themselves. Then she returned to what you might call the main issue.

'Bertie,' she said, 'you will go and see this girl again to-morrow, and this time you will do as I told you.'

'But, dash it! With this excellent alternative scheme, based firmly on the psychology of the individual—'

'That is quite enough, Bertie. You heard what I said. I am going. Good-bye.'

She buzzed off, little knowing of what stuff Bertram Wooster was made. The door had hardly closed before I was shouting for Jeeves.

'Jeeves,' I said, 'the recent aunt will have none of your excellent alternative schemes, but none the less I propose to go through with it unswervingly. I consider it a ball of fire. Can you get hold of this female and bring her here for lunch to-morrow?'

'Yes, sir.'

'Good. Meanwhile, I will be 'phoning Uncle George. We will do Aunt Agatha good despite herself. What is it the poet says, Jeeves?'

'The poet Burns, sir?'

'Not the poet Burns. Some other poet. About doing good by stealth.'

'"These little acts of unremembered kindness", sir?'

'That's it in a nutshell, Jeeves.'

I suppose doing good by stealth ought to give one a glow, but I can't say I found myself exactly looking forward to the binge in prospect. Uncle George by himself is a mouldy enough luncheon companion, being extremely apt to collar the conversation and confine it to a description of his symptoms, he being one of those birds who can never be brought to believe that the general public isn't agog to hear all about the lining of his stomach. Add the aunt, and you have a little gathering which might well dismay the stoutest. The moment I woke, I felt conscious of some impending doom, and the cloud, if you know what I mean, grew darker all the morning. By the time Jeeves came in with the cocktails, I was feeling pretty low.

'For two pins, Jeeves,' I said, 'I would turn the whole thing up and leg it to the Drones.'

'I can readily imagine that this will prove something of an ordeal, sir.'

'How did you get to know these people, Jeeves?'

'It was through a young fellow of my acquaintance, sir, Colonel Mainwaring-Smith's personal gentleman's gentleman. He and the young person had an understanding at the time, and he desired me to accompany him to Wistaria Lodge and meet her.'

'They were engaged?'

'Not precisely engaged, sir. An understanding.'

'What did they quarrel about?'

'They did not quarrel, sir. When his lordship began to pay his addresses, the young person, naturally flattered, began to waver between love and ambition. But even now she has not formally rescinded the understanding.'

'Then, if your scheme works and Uncle George edges out, it will do your pal a bit of good?'

'Yes, sir. Smethurst – his name is Smethurst – would consider it a consummation devoutly to be wished.'

'Rather well put, that, Jeeves. Your own?'

'No, sir. The Swan of Avon, sir.'

An unseen hand without tootled on the bell, and I braced myself to play the host. The binge was on.

'Mrs Wilberforce, sir,' announced Jeeves.

'And how I'm to keep a straight face with you standing behind and saying "Madam, can I tempt you with a potato?" is more than I know,' said the aunt, sailing in, looking larger and pinker and matier than ever. 'I know him, you know,' she said, jerking a thumb after Jeeves. 'He's been round and taken tea with us.'

'So he told me.'

She gave the sitting-room the once-over.

'You've got a nice place here,' she said. 'Though I like more pink about. It's so cheerful. What's that you've got there? Cocktails?'

'Martini with a spot of absinthe,' I said, beginning to pour.

She gave a girlish squeal.

'Don't you try to make me drink that stuff! Do you know what would happen if I touched one of those things? I'd be racked with pain. What they do to the lining of your stomach!'

'Oh, I don't know.'

'I do. If you had been a barmaid as long as I was, you'd know, too.'

'Oh – er – were you a barmaid?'

'For years, when I was younger than I am. At the Criterion.'

I dropped the shaker.

'There!' she said, pointing the moral. 'That's through drinking that stuff. Makes your hand wobble. What I always used to say to the boys was, "Port, if you like. Port's wholesome. I appreciate a drop of port myself. But these new-fangled messes from America, no." But they would never listen to me.'

I was eyeing her warily. Of course, there must have been thousands of barmaids at the Criterion in its time, but still it gave one a bit of a start. It was years ago that Uncle George's dash at a mesalliance had occurred – long before he came into the title – but the Wooster clan still quivered at the name of the Criterion.

'Er – when you were at the Cri.,' I said, 'did you ever happen to run into a fellow of my name?'

'I've forgotten what it is. I'm always silly about names.'

'Wooster.'

'Wooster! When you were there yesterday I thought you said Foster. Wooster! Did I run into a fellow named Wooster? Well! Why, George Wooster and me – Piggy, I used to call him – were going off to the registrar's, only his family heard of it and interfered. They offered me a lot of money to give him up, and, like a silly girl, I let them persuade me. If I've wondered once what became of him, I've wondered a thousand times. Is he a relation of yours?'

'Excuse me,' I said. 'I just want a word with Jeeves.'

I legged it for the pantry.

'Jeeves!'

'Sir?'

'Do you know what's happened?'

'No, sir.'

'This female—'

'Sir?'

'She's Uncle George's barmaid!'

'Sir?'

'Oh, dash it, you must have heard of Uncle George's barmaid. You know all the family history. The barmaid he wanted to marry years ago.'

'Ah, yes, sir.'

'She's the only woman he ever loved. He's told me so a million times. Every time he gets to the fourth whisky-and-potash, he always becomes maudlin about this female. What a dashed bit of bad luck! The first thing we know, the call of the past will be echoing in his heart. I can feel it, Jeeves. She's just his sort. The first thing she did when she came in was to start talking about the lining of her stomach. You see the hideous significance of that, Jeeves? The lining of his stomach is Uncle George's favourite topic of conversation. It means that he and she are kindred souls. This woman and he will be like—'

'Deep calling to deep, sir?'

'Exactly.'

'Most disturbing, sir.'

'What's to be done?'

'I could not say, sir.'

'I'll tell you what I'm going to do – 'phone him and say the lunch is off.'

'Scarcely feasible, sir. I fancy that is his lordship at the door now.'

And so it was. Jeeves let him in, and I followed him as he navigated down the passage to the sitting-room. There was a stunned silence as he went in, and then a couple of the startled yelps you hear when old buddies get together after long separation.

'Piggy!'

'Maudie!'

'Well, I never!'

'Well, I'm dashed!'

'Did you ever!'

'Well, bless my soul!'

'Fancy you being Lord Yaxley!'

'Came into the title soon after we parted.'

'Just to think!'

'You could have knocked me down with a feather!'

I hung about in the offing, now on this leg, now on that. For all the notice they took of me, I might just have well been the late Bertram Wooster, disembodied.

'Maudie, you don't look a day older, dash it!'

'Nor do you, Piggy.'

'How have you been all these years?'

'Pretty well. The lining of my stomach isn't all it should be.'

'Good Gad! You don't say so? I have trouble with the lining of *my* stomach.'

'It's a sort of heavy feeling after meals.'

'*I* get a sort of heavy feeling after meals. What are you trying for it?'

'I've been taking Perkins' Digestine.'

'My dear girl, no use! No use at all. Tried it myself for years and got no relief. Now, if you really want something that is some good—'

I slid away. The last I saw of them, Uncle George was down beside her on the Chesterfield, buzzing hard.

'Jeeves,' I said, tottering into the pantry.

'Sir?'

'There will only be two for lunch. Count me out. If they notice I'm not there, tell them I was called away by an urgent 'phone message. The situation has got beyond Bertram, Jeeves. You will find me at the Drones.'

'Very good, sir.'

It was lateish in the evening when one of the waiters came to me as I played a distrait game of snooker pool and informed me that Aunt Agatha was on the 'phone.

'Bertie!'

'Hullo?'

I was amazed to note that her voice was that of an aunt who feels that things are breaking right. It had the birdlike trill.

'Bertie, have you that cheque I gave you?'

'Yes.'

'Then tear it up. It will not be needed.'

'Eh?'

'I say it will not be needed. Your uncle has been speaking to me on the telephone. He is not going to marry that girl.'

'Not?'

'No. Apparently he has been thinking it over and sees how unsuitable it would have been. But what is astonishing is that he *is* going to be married!'

'He is?'

'Yes, to an old friend of his, a Mrs Wilberforce. A woman of a sensible age, he gave me to understand. I wonder which Wilberforces that would be. There are two main branches of the family – the Essex Wilberforces and the Cumberland Wilberforces. I believe there is also a cadet branch somewhere in Shropshire.'

'And one in East Dulwich.'

'What did you say?'

'Nothing,' I said. 'Nothing.'

I hung up. Then back to the old flat, feeling a trifle sandbagged.

'Well, Jeeves,' I said, and there was censure in the eyes. 'So I gather everything is nicely settled?'

'Yes, sir. His lordship formally announced the engagement between the sweet and cheese courses, sir.'

'He did, did he?'

'Yes, sir.'

I eyed the man sternly.

'You do not appear to be aware of it, Jeeves,' I said, in a cold, level voice, 'but this binge has depreciated your stock very considerably. I have always been accustomed to look upon you as a counsellor without equal. I have, so to speak, hung upon your lips. And now see what you have done. All this is the direct consequence of your scheme, based on the psychology of the individual. I should have thought, Jeeves, that, knowing the woman – meeting her socially, as you might say, over the afternoon cup of tea – you might have ascertained that she was Uncle George's barmaid.'

'I did, sir.'

'What!'

'I was aware of the fact, sir.'

'Then you must have known what would happen if she came to lunch and met him.'

'Yes, sir.'

'Well, I'm dashed!'

'If I might explain, sir. The young man Smethurst, who is greatly attached to the young person, is an intimate friend of mine. He applied to me some little while back in the hope that I might be able to do something to ensure that the young person followed the dictates of her heart and refrained from permitting herself to be lured by gold and the glamour of his lordship's position. There will now be no obstacle to their union.'

'I see. "Little acts of unremembered kindness", what?'

'Precisely, sir.'

'And how about Uncle George? You've landed him pretty nicely in the cart.'

'No, sir, if I may take the liberty of opposing your view. I fancy that Mrs Wilberforce should make an ideal mate for his lordship. If there was a defect in his lordship's mode of life, it was that he was a little unduly attached to the pleasures of the table—'

'Ate like a pig, you mean?'

'I would not have ventured to put it in quite that way, sir, but the expression does meet the facts of the case. He was also inclined to drink rather more than his medical adviser would have approved of. Elderly bachelors who are wealthy and without occupation tend somewhat frequently to fall into this error, sir. The future Lady Yaxley will check this. Indeed, I overheard her ladyship saying as much as I brought in the fish. She was commenting on a certain puffiness of the face which had been absent in his lordship's appearance in the earlier days of their acquaintanceship, and she observed that his lordship needed looking after. I fancy, sir, that you will find the union will turn out an extremely satisfactory one.'

It was – what's the word I want? – it was plausible, of course, but still I shook the onion.

'But, Jeeves!'

'Sir?'

'She *is*, as you remarked not long ago, definitely of the people.'

He looked at me in a reproachful sort of way.

'Sturdy lower middle class stock, sir.'

'H'm!'

'Sir?'

'I said "H'm!" Jeeves.'

'Besides, sir, remember what the poet Tennyson said: "Kind hearts are more than coronets".'

'And which of us is going to tell Aunt Agatha that?'

'If I might make the suggestion, sir, I would advise that we omitted to communicate with Mrs Spenser Gregson in any way.

I have your suitcase practically packed. It would be a matter of but a few minutes to bring the car round from the garage—'

'And off over the horizon to where men are men?'

'Precisely, sir.'

'Jeeves,' I said, 'I'm not sure that even now I can altogether see eye to eye with you regarding your recent activities. You think you have scattered light and sweetness on every side. I am not so sure. However, with this latest suggestion you have rung the bell. I examine it narrowly and I find no flaw in it. It is the goods. I'll get the car at once.'

'Very good, sir.'

'Remember what the poet Shakespeare said, Jeeves.'

'What was that, sir?'

'"Exit hurriedly, pursued by a bear". You'll find it in one of his plays. I remember drawing a picture of it on the side of the page, when I was at school.'

'What-ho, Jeeves!' I said, entering the room where he waded knee-deep in suitcases and shirts and winter suitings, like a sea-beast among rocks. 'Packing?'

'Yes, sir,' replied the honest fellow, for there are no secrets between us.

'Pack on!' I said approvingly. 'Pack, Jeeves, pack with care. Pack in the presence of the passenjare.' And I rather fancy I added the words 'Tra-la!' for I was in merry mood.

Every year, starting about the middle of November, there is a good deal of anxiety and apprehension among owners of the better class of country-house throughout England as to who will get Bertram Wooster's patronage for the Christmas holidays. It may be one or it may be another. As my Aunt Dahlia says, you never know where the blow will fall.

This year, however, I had decided early. It couldn't have been later than Nov. 10 when a sigh of relief went up from a dozen stately homes as it became known that the short straw had been drawn by Sir Reginald Witherspoon, Bart, of Bleaching Court, Upper Bleaching, Hants.

In coming to the decision to give this Witherspoon my custom, I had been actuated by several reasons, not counting the fact that, having married Aunt Dahlia's husband's younger sister Katherine, he is by way of being a sort of uncle of mine. In the first place, the Bart does one extraordinarily well, both browsing and sluicing being above criticism. Then, again, his stables always contain something worth riding, which is a consideration. And, thirdly, there is no danger of getting lugged into a party of amateur Waits and having to tramp the countryside in the rain, singing, 'When Shepherds Watched Their Flocks by Night'. Or for the matter of that, 'Noel! Noel!'

All these things counted with me, but what really drew me to Bleaching Court like a magnet was the knowledge that young Tuppy Glossop would be among those present.

I feel sure I have told you before about this black-hearted bird, but I will give you the strength of it once again, just to keep the records straight. He was the fellow, if you remember, who, ignoring a lifelong friendship in the course of which he had frequently eaten my bread and salt, betted me one night at the Drones that I wouldn't swing myself across the swimming-bath by the ropes and rings and then, with almost inconceivable treachery, went and looped back the last ring, causing me to drop into the fluid and ruin one of the nattiest suits of dress-clothes in London.

To execute a fitting vengeance on this bloke had been the ruling passion of my life ever since.

'You are bearing in mind, Jeeves,' I said, 'the fact that Mr Glossop will be at Bleaching?'

'Yes, sir.'

'And, consequently, are not forgetting to put in the Giant Squirt?'

'No, sir.'

'Nor the Luminous Rabbit?'

'No, sir.'

'Good! I am rather pinning my faith on the Luminous Rabbit, Jeeves. I hear excellent reports of it on all sides. You wind it up and put in it somebody's room in the night watches, and it shines in the dark and jumps about, making odd, squeaking noises the while. The whole performance being, I should imagine, well calculated to scare young Tuppy into a decline.'

'Very possibly, sir.'

'Should that fail, there is always the Giant Squirt. We must leave no stone unturned to put it across the man somehow,' I said. 'The Wooster honour is at stake.'

I would have spoken further on this subject, but just then the front-door bell buzzed.

'I'll answer it,' I said. 'I expect it's Aunt Dahlia. She 'phoned that she would be calling this morning.'

It was not Aunt Dahlia. It was a telegraph-boy with telegram. I opened it, read it, and carried it back to the bedroom, the brow a bit knitted.

'Jeeves,' I said. 'A rummy communication has arrived. From Mr Glossop.'

'Indeed, sir?'

'I will read it to you. Handed in at Upper Bleaching. Message runs as follows:

'"When you come to-morrow, bring my football boots. Also, if humanly possible, Irish water-spaniel. Urgent. Regards. Tuppy."

'What do you make of that, Jeeves?'

'As I interpret the document, sir, Mr Glossop wishes you, when you come to-morrow, to bring his football boots. Also, if humanly possible, an Irish water-spaniel. He hints that the matter is urgent, and sends his regards.'

'Yes, that's how I read it, too. But why football boots?'

'Perhaps Mr Glossop wishes to play football, sir.'

I considered this.

'Yes,' I said. 'That may be the solution. But why would a man, staying peacefully at a country-house, suddenly develop a craving to play football?'

'I could not say, sir.'

'And why an Irish water-spaniel?'

'There again I fear I can hazard no conjecture, sir.'

'What *is* an Irish water-spaniel?'

'A water-spaniel of a variety bred in Ireland, sir.'

'You think so?'

'Yes, sir.'

'Well, perhaps you're right. But why should I sweat about the place collecting dogs – of whatever nationality – for young Tuppy? Does he think I'm Santa Claus? Is he under the impression that my feelings towards him, after that Drones Club incident, are those of kindly benevolence? Irish water-spaniels, indeed! Tchah!'

'Sir?'

'Tchah, Jeeves.'

'Very good, sir.'

The front-door bell buzzed again.

'Our busy morning, Jeeves.'

'Yes, sir.'

'All right. I'll go.'

This time it was Aunt Dahlia. She charged in with the air of a woman with something on her mind – giving tongue, in fact, while actually on the very doormat.

'Bertie,' she boomed, in that ringing voice of hers which cracks window-panes and upsets vases, 'I've come about that young hound, Glossop.'

'It's quite all right, Aunt Dahlia,' I replied soothingly. 'I have the situation well in hand. The Giant Squirt and the Luminous Rabbit are even now being packed.'

'I don't know what you're talking about, and I don't for a moment suppose you do, either,' said the relative somewhat brusquely, 'but, if you'll kindly stop gibbering, I'll tell you what I mean. I have had a most disturbing letter from Katherine. About this reptile. Of course, I haven't breathed a word to Angela. She'd hit the ceiling.'

This Angela is Aunt Dahlia's daughter. She and young Tuppy are generally supposed to be more or less engaged, though nothing definitely 'Morning Posted' yet.

'Why?' I said.

'Why what?'

'Why would Angela hit the ceiling?'

'Well, wouldn't you, if you were practically engaged to a fiend in human shape and somebody told you he had gone off to the country and was flirting with a dog-girl?'

'With a what was that, once again?'

'A dog-girl. One of these dashed open-air flappers in thick boots and tailor-made tweeds who infest the rural districts and go about the place followed by packs of assorted dogs. I used to be one of them myself in my younger days, so I know how dangerous they are. Her name is Dalgleish. Old Colonel Dalgleish's daughter. They live near Bleaching.'

I saw a gleam of daylight.

'Then that must be what his telegram was about. He's just wired, asking me to bring down an Irish water-spaniel. A Christmas present for this girl, no doubt.'

'Probably. Katherine tells me he seems to be infatuated with her. She says he follows her about like one of her dogs, looking like a tame cat and bleating like a sheep.'

'Quite the private Zoo, what?'

'Bertie,' said Aunt Dahlia – and I could see her generous nature was stirred to its depths – 'one more crack like that out of you, and I shall forget that I am an aunt and hand you one.'

I became soothing. I gave her the old oil.

'I shouldn't worry,' I said. 'There's probably nothing in it. Whole thing no doubt much exaggerated.'

'You think so, eh? Well, you know what he's like. You remember the trouble we had when he ran after that singing-woman.'

I recollected the case. You will find it elsewhere in the archives. Cora Bellinger was the female's name. She was studying for Opera, and young Tuppy thought highly of her. Fortunately, however, she punched him in the eye during Beefy Bingham's clean, bright entertainment in Bermondsey East, and love died.

'Besides,' said Aunt Dahlia, 'There's something I haven't told you. Just before he went to Bleaching, he and Angela quarrelled.'

'They did?'

'Yes. I got it out of Angela this morning. She was crying her eyes out, poor angel. It was something about her last hat. As far as I could gather, he told her it made her look like a Pekingese, and she told him she never wanted to see him again in this world or the next. And he said "Right-ho!" and breezed off. I can see what has happened. This dog-girl has caught him on the rebound, and, unless something is done quick, anything may happen. So place the facts before Jeeves, and tell him to take action the moment you get down there.'

I am always a little piqued, if you know what I mean, at this assumption on the relative's part that Jeeves is so dashed essential on these occasions. My manner, therefore, as I replied, was a bit on the crisp side.

'Jeeves's services will not be required,' I said. 'I can handle this business. The programme which I have laid out will be quite sufficient to take young Tuppy's mind off love-making. It is my intention to insert the Luminous Rabbit in his room at the first opportunity that presents itself. The Luminous Rabbit shines in the dark and jumps about, making odd, squeaking noises. It will sound to young Tuppy like the Voice of Conscience, and I anticipate that a single treatment will make him retire into a nursing-home for a couple of weeks or so. At the end of which period he will have forgotten all about the bally girl.'

'Bertie,' said Aunt Dahlia, with a sort of frozen calm, 'you are the Abysmal Chump. Listen to me. It's simply because I am fond of you and have influence with the Lunacy Commissioners that you weren't put in a padded cell years ago. Bungle this business, and I withdraw my protection. Can't you understand that this thing is far too serious for any fooling about? Angela's whole happiness is at stake. Do as I tell you, and put it up to Jeeves.'

'Just as you say, Aunt Dahlia,' I said stiffly.

'All right, then. Do it now.'

I went back to the bedroom.

'Jeeves,' I said, and I did not trouble to conceal my chagrin, 'you need not pack the Luminous Rabbit.'

'Very good, sir.'

'Nor the Giant Squirt.'

'Very good, sir.'

'They have been subjected to destructive criticism, and the zest has gone. Oh, and, Jeeves.'

'Sir?'

'Mrs Travers wishes you, on arriving at Bleaching Court, to disentangle Mr Glossop from a dog-girl.'

'Very good, sir. I will attend to the matter and will do my best to give satisfaction.'

That Aunt Dahlia had not exaggerated the perilous nature of the situation was made clear to me on the following afternoon. Jeeves and I drove down to Bleaching in the two-seater, and we were tooling along about half-way between the village and the Court when suddenly there appeared ahead of us a sea of dogs and in the middle of it young Tuppy frisking round one of those largish, corn-fed girls. He was bending towards her in a devout sort of way, and even at a considerable distance I could see that his ears were pink. His attitude, in short, was unmistakably that of a man endeavouring to push a good thing along; and when I came closer and noted that the girl wore tailor-made tweeds and thick boots, I had no further doubts.

'You observe, Jeeves?' I said in a low, significant voice.

'Yes, sir.'

'The girl, what?'

'Yes, sir.'

I tootled amiably on the horn and yodelled a bit. They turned – Tuppy, I fancied, not any too pleased.

'Oh, hullo, Bertie,' he said.

'Hullo,' I said.

'My friend, Bertie Wooster,' said Tuppy to the girl, in what seemed to me rather an apologetic manner. You know – as if he would have preferred to hush me up.

'Hullo,' said the girl.

'Hullo,' I said.

'Hullo, Jeeves,' said Tuppy.

'Good afternoon, sir,' said Jeeves.

There was a somewhat constrained silence.

'Well, good-bye, Bertie,' said young Tuppy. 'You'll be wanting to push along, I expect.'

We Woosters can take a hint as well as the next man.

'See you later,' I said.

'Oh, rather,' said Tuppy.

I set the machinery in motion again, and we rolled off.

'Sinister, Jeeves,' I said. 'You noticed that the subject was looking like a stuffed frog?'

'Yes, sir.'

'And gave no indication of wanting us to stop and join the party?'

'No, sir.'

'I think Aunt Dahlia's fears are justified. The thing seems serious.'

'Yes, sir.'

'Well, strain the brain, Jeeves.'

'Very good, sir.'

It wasn't till I was dressing for dinner that night that I saw young Tuppy again. He trickled in just as I was arranging the tie.

'Hullo!' I said.

'Hullo!' said Tuppy.

'Who was the girl?' I asked, in that casual, snaky way of mine – off-hand, I mean.

'A Miss Dalgleish,' said Tuppy, and I noticed that he blushed a spot.

'Staying here?'

'No. She lives in that house just before you come to the gates of this place. Did you bring my football boots?'

'Yes. Jeeves has got them somewhere.'

'And the water-spaniel?'

'Sorry. No water-spaniel.'

'Dashed nuisance. She's set her heart on an Irish water-spaniel.'

'Well, what do you care?'

'I wanted to give her one.'

'Why?'

Tuppy became a trifle haughty. Frigid. The rebuking eye.

'Colonel and Mrs Dalgleish,' he said, 'have been extremely kind to me since I got here. They have entertained me. I naturally wish to make some return for their hospitality. I don't want them to look upon me as one of those ill-mannered modern young men you read about in the papers who grab everything they can lay their hooks on and never buy back. If people ask you to lunch and tea and what not, they appreciate it if you make them some little present in return.'

'Well, give them your football boots. In passing, why did you want the bally things?'

'I'm playing in a match next Thursday.'

'Down here?'

'Yes. Upper Bleaching versus Hockley-cum-Meston. Apparently it's the big game of the year.'

'How did you get roped in?'

'I happened to mention in the course of conversation the other day that, when in London, I generally turn out on Saturdays for the Old Austinians, and Miss Dalgleish seemed rather keen that I should help the village.'

'Which village?'

'Upper Bleaching, of course.'

'Ah, then you're going to play for Hockley?'

'You needn't be funny, Bertie. You may not know it, but I'm pretty hot stuff on the football field. Oh, Jeeves.'

'Sir?' said Jeeves, entering right centre.

'Mr Wooster tells me you have my football boots.'

'Yes, sir. I have placed them in your room.'

'Thanks. Jeeves, do you want to make a bit of money?'

'Yes, sir.'

'Then put a trifle on Upper Bleaching for the annual encounter with Hockley-cum-Meston next Thursday,' said Tuppy, exiting with swelling bosom.

'Mr Glossop is going to play on Thursday,' I explained as the door closed.

'So I was informed in the Servants' Hall, sir.'

'Oh? And what's the general feeling there about it?'

'The impression I gathered, sir, was that the Servants' Hall considers Mr Glossop ill-advised.'

'Why's that?'

'I am informed by Mr Mulready, Sir Reginald's butler, sir, that this contest differs in some respects from the ordinary football game. Owing to the fact that there has existed for many years considerable animus between the two villages, the struggle is conducted, it appears, on somewhat looser and more primitive lines than is usually the case when two teams meet in friendly rivalry. The primary object of the players, I am given to understand, is not so much to score points as to inflict violence.'

'Good Lord, Jeeves!'

'Such appears to be the case, sir. The game is one that would have a great interest for the antiquarian. It was played first in the reign of King Henry the Eighth, when it lasted from noon till sun-down over an area covering several square miles. Seven deaths resulted on that occasion.'

'Seven!'

'Not inclusive of two of the spectators, sir. In recent years, however, the casualties appear to have been confined to broken limbs and other minor injuries. The opinion of the Servants' Hall is that it would be more judicious on Mr Glossop's part, were he to refrain from mixing himself up in the affair.'

I was more or less aghast. I mean to say, while I had made it my mission in life to get back at young Tuppy for that business at the Drones, there still remained certain faint vestiges, if vestiges is the word I want, of the old friendship and esteem. Besides, there are limits to one's thirst for vengeance. Deep as my resentment was for the ghastly outrage he had perpetrated on me, I had no wish to see him toddle unsuspiciously into the arena and get all chewed up by wild villagers. A Tuppy scared stiff by a Luminous Rabbit – yes. Excellent business. The happy ending, in fact. But a Tuppy carried off on a stretcher in half a dozen pieces – no. Quite a different matter. All wrong. Not to be considered for a moment.

Obviously, then, a kindly word of warning, while there was yet time, was indicated. I buzzed off to his room forthwith, and found him toying dreamily with the football boots.

I put him in possession of the facts.

'What you had better do – and the Servants' Hall thinks the same,' I said, 'is fake a sprained ankle on the eve of the match.'

He looked at me in an odd sort of way.

'You suggest that, when Miss Dalgleish is trusting me, relying on me, looking forward with eager, girlish enthusiasm to seeing me help her village on to victory, I should let her down with a thud?'

I was pleased with his ready intelligence.

'That's the idea,' I said.

'Faugh!' said Tuppy – the only time I've ever heard the word.

'How do you mean, "Faugh!"?' I asked.

'Bertie,' said Tuppy, 'what you tell me merely makes me all the keener for the fray. A warm game is what I want. I welcome this sporting spirit on the part of the opposition. I shall enjoy a spot of roughness. It will enable me to go all out and give of my best. Do you realize,' said young Tuppy, vermilion to the gills, 'that She will be looking on? And do you know how that will make me feel? It will make me feel like some knight of old jousting under the eyes of his lady. Do you suppose that Sir Lancelot or Sir Galahad, when there was a tourney scheduled for the following Thursday, went and pretended they had sprained their ankles just because the thing was likely to be a bit rough?'

'Don't forget that in the reign of King Henry the Eighth—'

'Never mind about the reign of King Henry the Eighth. All I care about is that it's Upper Bleaching's turn this year to play in colours, so I shall be able to wear my Old Austinian shirt. Light blue, Bertie, with broad orange stripes. I shall look like something, I tell you.'

'But what?'

'Bertie,' said Tuppy, now becoming purely ga-ga, 'I may as well tell you that I'm in love at last. This is the real thing. I have found my mate. All my life I have dreamed of meeting some sweet, open-air girl with all the glory of the English countryside in her eyes, and I have found her. How different she is, Bertie, from these hot-house, artificial London girls! Would they stand in the mud on a winter afternoon, watching a football match? Would they know what to give an Alsatian for fits? Would they tramp ten miles a day across the fields and come back as fresh as paint? No!'

'Well, why should they?'

'Bertie, I'm staking everything on this game on Thursday. At the moment, I have an idea that she looks on me as something of a weakling, simply because I got a blister on my foot the other afternoon and had to take the bus back from Hockley. But when she sees me going through the rustic opposition like a devouring flame, will that make her think a bit? Will that make her open her eyes? What?'

'What?'

'I said "What?"'

'So did I.'

'I meant, "Won't it?"'

'Oh, rather.'

Here the dinner-gong sounded, not before I was ready for it.

Judicious enquiries during the next couple of days convinced me that the Servants' Hall at Bleaching Court, in advancing the suggestion that young Tuppy, born and bred in the gentler atmosphere of the metropolis, would do well to keep out of local disputes and avoid the football-field on which these were to be settled, had not spoken idly. It had weighed its words and said the sensible thing. Feeling between the two villages undoubtedly ran high, as they say.

You know how it is in these remote rural districts. Life tends at times to get a bit slow. There's nothing much to do in the long winter evenings but listen to the radio and brood on what a tick your neighbour is. You find yourself remembering how Farmer Giles did you down over the sale of your pig, and Farmer Giles finds himself remembering that it was your son, Ernest, who bunged the half-brick at his horse on the second Sunday before Septuagesima. And so on and so forth. How this particular feud had started, I don't know, but the season of peace and good will found it in full blast. The only topic of conversation in Upper Bleaching was Thursday's game, and the citizenry seemed to be looking forward to it in a spirit that can only be described as ghoulish. And it was the same in Hockley-cum-Meston.

I paid a visit to Hockley-cum-Meston on the Wednesday, being rather anxious to take a look at the inhabitants and see how formidable they were. I was shocked to observe that practically every second male might have been the Village Blacksmith's big brother. The muscles of their brawny arms were obviously strong as iron bands, and the way the company at the Green Pig, where I looked in incognito for a spot of beer, talked about the forthcoming sporting contest was enough to chill the blood of anyone who had a pal who proposed to fling himself into the fray. It sounded rather like Attila and a few of his Huns sketching out their next campaign.

I went back to Jeeves with my mind made up.

'Jeeves,' I said, 'you, who had the job of drying and pressing those dress-clothes of mine, are aware that I have suffered much at young Tuppy Glossop's hands. By rights, I suppose, I ought to be welcoming the fact that the Wrath of Heaven is now hovering over him in this fearful manner. But the view I take of it is that Heaven looks like overdoing it. Heaven's idea of a fitting retribution is not mine. In my most unrestrained moments I never wanted the poor blighter assassinated. And the idea in Hockley-cum-Meston seems to be that a good opportunity has arisen of making it a bumper Christmas for the local undertaker. There was a fellow with red hair at the Green Pig this afternoon who might have been the undertaker's partner, the way he talked. We must act, and speedily, Jeeves. We must put a bit of a jerk in it and save young Tuppy in spite of himself.'

'What course would you advocate, sir?'

'I'll tell you. He refuses to do the sensible thing and slide out, because the girl will be watching the game and he imagines, poor lizard, that he is going to shine and impress her. So we must employ guile. You must go up to London to-day, Jeeves, and to-morrow morning you will send a telegram, signed "Angela", which will run as follows. Jot it down. Ready?'

'Yes, sir.'

' "So sorry—" . . .' I pondered. 'What would a girl say, Jeeves, who, having had a row with the bird she was practically engaged to because he told her she looked like a Pekingese in her new hat, wanted to extend the olive-branch?'

' "So sorry I was cross", sir, would, I fancy, be the expression.'

'Strong enough, do you think?'

'Possibly the addition of the word "darling" would give the necessary verisimilitude, sir.'

'Right. Resume the jotting. "So sorry I was cross, darling . . ." No, wait, Jeeves. Scratch that out. I see where we have gone off the rails. I see where we are missing a chance to make this the real tabasco. Sign the telegram not "Angela" but "Travers". '

'Very good, sir.'

'Or, rather, "Dahlia Travers". And this is the body of the communication. "Please return at once." '

' "Immediately" would be more economical, sir. Only one word. And it has a stronger ring.'

'True. Jot on, then. "Please return immediately. Angela in a hell of a state." '

'I would suggest "seriously ill", sir.'

'All right. "Seriously ill". "Angela seriously ill. Keeps calling for you and says you were quite right about hat." '

'If I might suggest, sir—?'

'Well, go ahead.'

'I fancy the following would meet the case. "Please return immediately. Angela seriously ill. High fever and delirium. Keeps calling your name piteously and saying something about a hat and that you were quite right. Please catch earliest possible train. Dahlia Travers."'

'That sounds all right.'

'Yes, sir.'

'You like that "piteously"? You don't think "incessantly"?'

'No, sir. "Piteously" is the *mot juste*.'

'All right. You know. Well, send it off in time to get here at two-thirty.'

'Yes, sir.'

'Two-thirty, Jeeves. You see the devilish cunning?'

'No, sir.'

'I will tell you. If the telegram arrived earlier, he would get it before the game. By two-thirty, however, he will have started for the ground. I shall hand it to him the moment there is a lull in the battle. By that time he will have begun to get some idea of what a football match between Upper Bleaching and Hockley-cum-Meston is like, and the thing ought to work like magic. I can't imagine anyone who has been sporting awhile with those thugs I saw yesterday not welcoming any excuse to call it a day. You follow me?'

'Yes, sir.'

'Very good, Jeeves.'

'Very good, sir.'

You can always rely on Jeeves. Two-thirty I had said, and two-thirty it was. The telegram arrived almost on the minute. I was going to my room to change into something warmer at the moment, and I took it up with me. Then into the heavy tweeds and off in the car to the field of play. I got there just as the two teams were lining up, and half a minute later the whistle blew and the war was on.

What with one thing and another – having been at a school where they didn't play it and so forth – Rugby football is a game I can't claim absolutely to understand in all its niceties, if you know what I mean. I can follow the broad, general principles, of course. I mean to say, I know that the main scheme is to work the ball down the field somehow and deposit it over the line at the other end, and that, in order to squelch this programme, each side is allowed to put in a certain amount of assault and battery and do things to its fellow-man which, if done elsewhere, would result in fourteen days without the option, coupled with some strong remarks from the Bench. But there I stop. What you might call the science of the thing is to Bertram Wooster a sealed book. However, I am informed by experts that on this occasion there was not enough science for anyone to notice.

There had been a great deal of rain in the last few days, and the going appeared to be a bit sticky. In fact, I have seen swamps that were drier than this particular bit of ground. The red-haired bloke whom I had encountered in the pub paddled up and kicked off amidst cheers from the populace, and the ball went straight to where Tuppy was standing, a pretty colour-scheme in light blue and orange. Tuppy caught it neatly, and hoofed it back, and it was at this point that I understood that an Upper Bleaching versus Hockley-cum-Meston game had certain features not usually seen on the football-field.

For Tuppy, having done his bit, was just standing there, looking modest, when there was a thunder of large feet and the red-haired bird, galloping up, seized him by the neck, hurled him to earth, and fell on him. I had a glimpse of Tuppy's face, as it registered horror, dismay, and a general suggestion of stunned dissatisfaction with the scheme of things, and then he disappeared. By the time he had come to the surface, a sort of mob-warfare was going on at the other side of the field. Two assortments of sons of the soil had got their heads down and were shoving earnestly against each other, with the ball somewhere in the middle.

Tuppy wiped a fair portion of Hampshire out of his eye, peered round him in a dazed kind of way, saw the mass-meeting and ran towards it, arriving just in time for a couple of heavy-weights to gather him in and give him the mud-treatment again. This placed him in an admirable position for a third heavyweight to kick him in the ribs with a boot like a violin-case. The red-haired man then fell on him. It was all good, brisk play, and looked fine from my side of the ropes.

I saw now where Tuppy had made his mistake. He was too dressy. On occasions such as this it is safest not to be conspicuous, and that blue and orange shirt rather caught the eye. A sober beige, blending with the colour of the ground, was what his best friends would have recommended. And, in addition to the fact that his costume attracted attention, I rather think that the men of Hockley-cum-Meston resented his being on the field at all. They felt that, as a non-local, he had butted in on a private fight and had no business there.

At any rate, it certainly appeared to me that they were giving him preferential treatment. After each of those shoving-bees to which I have alluded, when the edifice caved in and tons of humanity wallowed in a tangled mass in the juice, the last soul to be excavated always seemed to be Tuppy. And on the rare occasions when he actually managed to stand upright for a moment, somebody – generally the red-haired man – invariably sprang to the congenial task of spilling him again.

In fact, it was beginning to look as though that telegram would come too late to save a human life, when an interruption occurred. Play had worked round close to where I was standing, and there had been the customary collapse of all concerned, with Tuppy at the bottom of the basket, as usual; but this time, when they got up and started to count the survivors, a sizeable cove in what had once been a white shirt remained on the ground. And a hearty cheer went up from a hundred patriotic throats as the news spread that Upper Bleaching had drawn first blood.

The victim was carried off by a couple of his old chums, and the rest of the players sat down and pulled their stockings up and thought of life for a bit. The moment had come, it seemed to me, to remove Tuppy from the *abattoir*, and I hopped over the ropes and toddled to where he sat scraping mud from his wishbone. His air was that of a man who has been passed through a wringer, and his eyes, what you could see of them, had a strange, smouldering gleam. He was so crusted with alluvial deposits that one realized how little a mere bath would ever be able to effect. To fit him to take his place once more in polite society, he would certainly have to be sent to the cleaner's. Indeed, it was a moot point whether it wouldn't be simpler just to throw him away.

'Tuppy, old man,' I said.

'Eh?' said Tuppy.

'A telegram for you.'

'Eh?'

'I've got a wire here that came after you left the house.'

'Eh?' said Tuppy.

I stirred him up a trifle with the ferule of my stick, and he seemed to come to life.

'Be careful what you're doing, you silly ass,' he said, in part. 'I'm one solid bruise. What are you gibbering about?'

'A telegram has come for you. I think it may be important.'

He snorted in a bitter sort of way.

'Do you suppose I've time to read telegrams now?'

'But this one may be frightfully urgent,' I said. 'Here it is.'

But, if you understand me, it wasn't. How I had happened to do it, I don't know, but apparently, in changing the upholstery, I had left it in my other coat.

'Oh, my gosh,' I said, 'I've left it behind.'

'It doesn't matter.'

'But it does. It's probably something you ought to read at once. Immediately, if you know what I mean. If I were you, I'd just say a few words of farewell to the murder-squad and come back to the house right away.'

He raised his eyebrows. At least, I think he must have done, because the mud on his forehead stirred a little, as if something was going on underneath it.

'Do you imagine,' he said, 'that I would slink away under her very eyes? Good God! Besides,' he went on, in a quiet, meditative voice, 'there is no power on earth that could get me off this field until I've thoroughly disembowelled that red-haired bounder. Have you noticed how he keeps tackling me when I haven't got the ball?'

'Isn't that right?'

'Of course it's not right. Never mind! A bitter retribution awaits that bird. I've had enough of it. From now on I assert my personality.'

'I'm a bit foggy as to the rules of this pastime,' I said. 'Are you allowed to bite him?'

'I'll try, and see what happens,' said Tuppy, struck with the idea and brightening a little.

At this point, the pall-bearers returned, and fighting became general again all along the Front.

There's nothing like a bit of rest and what you might call folding of the hands for freshening up the shop-soiled athlete. The dirty work, resumed after this brief breather, started off with an added vim which it did one good to see. And the life and soul of the party was young Tuppy.

You know, only meeting a fellow at lunch or at the races or loafing round country-houses and so forth, you don't get on to his hidden depths, if you know what I mean. Until this moment, if asked, I would have said that Tuppy Glossop was, on the whole, essentially a pacific sort of bloke, with little or nothing of the tiger of the jungle in him. Yet here he was, running to and fro with fire streaming from his nostrils, a positive danger to traffic.

Yes, absolutely. Encouraged by the fact that the referee was either filled with the spirit of Live and Let Live or else had got his whistle choked up with mud, the result being that he appeared to regard the game with a sort of calm detachment, Tuppy was putting in some very impressive work. Even to me, knowing nothing of the finesse of the thing, it was plain that if Hockley-cum-Meston wanted the happy ending they must eliminate young Tuppy at the earliest possible moment. And I will say for them that they did their best, the red-haired man being particularly assiduous. But Tuppy was made of durable material. Every time the opposition talent ground him into the mire and sat on his head, he rose on stepping-stones of his dead self, if you follow me, to higher things. And in the end it was the red-haired bloke who did the dust-biting.

I couldn't tell you exactly how it happened, for by this time the shades of night were drawing in a bit and there was a dollop of mist rising, but one moment the fellow was hareing along, apparently without a care in the world, and then suddenly Tuppy had appeared from nowhere and was sailing through the air at his neck. They connected with a crash and a slither, and a little later the red-haired bird was hopping off, supported by a brace of friends, something having gone wrong with his left ankle.

After that, there was nothing to it. Upper Bleaching, thoroughly bucked, became busier than ever. There was a lot of earnest work in a sort of inland sea down at the Hockley end of the field, and then a kind of tidal wave poured over the line, and when the bodies had been removed and the tumult and the shouting had died, there was young Tuppy lying on the ball. And that, with the exception of a few spots of mayhem in the last five minutes, concluded the proceedings.

I drove back to the Court in rather what you might term a pensive frame of mind. Things having happened as they had happened, there seemed to me a goodish bit of hard thinking to be done. There was a servitor of sorts in the hall, when I arrived, and I asked him to send up a whisky-and-soda, strong-ish, to my room. The old brain, I felt, needed stimulating. And about ten minutes later there was a knock at the door, and in came Jeeves, bearing tray and materials.

'Hullo, Jeeves,' I said, surprised. 'Are you back?'

'Yes, sir.'

'When did you get here?'

'Some little while ago, sir. Was it an enjoyable game, sir?'

'In a sense, Jeeves,' I said, 'yes. Replete with human interest and all that, if you know what I mean. But I fear that, owing to a touch of carelessness on my part, the worst has happened. I left the telegram in my other coat, so young Tuppy remained in action throughout.'

'Was he injured, sir?'

'Worse than that, Jeeves. He was the star of the game. Toasts, I should imagine, are now being drunk to him at every pub in the village. So spectacularly did he play – in fact, so heartily did he joust – that I can't see the girl not being all over him. Unless I am greatly mistaken, the moment they meet, she will exclaim "My hero!" and fall into his bally arms.'

'Indeed, sir?'

I didn't like the man's manner. Too calm. Unimpressed. A little leaping about with fallen jaw was what I had expected my words to produce, and I was on the point of saying as much when the door opened again and Tuppy limped in.

He was wearing an ulster over his football things, and I wondered why he had come to pay a social call on me instead of proceeding straight to the bathroom. He eyed my glass in a wolfish sort of way.

'Whisky?' he said, in a hushed voice.

'And soda.'

'Bring me one, Jeeves,' said young Tuppy. 'A large one.'

'Very good, sir.'

Tuppy wandered to the window and looked out into the gathering darkness, and for the first time I perceived that he had got a grouch of some description. You can generally tell by a fellow's back. Humped. Bent. Bowed down with weight of woe, if you follow me.

'What's the matter?' I asked.

Tuppy emitted a mirthless.

'Oh, nothing much,' he said. 'My faith in woman is dead, that's all.'

'It is?'

'You jolly well bet it is. Women are a wash-out. I see no future for the sex, Bertie. Blisters, all of them.'

'Er – even the Dogsbody girl?'

'Her name,' said Tuppy, a little stiffly, 'is Dalgleish, if it happens to interest you. And, if you want to know something else, she's the worst of the lot.'

'My dear chap!'

Tuppy turned. Beneath the mud, I could see that his face was drawn and, to put it in a nutshell, wan.

'Do you know what happened, Bertie?'

'What?'

'She wasn't there.'

'Where?'

'At the match, you silly ass.'

'Not at the match?'

'No.'

'You mean, not among the throng of eager spectators?'

'Of course I mean not among the spectators. Did you think I expected her to be playing?'

'But I thought the whole scheme of the thing—'

'So did I. My gosh!' said Tuppy, laughing another of those hollow ones. 'I sweat myself to the bone for her sake. I allow a mob of homicidal maniacs to kick me in the ribs and stroll about on my face. And then, when I have braved a fate worse than death, so to speak, all to please her, I find that she didn't bother to come and watch the game. She got a 'phone-call from

London from somebody who said he had located an Irish water-spaniel, and up she popped in her car, leaving me flat. I met her just now outside her house, and she told me. And all she could think of was that she was as sore as a sun-burnt neck because she had had her trip for nothing. Apparently it wasn't an Irish water-spaniel at all. Just an ordinary English water-spaniel. And to think I fancied I loved a girl like that. A nice life-partner she would make! "When pain and anguish wring the brow, a ministering angel thou" – I don't think! Why, if a man married a girl like that and happened to get stricken by some dangerous illness, would she smooth his pillow and press cooling drinks on him? Not a chance! She'd be off somewhere trying to buy Siberian eel-hounds. I'm through with women.'

I saw that the moment had come to put in a word for the old firm.

'My cousin Angela's not a bad sort, Tuppy,' I said, in a grave elder-brotherly kind of way. 'Not altogether a bad egg, Angela, if you look at her squarely. I had always been hoping that she and you . . . and I know my Aunt Dahlia felt the same.'

Tuppy's bitter sneer cracked the top-soil.

'Angela!' he woofed. 'Don't talk to me about Angela. Angela's a rag and a bone and a hank of hair and an A1 scourge, if you want to know. She gave me the push. Yes, she did. Simply because I had the manly courage to speak out candidly on the subject of that ghastly lid she was chump enough to buy. It made her look like a Peke, and I told her it made her look like a Peke. And instead of admiring me for my fearless honesty she bunged me out on my ear. Faugh!'

'She did?' I said.

'She jolly well did,' said young Tuppy. 'At four-sixteen p.m. on Tuesday the seventeenth.'

'By the way, old man,' I said, 'I've found that telegram.'

'What telegram?'

'The one I told you about.'

'Oh, that one?'

'Yes, that's the one.'

'Well, let's have a look at the beastly thing.'

I handed it over, watching him narrowly. And suddenly, as he read, I saw him wobble. Stirred to the core. Obviously.

'Anything important?' I said.

'Bertie,' said young Tuppy, in a voice that quivered with strong emotion, 'my recent remarks *re* your cousin Angela. Wash them out. Cancel them. Look on them as not spoken. I tell you, Bertie, Angela's all right. An angel in human shape, and that's official. Bertie, I've got to get up to London. She's ill.'

'Ill?'

'High fever and delirium. This wire's from your aunt. She wants me to come up to London at once. Can I borrow your car?'

'Of course.'

'Thanks,' said Tuppy, and dashed out.

He had only been gone about a second when Jeeves came in with the restorative.

'Mr Glossop's gone, Jeeves.'

'Indeed, sir?'

'To London.'

'Yes, sir?'

'In my car. To see my cousin Angela. The sun is once more shining, Jeeves.'

'Extremely gratifying, sir.'

I gave him the eye.

'Was it you, Jeeves, who 'phoned to Miss What's-her-bally-name about the alleged water-spaniel?'

'Yes, sir.'

'I thought as much.'

'Yes, sir?'

'Yes, Jeeves, the moment Mr Glossop told me that a Mysterious Voice had 'phoned on the subject of Irish water-spaniels, I thought as much. I recognized your touch. I read your motives like an open book. You knew she would come buzzing up.'

'Yes, sir.'

'And you knew how Tuppy would react. If there's one thing that gives a jousting knight the pip, it is to have his audience walk out on him.'

'Yes, sir.'

'But, Jeeves.'

'Sir?'

'There's just one point. What will Mr Glossop say when he finds my cousin Angela full of beans and not delirious?'

'The point had not escaped me, sir. I took the liberty of ringing Mrs Travers up on the telephone and explaining the circumstances. All will be in readiness for Mr Glossop's arrival.'

'Jeeves,' I said, 'you think of everything.'

'Thank you, sir. In Mr Glossop's absence, would you care to drink this whisky-and-soda?'

I shook the head.

'No, Jeeves, there is only one man who must do that. It is you. If ever anyone earned a refreshing snort, you are he. Pour it out, Jeeves, and shove it down.'

'Thank you very much, sir.'

'Cheerio, Jeeves!'

'Cheerio, sir, if I may use the expression.'

THE END

P. G. Wodehouse

IN ARROW BOOKS

If you have enjoyed Jeeves and Wooster, you'll love Blandings

FROM

Blandings Castle

THE morning sunshine descended like an amber shower-bath on Blandings Castle, lighting up with a heartening glow its ivied walls, its rolling parks, its gardens, outhouses, and messuages, and such of its inhabitants as chanced at the moment to be taking the air. It fell on green lawns and wide terraces, on noble trees and bright flower-beds. It fell on the baggy trousers-seat of Angus McAllister, head-gardener to the ninth Earl of Emsworth, as he bent with dour Scottish determination to pluck a slug from its reverie beneath the leaf of a lettuce. It fell on the white flannels of the Hon. Freddie Threepwood, Lord Emsworth's second son, hurrying across the water-meadows. It also fell on Lord Emsworth himself and on Beach, his faithful butler. They were standing on the turret above the west wing, the former with his eye to a powerful telescope, the latter holding the hat which he had been sent to fetch.

'Beach,' said Lord Emsworth.

'M'lord?'

'I've been swindled. This dashed thing doesn't work.'

'Your lordship cannot see clearly?'

'I can't see at all, dash it. It's all black.'

The butler was an observant man.

'Perhaps if I were to remove the cap at the extremity of the instrument, m'lord, more satisfactory results might be obtained.'

'Eh? Cap? Is there a cap? So there is. Take it off, Beach.'

'Very good, m'lord.'

'Ah!' There was satisfaction in Lord Emsworth's voice. He twiddled and adjusted, and the satisfaction deepened. 'Yes, that's better. That's capital. Beach, I can see a cow.'

'Indeed, m'lord?'

'Down in the water-meadows. Remarkable. Might be two yards away. All right, Beach. Shan't want you any longer.'

'Your hat, m'lord?'

'Put it on my head.'

'Very good, m'lord.'

The butler, this kindly act performed, withdrew. Lord Emsworth continued gazing at the cow.

The ninth Earl of Emsworth was a fluffy-minded and amiable old gentleman with a fondness for new toys. Although the main interest of his life was his garden, he was always ready to try a side line, and the latest of these side lines was this telescope of his. Ordered from London in a burst of enthusiasm consequent upon the reading of an article on astronomy in a monthly magazine, it had been placed in position on the previous evening. What was now in progress was its trial trip.

Presently, the cow's audience-appeal began to wane. It was a fine cow, as cows go, but, like so many cows, it lacked sustained dramatic interest. Surfeited after awhile by the spectacle of it chewing the cud and staring glassily at nothing, Lord Emsworth decided to swivel the apparatus round in the hope of picking up something a trifle more sensational. And he was just about to do so, when into the range of his vision there came the Hon. Freddie. White and shining, he tripped along over the turf like a Theocritan shepherd hastening to keep an appointment with a nymph, and a sudden frown marred the serenity of Lord Emsworth's brow. He generally frowned when he saw Freddie, for with the passage of the years that youth had become more and more of a problem to an anxious father.

Unlike the male codfish, which, suddenly finding itself the parent of three million five hundred thousand little codfish, cheerfully resolves to love them all, the British aristocracy is apt to look with a somewhat jaundiced eye on its younger sons. And Freddie Threepwood was one of those younger sons who rather invite the jaundiced eye. It seemed to the head of the family that there was no way of coping with the boy. If he was allowed to live in London, he piled up debts and got into mischief; and when you jerked him back into the purer sur-roundings of Blandings Castle, he just mooned about the place, moping broodingly. Hamlet's society at Elsinore must have had much the same effect on his stepfather as did that of Freddie Threepwood at Blandings on Lord Emsworth. And it is prob-able that what induced the latter to keep a telescopic eye on him at this moment was the fact that his demeanour was so myster-iously jaunty, his bearing so intriguingly free from its customary crushed misery. Some inner voice whispered to Lord Emsworth that this smiling, prancing youth was up to no good and would bear watching.

The inner voice was absolutely correct. Within thirty seconds its case had been proved up to the hilt. Scarcely had his lordship had time to wish, as he invariably wished on seeing his offspring, that Freddie had been something entirely different in manners, morals, and appearance, and had been the son of somebody else living a considerable distance away, when out of a small spinney near the end of the meadow there bounded a girl. And Freddie, after a cautious glance over his shoulder, immediately proceeded to fold this female in a warm embrace.

Lord Emsworth had seen enough. He tottered away from the telescope, a shattered man. One of his favourite dreams was of some nice, eligible girl, belonging to a good family, and possessing a bit of money of her own, coming along some day and taking Freddie off his hands; but that inner voice, more confident now than ever, told him that this was not she. Freddie would not sneak off in this furtive fashion to meet eligible girls, nor could he imagine any eligible girl, in her right senses, rushing into Freddie's arms in that enthusiastic way. No, there was only one explanation. In the cloistral seclusion of Blandings, far from the Metropolis with all its conveniences for that sort of thing, Freddie had managed to get himself entangled. Seething with anguish and fury, Lord Emsworth hurried down the stairs and out on to the terrace. Here he prowled like an elderly leopard waiting for feeding-time, until in due season there was a flicker of white among the trees that flanked the drive and a cheerful whistling announced the culprit's approach.

It was with a sour and hostile eye that Lord Emsworth watched his son draw near. He adjusted his pince-nez, and with their assistance was able to perceive that a fatuous smile of self-satisfaction illumined the young man's face, giving him the appearance of a beaming sheep. In the young man's buttonhole there shone a nosegay of simple meadow flowers, which, as he walked, he patted from time to time with a loving hand.

'Frederick!' bellowed his lordship.

The villain of the piece halted abruptly. Sunk in a roseate trance, he had not observed his father. But such was the sunniness of his mood that even this encounter could not damp him. He gambolled happily up.

'Hullo, guv'nor!' he carolled. He searched in his mind for a pleasant topic of conversation – always a matter of some little difficulty on these occasions. 'Lovely day, what?'

His lordship was not to be diverted into a discussion of the weather. He drew a step nearer, looking like the man who smothered the young princes in the Tower.

'Frederick,' he demanded, 'who was that girl?'

The Hon. Freddie started convulsively. He appeared to be swallowing with difficulty something large and jagged.

'Girl?' he quavered. 'Girl? Girl, guv'nor?'

'That girl I saw you kissing ten minutes ago down in the water-meadows.'

'Oh!' said the Hon. Freddie. He paused. 'Oh, ah!' He paused again. 'Oh, ah, yes! I've been meaning to tell you about that, guv'nor.'

'You have, have you?'

'All perfectly correct, you know. Oh, yes, indeed! All most absolutely correct-o! Nothing fishy, I mean to say, or anything like that. She's my *fiancée*.'

A sharp howl escaped Lord Emsworth, as if one of the bees humming in the lavender-beds had taken time off to sting him in the neck.

'Who is she?' he boomed. 'Who is this woman?'

'Her name's Donaldson.'

'Who is she?'

'Aggie Donaldson. Aggie's short for Niagara. Her people spent their honeymoon at the Falls, she tells me. She's American and all that. Rummy names they give kids in America,' proceeded Freddie, with hollow chattiness. 'I mean to say! Niagara! I ask you!'

'Who is she?'

'She's most awfully bright, you know. Full of beans. You'll love her.'

'Who is she?'

'And can play the saxophone.'

'Who,' demanded Lord Emsworth for the sixth time, 'is she? And where did you meet her?'

Freddie coughed. The information, he perceived, could no longer be withheld, and he was keenly alive to the fact that it scarcely fell into the class of tidings of great joy.

'Well, as a matter of fact, guv'nor, she's a sort of cousin of Angus McAllister's. She's come over to England for a visit, don't you know, and is staying with the old boy. That's how I happened to run across her.'

Lord Emsworth's eyes bulged and he gargled faintly. He had had many unpleasant visions of his son's future, but they had never included one of him walking down the aisle with a sort of cousin of his head-gardener.

'Oh!' he said. 'Oh, indeed?'

'That's the strength of it, guv'nor.'

Lord Emsworth threw his arms up, as if calling on Heaven to witness a good man's persecution, and shot off along the terrace at a rapid trot. Having ranged the grounds for some minutes, he ran his quarry to earth at the entrance to the yew alley.

The head-gardener turned at the sound of his footsteps. He was a sturdy man of medium height, with eyebrows that would have fitted a bigger forehead. These, added to a red and wiry beard, gave him a formidable and uncompromising expression. Honesty Angus McAllister's face had in full measure, and also intelligence; but it was a bit short on sweetness and light.

'McAllister,' said his lordship, plunging without preamble

into the matter of his discourse. 'That girl. You must send her away.'

A look of bewilderment clouded such of Mr McAllister's features as were not concealed behind his beard and eyebrows.

'Gurrul?'

'That girl who is staying with you. She must go!'

'Gae where?'

Lord Emsworth was not in the mood to be finicky about details.

'Anywhere,' he said. 'I won't have her here a day longer.'

'Why?' inquired Mr McAllister, who liked to thresh these things out.

'Never mind why. You must send her away immediately.'

Mr McAllister mentioned an insuperable objection.

'She's payin' me twa poon' a week,' he said simply.

Lord Emsworth did not grind his teeth, for he was not given to that form of displaying emotion; but he leaped some ten inches into the air and dropped his pince-nez. And, though normally a fair-minded and reasonable man, well aware that modern earls must think twice before pulling the feudal stuff on their *employés*, he took on the forthright truculence of a large landowner of the early Norman period ticking off a serf.

'Listen, McAllister! Listen to me! Either you send that girl away to-day or you can go yourself. I mean it!'

A curious expression came into Angus McAllister's face – always excepting the occupied territories. It was the look of a man who has not forgotten Bannockburn, a man conscious of belonging to the country of William Wallace and Robert the Bruce. He made Scotch noises at the back of his throat.

'Y'r lorrudsheep will accept ma notis,' he said, with formal dignity.

'I'll pay you a month's wages in lieu of notice and you will leave this afternoon,' retorted Lord Emsworth with spirit.

'Mphm!' said Mr McAllister.

Lord Emsworth left the battle-field with a feeling of pure exhilaration, still in the grip of the animal fury of conflict. No twinge of remorse did he feel at the thought that Angus McAllister had served him faithfully for ten years. Nor did it cross his mind that he might miss McAllister.

But that night, as he sat smoking his after-dinner cigarette, Reason, so violently expelled, came stealing timidly back to her throne, and a cold hand seemed suddenly placed upon his heart.

With Angus McAllister gone, how would the pumpkin fare?

'Had P. G. Wodehouse's only contribution to literature been Lord Emsworth and Blandings Castle, his place in history would have been assured. Had he written of none but Mike and Psmith, he would be cherished today as the best and brightest of our comic authors. If Jeeves and Wooster had been his solitary theme, still he would be hailed as The Master. If he had given us only Ukridge, or nothing but the recollections of the Mulliner family, or a pure diet of golfing stories, Wodehouse would nonetheless be considered immortal. That he gave us all those and more – so much more – is our good fortune and a testament to the most industrious, prolific and beneficent author ever to have sat down, scratched his head and banged out a sentence.'   Stephen Fry

We hope you have enjoyed this book. With over ninety novels and around 300 short stories to choose from, you may be wondering which Wodehouse to choose next. It is our pleasure to introduce...

UNCLE FRED

Uncle Dynamite

Meet Frederick Altamount Cornwallis Twistleton, Fifth Earl of Ickenham. Better known as Uncle Fred, an old boy of such a sunny and youthful nature that explosions of sweetness and light detonate all around him.

Cocktail Time

Frederick, Earl of Ickenham, remains young at heart. So his jape of using a catapult to ping the silk top hat off his grumpy half-brother-in-law, is nothing out of the ordinary – but the consequences abound with possibilities.

UKRIDGE

Ukridge

Money makes the world go round for Stanley Featherstonehaugh Ukridge – looking like an animated blob of mustard in his bright yellow raincoat – and when there isn't enough of it, the world just has to spin a bit faster.

MR MULLINER

Meet Mr Mulliner

Sitting in the Angler's Rest, drinking hot scotch and lemon, Mr Mulliner has fabulous stories to tell of the extraordinary behaviour of his far-flung family. This includes Wilfred, whose formula for Buck-U-Uppo enables elephants to face tigers with the necessary nonchalance.

Mr Mulliner Speaking

Holding court in the bar-parlour of the Angler's Rest, Mr Mulliner reveals what happened to The Man Who Gave Up Smoking, what the Something Squishy was that the butler delivered on a silver salver, and what caused the dreadful Unpleasantness at Bludleigh Court.

MONTY BODKIN

The Luck of the Bodkins

Monty Bodkin, besotted with 'precious dream-rabbit' Gertrude Butterwick, Reggie and Ambrose Tennyson (the latter mistaken for the late Poet Laureate), and Hollywood starlet Lotus Blossom, complete with pet alligator, all embark on a voyage of personal discovery aboard the luxurious liner, *S.S. Atlantic*.

JEEVES
The Novels

Thank You, Jeeves

Bertie disappears to the country as a guest of his chum Chuffy – only to find his peace shattered by the arrival of his ex-fiancée Pauline Stoker, her formidable father and the eminent loony-doctor Sir Roderick Glossop. When Chuffy falls in love with Pauline and Bertie seems to be caught in flagrante, a situation boils up which only Jeeves (whether employed or not) can simmer down . . .

Jeeves and the Feudal Spirit

A moustachioed Bertie must live up to 'Stilton' Cheesewright's expectations in the Drones Club darts tournament, or risk being beaten to a pulp by 'Stilton', jealous of his fiancée Florence's affections . . .

Much Obliged, Jeeves

What happens when the Book of Revelations, the Junior Ganymede Club's recording of their masters' less than perfect habits, falls into potentially hostile hands?

Aunts Aren't Gentlemen

Under doctor's orders, Bertie moves with Jeeves to a countryside cottage. But Jeeves can cope with anything – even Aunt Dahlia.

Jeeves in the Offing

When Jeeves goes on holiday to Herne Bay, Bertie's life collapses; finding his mysterious engagement announced in *The Times* and encountering his nemesis Sir Roderick Glossop in disguise, Bertie hightails it to Herne Bay. Then the fun really starts . . .

The Code of the Woosters

Purloining an antique cow creamer under the instruction of the indomitable Aunt Dahlia is the least of Bertie's tasks, for he has to play Cupid while feuding with Spode.

The Mating Season

In an idyllic Tudor manor in a picture-perfect English village, Bertie is in disguise as Gussie Fink-Nottle, Gussie is in disguise as Bertram Wooster and Jeeves, also in disguise, is the only one who can set things right . . .

Ring for Jeeves

Patch Perkins and his clerk are not the 'honest bookies' they seem, but Bill, the rather impoverished Ninth Earl of Rowcester, and his temporary butler Jeeves. When they abscond with the freak winnings of Captain Biggar, Jeeves's resourcefulness is put to the test . . .

Stiff Upper Lip, Jeeves

Bertie Wooster visits Major Plank in an attempt to return a work of art which Stiffy had told Bertie had been effectively stolen from Plank by Sir Watkyn Bassett. Thank goodness for Chief Inspector Witherspoon – but is he all he seems?

Right Ho, Jeeves

Bertie assumes his alter ego of Cupid and arranges the engagement of Gussie Fink-Nottle to Tuppy Glossop. Thankfully, Jeeves is ever present to correct the blundering plans hatched by his master.

Joy in the Morning

Trapped in rural Steeple Bumpleigh with old flame Florence Craye, her new and suspicious fiancé Stilton Cheesewright, and two-faced Edwin the Boy Scout, Bertie desperately needs Jeeves to save him . . .

JEEVES

The Collections

Carry on, Jeeves

In his new role as valet to Bertie Wooster, Jeeves's first duty is to create a miracle hangover cure. From that moment, the partnership that is Jeeves and Wooster never looks back . . .

Very Good, Jeeves

Endeavouring to give satisfaction, Jeeves embarks on a number of rescue missions, including rescuing Bingo Little and Tuppy Glossop from the soup . . . Twice each.

The Inimitable Jeeves

In pages stalked by the carnivorous Aunt Agatha, Bingo Little embarks on a relationship roller coaster and Bertie needs Jeeves's help to narrowly evade the clutches of terrifying Honoria Glossop . . .

The World of Jeeves

A complete collection of the Jeeves and Wooster short stories, described by Wodehouse as 'the ideal paperweight'.

BLANDINGS

Something Fresh

The first Blandings novel, featuring the delightfully dotty Lord Emsworth and introducing the first of many impostors who are to visit the Castle.

Pigs Have Wings

Can the Empress of Blandings avoid a pignapping to win the Fat Pigs class at the Shropshire Show for the third year running?

Leave it to Psmith

Lady Constance Keeble, sister of Lord Emsworth of Blandings Castle, has both an imperious manner and a valuable diamond necklace. The precarious peace of Blandings is shattered when her necklace becomes the object of dark plottings, for within the castle lurk some well-connected jewel thieves. Among them, a pair of American crooks: Lord Emsworth's younger son Freddie, desperate for money to establish a bookie's business, and Psmith, hoping to use a promised commission to finance his old school friend Mike's purchase of a farm to secure his future happiness.

Service with a Smile

When Clarence, Ninth Earl of Emsworth, must travel to London for the opening of Parliament, he grudgingly leaves his beloved pig, the Empress of Blandings, at home. When he returns, he must call upon Uncle Fred to restore normality to the chaos instilled during his absence . . .

Summer Lightning

The first appearance in a novel of the Empress of Blandings, the prize-winning pig and all-consuming passion of Clarence, Ninth Earl of Emsworth, which has disappeared. Suspects within the Castle abound . . . Did the butler do it?

Full Moon

When the moon is full at Blandings, strange things happen. Including a renowned painter being miraculously revivified decades after his death to paint a portrait of the beloved pig, the Empress of Blandings . . .

Uncle Fred in the Springtime

Uncle Fred believes he can achieve anything in the springtime. However, disguised as a loony doctor and trying to prevent prize pig, the Empress of Blandings, from falling into the hands of the unscrupulous Duke of Dunstable, he is stretched to his limit . . .

A Pelican at Blandings

Skulduggery is afoot, involving the sale of a modern nude painting, which, in Lord Emsworth's eyes, resembles a pig. Inundated with unwelcome guests, Clarence embarks on the short journey to the end of his wits. Fortunately Galahad Threepwood is on hand to solve all the mysteries . . .

The World of Blandings (Omnibus)

This wonderfully fat omnibus (containing three short stories and two full novels) spans the dimensions of the Empress of Blandings herself, surely the fattest pig in England . . .

Blandings Castle

The Empress of Blandings, potential silver medal winner in the Fat Pigs Class at the Shropshire Agricultural show, is off her food. Clarence, absent-minded Ninth Earl of Emsworth, is engaged in a feud with Head Gardener McAllister. But first of all, the vexed matter of the custody of the pumpkin must be resolved. This collection also includes Mr Mulliner's stories about Hollywood.

And Some Other Treats...

What Ho!

Introduced by Stephen Fry, this is a bumper anthology, providing the cream of the crop of Wodehouse's hilarious stories, together with verse, articles and all manner of treasures.

The Heart of a Goof

From his favourite chair on the terrace above the ninth hole, the Oldest Member reveals the stories behind his club's players, from notorious 'golfing giggler' Evangeline to poor, inept Rollo Podmarsh.

The Clicking of Cuthbert

A collection of stories, including that of Cuthbert, golfing ace, hopelessly in love with Adeline, who only cares for rising young writers. But enter a Great Russian Novelist with a strange passion, and Cuthbert's prospects might be looking up . . .

Big Money

Berry Conway, employee of dyspeptic American millionaire Torquil Patterson Frisby, has inherited a large number of shares in the Dream Come True copper mine. Of course they're worthless . . . aren't they?

Hot Water

In the heady atmosphere of a 1930s French chateau, J. Wellington Gedge only wants to return to his life in California, where everything is as it seems . . .

Laughing Gas

Joey Cooley, golden-curled Hollywood child film star, and six-foot-tall boxer Reginald, Earl of Havershot, are both under anaesthetic at the dentist's when their identities are swapped in the fourth dimension.

The Small Bachelor

It's Prohibition America and shy young George Finch is setting out as an artist – without the encumbrance of a shred of talent. Will George triumph over the social snob Mrs Waddington and successfully woo her stepdaughter?

Money for Nothing

Two households, both alike in dignity, in fair Rudge-in-the-Vale, where we lay our scene . . . Will the love of John Carmody and Pat Wyvern survive the bitter feud between their fathers, miserly Lester Carmody and peppery Colonel Wyvern?

Summer Moonshine

Poor Sir Buckstone Abbott owns in Walsingford Hall one of the least attractive stately homes in the country, so when a rich continental princess seems willing to buy it, he's overjoyed. But will the deal be completed?

The Adventures of Sally

When Sally Nicholas inherits some money, her life becomes increasingly complicated; with a needy brother, a handsome fiancé, who is not all he seems, and a naive generosity of spirit, Sally must turn to doting, clueless Ginger Kemp to set things right . . .

Young Men in Spats

Meet the Young Men in Spats – all innocent members of the Drones Club, all hopeless suitors, and all busy betting their sometimes non-existent fortunes on highly improbable outcomes. That is when they're not recovering from driving their sports cars *through* Marble Arch . . .

Piccadilly Jim

It takes a lot of effort for Jimmy Crocker to become Piccadilly Jim – nights on the town roistering, and a string of broken hearts. When he eventually succeeds, Jimmy ends up having to pretend he's himself, possibly the hardest pretence of all …

A Damsel in Distress

The Earl of Marshmoreton just wants a quiet life pottering around his garden, supported by his portly butler Keggs. However, when his spirited daughter, Lady Maud, is placed under house-arrest due to an unfortunate infatuation, and the American, George Bevan, determines to claim her heart, the Earl is allowed no such reprieve …

The Girl in Blue

Young Jerry West has a few problems, including uncles with butlers who aren't all they seem, and a love for the woman he is not due to marry. When his uncle's miniature Gainsborough, *The Girl in Blue*, is stolen, Jerry sets out on a mission to find her … Will everything come right in the process?